CONSPIRACY TO MURDER

ADRIANO BIASINI

ISBN: 978-1-61296-580-2

PUBLISHED BY BLACK ROSE WRITING

www.blackrosewriting.com

Printed in the United States of America

Suggested retail price $18.95

Conspiracy to Murder is printed in Adobe Caslon Pro

Cover Design by David F. Di Benedetto

I wish to acknowledge those instrumental
for making this book possible:

To Angela, Nicholas, and Alexander Biasini, you are truly the
"beacons of light" that inspire me each and every day.
To Paul for providing me with the final "roadmap" to my success.
And to Eddie, for introducing me to everything that is "JFK".

To my wonderful friend James
Ferlisi

Thanks for your continued support.

Yours Truly,

CONSPIRACY TO MURDER

CHAPTER 1

The three men stood around a large table in a dimly lit room. The conversation they were engaged in soon became quite animated. The heaviest set individual had clearly taken over the conversation. "I am sick and tired of everything that is going on in this country. Since when do two people decide how we are going to run our business? Who died and made them boss? I mean, we're the ones who helped get him into office to begin with!"

The second of the three men, in a somewhat desperate plea countered. "Tell me then; what can we do about it?" "We get rid of him!" replied the first man. The other two men now stared at one another. The third man now factored into the conversation. "Just how do you intend to pull that off?" he replied, "Do you realize who we are talking about here?"

The man at the forefront of the conversation responded to his detractor. In a very stern voice he proclaimed, "Like I've always said, anything is possible, if you have the right circumstance and the right people in place!" His declaration had caught the others by surprise. Both of them were stunned by his assertion. From the look on their faces, it was clear that the mere notion of what he had suggested represented quite a monumental task. The reverberations of this plan, if carried out would be felt by many.

The sequence ended as I awoke from the dream I had just experienced. I glanced back at the alarm clock by my bed. It was not quite 4am. I tossed and turned for the next three hours. Certain elements of what I had dreamt about swirled in my mind as I subconsciously tried to make sense of all that had taken place throughout the dream.

Everything I had witnessed in my mind stayed with me that entire morning. Never before had I witnessed such an intense dream in my life. I couldn't help but wonder who these three men were. More importantly, what were the circumstances they so vehemently spoke of?

As I made my way to school, I fought the continuous urge to try and make sense all that I had dreamt of that morning. This was perhaps the most important day of my high school tenure. It was the day I was to choose the subject of my final essay of my school year. This one assignment comprised 50% of my overall grade! School had always come naturally to me. My parents had invested a great deal of resources in putting me through private school. I wasn't about to waste the opportunity I had been given.

My grades had slipped and I was in jeopardy of not making the honor role for the first time in my academic career. This was something totally new to me; I had always been able to control whatever situation I found myself in. Any chance of salvaging the hope of one day entering Harvard University now hinged upon my ability to do just that. As I was to discover later that morning, the subject I had been assigned would prove to be quite interesting.

Mrs. Harrison, my English teacher, had hinted to me throughout the week that the topic she had chosen for me was to be my most challenging one to date. I knew she had chosen this particular one for me in part because she wanted me to succeed. In my mind she knew I was the one person she felt could take on such a complex subject and be successful in it. I soon stared at the subject chosen for me. "John Fitzgerald Kennedy: the man and the myth."

I had heard about the lore of John F. Kennedy in passing a number of times. His presidency seemed to be one that endured the test of time. For some strange reason I found myself eager to delve into the world that was JFK. Given everything at stake I wasted no time in starting the research into the subject I had now been assigned to.

I sat in front of my computer and proceeded to type in the call letters JFK. I waited for a response; moments later thousands of sites came up! It became immediately obvious to me, there was not going to be any shortage of information on the subject I was chosen to write about.

The story of John Fitzgerald Kennedy was one that promised to have the pomp and pageantry one would expect from one of the most recognizable figures in American history. It began with his inauguration, which, as I immediately discovered, was an event in itself. I began to view a video extract of President Kennedy's inauguration. The oath of office was administered to John F. Kennedy on Friday January 20, 1961 by Chief Justice Earl Warren. Kennedy's inaugural address arrived with great anticipation. Famous British author Robert Frost spoke during the ceremony. I was immediately struck by the words that he spoke that day.

Kennedy began to speak, "Vice President Johnson, Mr. Speaker, Mr. Chief Justice, President Eisenhower, Vice President Nixon, President Truman, reverend clergy, fellow citizens, we observe today not a victory of party, but a celebration of freedom-symbolizing an end, as well as a beginning-signifying renewal, as well as change." Let every nation know, whether it wishes us well or till, that we shall pay any price, bear any burden, meet any hardship, support any friend, oppose any foe, in order to assure the survival and the success of liberty…..Let all our neighbors know that we shall join with them to oppose aggression or subversion anywhere in the Americas. And let every other power know that this hemisphere intends to remain the master of its own house." *(fn)*

I continued to read on as Kennedy's speech continued. "In the long history of the world, only a few generations have been granted the role of defending freedom in its hour of maximum danger. I do not shrink from this responsibility- I welcome it.…And so, my fellow Americans: ask not what your country can do for you-ask what you can do for your country. My fellow citizens of the world: ask not what America will do for you, but what together we can do for the freedom of man." *(fn)*

Although written years earlier, the last few sentences of President

Kennedy's inaugural speech immediately "struck a chord" with me. As I was soon to discover, the message Kennedy spoke of would become forever immortalized in history. My instincts had never failed me before; something inside was now telling me that I had only skimmed the surface of what lay ahead. The story of JFK now seemed to offer more than I had first anticipated. I made my way back to the library the next day after school and immediately logged onto one of the library computers.

I typed in the key words "JFK-CAMELOT". It was a phrase I had heard previously to describe President Kennedy's term in office. I came across a host of internet sites, all of which spoke of Kennedy in an almost god-like manner. All the brief images I saw in Kennedy's inaugural speech, as well as his personal life were proof of the appeal that President Kennedy had to the American people. Here was a brash, good-looking young man who had literally taken the country by storm. He seemed to resonate with all Americans.

Kennedy's inaugural speech spoke of promise and hope, on so many levels. Kennedy hoped to usher legislation that would, amongst other things, provide improved medical care for the elderly, aid for depressed areas of the country, cut unemployment, and create economic growth.

I began to read about the many causes brought forward by the Kennedy administration including his fight for civil rights. Kennedy broke the mould by appointing his brother Robert Kennedy as Attorney General. Together they worked to create laws that fought to uphold the civil rights of those who protested the racial discrimination that was still rampant in the American south.

I was immediately struck by the many "firsts" that this man ushered in as President. They all proved to secure his place in American history. John F. Kennedy was the first President to serve in the US Navy. He was the first Roman Catholic President elected to office. Surprisingly, Kennedy was the first President to have been born in the 20th century. The more I delved into the Kennedy mystique, the more intriguing it became.

Like his father before him John F. Kennedy possessed the charisma required to enter into politics. He fulfilled the potential many saw in him as early as 1946 when he successfully ran for the U.S. House of Representatives. By 1952 Kennedy was successful in entering the U.S. Senate.

Upon becoming President of the United States of America, Kennedy brought something to the political table that had not been seen before. He brought with him an energy level that had never been seen in any other President before him. He stood firm on his beliefs, and was not afraid to introduce tough legislation if the issue called for such. The fact that he was such a young President further enhanced the notion of change; his Presidency seemed to usher in hope for all Americans. John F. Kennedy's wife Jacqueline shared the same vigor and energy that her husband exhibited.

In every aspect, the Kennedys represented the closest thing to royalty Americans had ever experienced before. Having spent several hours researching all that I could on JFK I took a break and simply laid on my bed for a few minutes.

I now found myself suddenly re-energized. The story of JFK promised so much in terms of excitement. I had only spent a couple of hours researching JFK but there seemed so much more that lay ahead for me. I couldn't wait to discover everything else that surrounded John F. Kennedy's life both as President and as an individual. My mind now seemed to drift, moments later sudden images came to me, images I had never seen before.

A group of military personnel entered the room carrying a number of photos they indicated were taken recently. From what I could see it was clear that these photos were taken from a plane. Each photo contained a circle with a particular point of interest associated to it.

Those present included President Kennedy and members of his chiefs of staff including his brother Robert Kennedy. The meeting appeared to go on for several hours and ended with the President and his staff staring at the photos before them. The image suddenly disappeared as quickly as it came. I had never experienced images so real and detailed before, none had left such an indelible mark on me. It seemed as if the images I had just witnessed appeared to be real, almost to the point of being an actual event that had taken place in the past.

For the first time in a long time I found myself at a loss to explain the events I had seemingly witnessed in my mind. I quickly got up from my bed and sat in front of my computer once again. I spent the next hour or so reading through a host of internet sites until I stumbled across what I had hoped to find. The information I came across opened up a whole new avenue in my research of President Kennedy. As I would soon discover, Kennedy's tenure as President would prove to be quite tumultuous.

On Sunday October 14, 1962, U-2 reconnaissance flights over Cuba picked up the existence of Soviet medium-range ballistic missiles in Cuba. It was clear that a military site was in the process of being completed. The initial concern was whether or not the missiles were armed with nuclear warheads. President Kennedy was informed by his chiefs of staff of the military options that were open to them; they included air strikes as well as the invasion of Cuba. The President was warned of the fact that an air strike on the missile sites could lead to nuclear war, assuming the warheads found were in fact "armed".

On the advice of his top advisors, Kennedy ordered his staff to continue reconnaissance flights in Cuba. As I read on I couldn't help but wonder what John F. Kennedy must have felt at the time. Since the dawn of the nuclear age in 1945 never had any one leader held the fate of the entire world in his hands. The decisions that were now to be made by President Kennedy would determine if the world would soon find itself at the brink of nuclear Armageddon.

I tried to make sense of all that I had envisioned earlier that day. Was it somehow possible that the images I had witnessed somehow represented actual events in history? Perhaps I was simply day dreaming and had merely witnessed what I felt might have been said given the events I had read about. I walked over to my computer and searched through a number of internet sites.

Moments later, the answers to my questions were answered. I came across a document of transcripts that contained conversations that had taken place between John and Robert Kennedy during the Cuban Missile Crisis. I read through them for several minutes. As I did so, it became more and more apparent that the images I had envisioned matched the transcripts of conversations that had actually taken place in 1962. A sudden chill ran through my entire body. Had I really witnessed events of the past in my mind? Were these events that I had no prior knowledge of as real as the day they took place?

It was at that moment that I realized I would have to familiarize myself with all that was taking place in history during the Kennedy administration. I immersed myself in the events of 1962. As I was soon to discover, events during this time began to quickly unfold!

It was clear on the morning of October 18, 1962 analysts had discovered the presence of intermediate-range ballistic missiles being installed by the Russians with twice the range of the original medium-range ballistic missiles first detected. On the evening of October 22, 1962 President Kennedy announced to the nation that the U.S. was to impose a blockade on Cuba immediately as a response to the missiles that had been discovered in Cuba. Five days later, on the evening of Saturday Oct 27, 1962 Kennedy accepted the initial proposal sent by the Russians. He then instructed Attorney General Robert Kennedy to inform Russian diplomats of America's willingness to remove American Jupiter missiles placed in Turkey.

Khrushchev inevitably accepted Kennedy's response and agreed to the removal of all Soviet missiles in Cuba. Kennedy was praised by all as the leader who met the Russian Bear "head on" and came away the victor. The Kennedy administration had averted nuclear war. Having now spent mere days researching my paper it was becoming clear that everything I had initially read about John F. Kennedy was indeed true.

President Kennedy's actions during the Cuban Missile crisis were further proof of the appeal that Kennedy exhibited during his tenure as President. The Kennedy administration was faced with the prospect of having long-range nuclear weapons within arms reach of their country. America was in the line of fire; in the middle of it all was John F. Kennedy.

Faced with the decisions before it, the Kennedy administration under the guidance of its President met the crisis head on. In the end, a nuclear war with Russia had been averted in America's favor. In my mind, it was clear that Kennedy had indeed "made good" on the promises set forth in his inaugural speech.

The Cuban Missile Crisis proved to be a true test of President Kennedy's resolve to stop the spread of communism as promised in his inaugural speech. As far as I was concerned, Kennedy did not want to be responsible for leading the world to the brink of nuclear Armageddon.

Still, something was telling me that history was not going to treat either leader well. As I continued to read on it soon became evident that my suspicions were indeed correct. Nikita Khrushchev would never recover from events that took place that year. His place in Russian history had been cemented through this crisis, but he was never able to keep hold of his power. He was removed from office and retired to a life of anonymity forever known as the person who had buckled to American pressure.

In sharp contrast American reaction to the Cuban Missile Crisis was swift and succinct. Praise poured in throughout America. John F. Kennedy had become an American hero overnight. The Kennedy mystique was alive and well early during his time as President.

As I sat in third class that afternoon, I could think of only one thing. I began to realize why Mrs. Harrison had chosen the subject of JFK for me. The life of JFK had all the elements of a great story. All I could think of was what I would research next!

CHAPTER 2

I spent my entire spare class in the library combing through the events that took place during Kennedy's initial time in office. As was the case with the Cuban Missile Crisis in 1962, events continued to unfold throughout President Kennedy's term in office.

The race to space was front and central during the early 1960s. On April 12, 1961, Yuri Cagarin became the first man in space. On May 5, 1961 the United States responded by making Alan Sheppard Jr. the first American in space. Weeks later on May 25, 1961, in an address to Congress, President Kennedy pledged that the United States would land a man on the surface of the moon by the end of the decade. On June 3, 1961 Kennedy met with Soviet premier Nikita Khrushchev in Vienna; the conference failed to resolve conflicts over the status of Berlin.

From all that I had read so far, the overlying theme was the premise that the United States and the Soviet Union were becoming adversaries in the arena of both domestic and foreign policy. On Aug 1, 1961 East Germany, supported by the Soviet Union, began construction of the Berlin Wall, thereby halting the flow of refugees to the West, a clear sign the Cold War was entering its Zenith.

I walked home that afternoon taking the route I had taken so many times before. As I approached my house my attention was immediately drawn towards the newspaper stand located across the street. I made my way towards it and noticed there was one copy left.

The print on the newspaper was not the clear blue color that had always been the stalwart of the local newspaper. The paper that lay in the box was completely printed in black in white; the first thought that came to mind was that this was a special commemorative edition. I now glanced down at it. The headline announced that the Russians were to remove their nuclear basses from Cuba. Looking around me I immediately grabbed the copy still in the box. I anxiously folded it and made my way back to my room.

I entered my room and quickly closed the door behind me. I then unfolded the newspaper. It appeared to be a copy of The Washington Post newspaper dated October 29, 1962. It was in pristine condition, as if it had come straight off the press the day it was printed. On the right corner of it was the cost, a mere 10 cents. *(fn)*

The obvious question immediately came to mind. How was it possible that a newspaper copy identical to one that was printed years earlier could somehow turn up years later in pristine condition? Logic suggested it wasn't possible; yet I now stared at the copy before me. Just as they had done in the past, events were beginning to unfold before me in a manner I could have never anticipated!

The copy of the newspaper lay beside my computer as I typed in the call words- "Cuban Missile Crisis". Hundreds of results came up covering a myriad of topics surrounding it. The Cuban Missile Crisis dominated the first several pages of the newspaper. Each subsequent headline and article I read fueled my curiosity even more. The writing style and words used were far different from what was being printed by today's standards.

I held the copy of the newspaper I had miraculously come across. I stared at it for, what seemed like an eternity. I continued to ponder its significance; a number of thoughts now ran through my mind. The story of John F. Kennedy, it seemed was truly one for the ages. His stamp on history was no myth. I tried to place myself in the mindset of how Americans were feeling at the time of Kennedy's rise to power. He entered the Presidency with promise and vigor and met the biggest crisis of his administration head on. His popularity following the Cuban Missile Crisis was at an all time high.

I began to think back to all that I had read about over the past few days. Soon after more images began to appear in my mind, images that would prove to be more intriguing than those I had seen before. I clearly saw what appeared to be a small army of men being trained in a makeshift camp. From what I could see, they were being trained by American army personnel, though the purpose was not immediately clear to me. The images ended as quickly as they had come.

As I would soon discover, the Cuban Missile Crisis was not the only incident involving the U.S. and Cuba. I began to read through a host of articles that shed light on a number of new revelations. My initial research was now taking me on a journey through American history I would have never anticipated. Yet each piece of historical information I came across created my appetite for more. As I would now discover, it began with the first major incident President Kennedy was forced to deal with shortly after taking office.

On April 17, 1961, a small army of Cuban refugees, exiled following the 1959 Cuban revolution, invaded Playa Giron (Bay of Pigs) in Cuba. As I read on it quickly became evident to me that the images I had seen the previous evening were based on events I had just read about. For the moment, I tossed aside all doubts of the validity of the images I had seen in my mind over the past few days.

I couldn't help but wonder as to the timing of these images and their importance to the information I had now stumbled across. With every site I visited, the importance of this event as it related to the JFK story became evident. Once again I found myself compelled to familiarize myself with the events that had surrounded the Kennedy administration. As I was soon to discover, these events were not without their own controversy.

The Cold War was in full effect by the late 1950s. The United States had fostered the policy of communist containment in Latin America. Cuba represented a problem and threat to the United States. Fidel Castro was seen as a threat to democracy in Latin America. For a host of reasons, the removal of Fidel Castro as leader of Cuba was quickly becoming a top priority of the American government.

The core of this American stance culminated in the Bay of Pigs invasion. The success of this operation was predicated on its ability to create subsequent uprisings in Cuba that would further aid in the overthrow of the Castro government. The invaders also felt that they had been given assurances that they would have both air and naval support from the United States. It never materialized. *(fn)*

Within three days, the invasion force began to run out of supplies and ammunition. Castro's forces eventually surrounded and captured the invading rebel army. The operation proved to be a dismal failure. The Bay of Pigs invasion was a major embarrassment for the Kennedy administration. Kennedy had committed his Presidency to the fight against the spread of communism throughout the free world.

Less than 100 days in office President Kennedy accepted responsibility for the failed invasion during an address to the American Association of Newspaper Editors. Having accepted responsibility for Bay of Pigs invasion the Kennedy administration attempted to detract blame for the failed operation. Kennedy blamed the CIA as well as the Joint Chiefs of Staff for poor planning and training. *(fn)*

The ill-fated invasion proved to have a number of negative repercussions. Not only did the failed coup serve to alienate Kennedy from Fidel Castro, it also created a rift between the President and his own military establishment. Kennedy blamed the CIA for substandard training. The CIA in turn blamed Kennedy for allowing such an ill-planned operation to go ahead.

From all that I had read, it was becoming clear that, within mere months of entering the office of the President, John F. Kennedy had made enemies. For the first time it seemed that the Kennedy mystique had been shaken. I spent the majority of that Saturday doing something I wouldn't have dreamed of ever doing. I spent the entire day at the library consumed with the idea of researching all that I could on the events that surrounded the Kennedy presidency. As was the case with everything I had encountered thus far, it wasn't without its intrigue.

With the failure of the Bay of Pigs invasion months earlier, on Feb 3, 1962 President Kennedy cancelled all trade with Cuba, effectively severing all ties with that country. At home the fight for civil rights was a key issue facing the Kennedy administration. On February 26,

1962, the U.S. Supreme Court ruled that segregation in transportation facilities was unconstitutional.

On September 30, 1962 the US Supreme Court ordered the University of Mississippi to admit James H Meredith, its first African-American student. After Governor Ross Barnett attempted to block his admission, President Kennedy ordered US Marshalls to escort Meredith to campus. Federal National Guardsmen were called in to ensure that riots did not ensue.

The space race continued in full force. On Feb 30, 1962, astronaut John Glenn became the first American to orbit the earth. On Sept 12, 1962 Kennedy furthered his cause when he delivered a speech at Rice University in Houston, Texas. It was during this speech that Kennedy announced his goal of putting a man on the moon.

The story that surrounded the life of John F. Kennedy now consumed every moment of my day. I found myself constantly daydreaming and thinking about all I had read and seen the previous day. These thoughts consumed me as I sat in class the next day. Once again, my mind began to wander as more thoughts appeared.

American troupes began to surround the border area; they were immediately met with heavy resistance from all sides. It was clear American casualties were high on both sides. Moments later I became cognizant of those around me.

Was I daydreaming again, or had I again witnessed another important event in my mind? I began to shut out everything around me as I tried to figure out how it was possible for me to witness these visions with increasing regularity. Not only did they all appear to be real, they all seemed to be a precursor of something to come. More images appeared.

The crowd increased in number with each passing minute. It was a mixture of young and old. A number of them were students holding up signs. It was peaceful, yet defiant. Riot police were stationed to the side of the street waiting for the moment at which they would be called in.

The signs that many on hand were holding all related to the same issue, "VIETNAM". I opened my eyes. The images I had just witnessed were as vivid as ever. The question still remained, what did it all mean? I found myself immersed in the history of events that began to unfold around John F. Kennedy during his time as President. Although I have never had an interest in history before, the information I had come across was as compelling as it was significant.

It soon became apparent that Vietnam was to be the centerpiece of US foreign policy for years to come. Northern Vietnam had turned into a communist state in the middle of the 20th century. The historical information I had come across was as compelling as any I continued to read.

Southern Vietnam remained a democratic state. In the years that followed, Northern Vietnam threatened to take over Southern Vietnam thereby turning it into a communist state. Military advisors pressed for American military intervention in order to stop the spread of communism into South Vietnam. John F. Kennedy had personally opposed the spread of communism anywhere in the free world. Clearly, North Vietnam was yet another threat to this. Reports indicated that the North was scaling its forces to prepare for the takeover of Southern Vietnam.

I spent the next several hours sifting through a number of articles on U.S. foreign policy during the 1950s and 1960s. The entire JFK story was now starting to become larger than life. My desire for more information was now becoming an obsession with each passing day.

Vietnam proved to be just as compelling as the Cuban Missile Crisis. From all that I read, it was clear that the issue of Vietnam had begun long before America's involvement. Kennedy inherited the Vietnam problem upon entering office in 1961. Early into Kennedy's presidency some 2000 U.S. forces occupied Vietnam; by 1963 that number had swelled to 15,000. Up to that point the support of the Diem government of South Vietnam had been seen as the only solution to stop the communist insurgence into this sensitive area of Vietnam. (fn)

By the spring of 1963 everything seemed to change. A group of top officials representing the Army of the Republic of Vietnam (ARVN) plotted to overthrow their leader. Given the strain that the Diem government was causing to the American effort in Vietnam, the

Kennedy administration offered covert assistance to this group. The result of this was the assassination of Diem during a coup on Nov 1, 1963. [fn]

It was becoming quite clear that Kennedy was faced with two major problems shortly after entering office in January of 1961. The similarities of both issues were becoming more apparent. As was the case with the Bay of Pigs invasion, Vietnam was a problem Kennedy had inherited based on decisions made by a previous administration. Both situations also required a great deal of damage control in order to justify the involvement by the U.S. government.

I wondered how comfortable John F Kennedy was with his country's involvement in either part of the world. In my mind, Kennedy probably felt the necessity to continue on the policies that had been previously adopted by his predecessors. He had to ensure that his administration had not left itself open to criticism should communism spread further into Latin America as well as other parts of the world!

With each day that passed one thing was becoming abundantly clear. My essay, the impetus for all the events and strange visions that I was witnessing, was now almost becoming an afterthought. I was coming across information that pulled me to a number of different directions, yet all of them revolved around John F Kennedy and the decisions he was faced with shortly after having become President.

The history that surrounded Kennedy's initial term in office was now the focal point of everything. I had come to the conclusion that it became imperative I familiarize myself with all the events surrounding President Kennedy's term. I began to realize the importance of the events that plagued him during his initial time as President. My days were now becoming consumed by more visions, their clarity and repercussions were affecting my every thought.

I scrolled down the many sites that were now becoming commonplace for me. I stumbled onto a particular site and found myself staring at one photo in particular. I later discovered that the photo was that of Allen Dulles, then Director of the CIA. What was this man's connection to President Kennedy? Something inside told me the CIA represented another piece to the ever- growing JFK puzzle. As I began to read articles and de-classified documentation, more revelations came to light.

CHAPTER 3

In its early inception the CIA was given far-reaching powers which gave its agents the authority to partake in operations in and out of the U.S. The CIA was involved in covert operations that led to the assassination of the leaders of countries throughout the world. *(fn)*

During this period the CIA had free reign of covert activity in and outside of the United States. The more I read, the more it became clear that this was truly an entity into itself with the resources and the authority to take part in secret operations that went far beyond the borders of the United States. This included the Bay of Pigs invasion. However, following the failure of the Bay of Pigs invasion, Kennedy made his displeasure of the CIA known to many circles. He quickly sought to minimize the authority and the autonomy the CIA had. His comments and actions did not sit well with the upper hierarchy in the CIA. Relations soon became strained. This became quite evident the more I read.

The net result of the increasing feud between the Whitehouse and the CIA was the resignation of Director Allen Dulles and the subsequent firing of Deputy Director Charles Cabell. These actions did not sit well with the remaining members of the CIA; they saw their power eroding under the Kennedy presidency. *(fn)*

Not only was the CIA at odds with the Kennedy administration's stand on the Bay of Pigs fiasco, it shared the same level of disappointment with members of the military establishment with respect to the issue of Vietnam. I decided to revisit the issue of

President Kennedy and Vietnam. More information soon came to light. The more I read into America's involvement in Vietnam, the more it became evident that President Kennedy's stance towards Vietnam seemed to change dramatically with each month that passed.

Following the assassination of Diem in the fall of 1963, events in Vietnam seemed to have taken a turn for the worse. Kennedy now opposed the full-scale participation of the U.S. army into Vietnam. National Security Action Memorandum no. 263 was to be announced by Kennedy late in 1963. It called for the gradual withdrawal of U.S troupes in Vietnam; the withdrawal program was to begin early in 1964. *(fn)*

High-ranking members of the military establishment were unhappy with the prospect of the United States pulling out. Vietnam was the symbol of communist insurgence. In the minds of many, it had to be stopped at all costs. Vietnam represented a long chain of Presidential decisions that had originally started with the ill-fated Bay of Pigs invasion. As I was soon to discover, the FBI was also a factor in the Vietnam War.

My research into the life of John F Kennedy was now moving in a totally different direction. While the historical revelations that surrounded the Kennedy Presidency were becoming more prevalent in my research, I began to realize that their origins were to provide the backdrop for later events.

J Edgar Hoover, head of the FBI and the President were at odds with one another since Kennedy's earlier days prior to entering political office. Hoover began to monitor his actions during his duty in the U.S. Navy. The information that J. Edgar Hoover possessed during his tenure had far-reaching repercussions. The election of 1960 was one of the closest in American history, the information that the FBI had in its possession posed a threat to President Kennedy's political career. *(fn)*

The very fact that Hoover continued to collect this derogatory evidence against Kennedy illustrated his distrust and dislike of the President. This clearly made their working relationship tenuous at best. I couldn't help but feel a certain sense of apprehension. The Kennedy mystique I had first admired now seemed somewhat tainted with the ever-growing evidence of rifts that clearly existed between Kennedy and the agencies he ultimately ruled over.

I dozed off for several moments, a series of peculiar images made their way into my mind. "Damn civil rights! Who the hell does he think he is, Martin Luther King?" Two individuals stood in an office and were both visibly upset as they spoke. "What did we vote him in for, black rights?" "Black rights, my ass!" The images continued. A host of individuals were questioned one by one before what appeared to be a tribunal of some sort. What I was now witnessing in my mind included some of the same individuals I had seen in previous dreams.

Moments later, I awoke. I stared at the darkness around me and immediately walked to my computer to search the internet for the next couple of hours. I scrolled through a number of newspaper articles of this period in American history. I immediately stumbled upon one that promised to shed some light on my recent dreams. "Mob Hearings to Begin Today" I spent the next several minutes reading a host of articles covering this latest piece of the Kennedy puzzle.

I made my way back to the library the next day and began to sift through a host of articles that covered the latest angle into the ever-growing story that was JFK. As I soon discovered, the Kennedy administration was the first in its attempt to convict mob leaders of crimes they had committed. The mob hearings went on for weeks. Their impact was immediate and far reaching.

As I finished reading the article on these hearings, I noticed that it made reference to film archives. The symbol beside it indicated that the film footage was available to view. I quickly approached the librarian and asked if she could assist me in finding the video. Within minutes, she returned with the subsequent videos in hand.

I made my way to one of the viewing rooms in the library. I looked on as each organized crime figure testified before Robert Kennedy. With every question asked, the response was the same. Kennedy was stern and forthright in his questioning. However, no pertinent information was given by any of the individuals questioned. I couldn't help but feel that Kennedy's attempts were futile. Moments later

Jimmy Hoffa entered the hearings. As they continued the images that I witnessed in my previous thoughts were now coming to life. Each image I had seen was a repeat of the actual events as they had occurred in 1961.

I paused to think about the relevance of what my latest dreams had once again proven. It was clear that I had somehow been given the ability to see events in the past that no one else would have been witness to, except for those present at the time they occurred. What was it that now suddenly made me able to revisit events that had taken place years earlier? It was at the moment that I felt I needed a break from everything I had had now come across. I walked outside and made my way to the vendor across the street. I sat down on the curb and began to eat the hot dog I had purchased from him.

An uneasy feeling suddenly came over me. I glanced over my shoulder across the street. A man stood directly across the street from where I now sat; he stared at me for several moments. His attention was completely focused squarely on me. I felt somewhat uncomfortable at the fact that he hadn't broken his stare. We continued to stare at one another for several more moments until I finally broke my stare. I glanced over at him once more. Although the individual continued to stare at me, for some strange reason I did not feel threatened in any way by him.

I got up and began to walk toward the entrance to the library. I took one last look at the man across the street. He put his head down for a moment then glanced at me once last time. I proceeded to make my way back into the library so as to continue my research.

I spent the remainder of that afternoon combing through articles on the Senate hearings. It soon became apparent that these hearings, while having no real effect on organized crime in America, would be the catalyst of other events that would later transpire in history. I couldn't help but think that there was a reason why I had relived these events years after they had first taken place.

From all I had read many Americans praised the Kennedy administration for the courage it showed in attempting to bring these mob figures to justice, however, the "war against organized crime" created a network of enemies that grew in number with each passing day.

One simple question remained; why did John and Robert Kennedy orchestrate such a "witch hunt" that, in my mind, presented no real chance of success? The JFK story was now becoming more involved and more intense with each passing day. The visions I was seeing with increasing regularity were beginning to have an onerous "feel" to them. With each subsequent dream, it appeared that Kennedy's hold on power was being challenged from every corner. It was becoming clear that the historical information I now came across was leading me towards a path I would have never dreamed of.

I thought back to the individual that had stared at me. His presence did not seem to have an onerous overtone; I wondered inside why I had garnered his attention. It was as if he wanted me to be aware of the fact that I had noticed him looking at me. His presence there was somewhat disconcerting to me simply because of the fact that I was as of yet unaware of whom he was.

A number of revelations began to take shape that "begged" more questions. As I discovered that day, the ties between the Kennedy and the mob were fascinating, to say the least. Many historians hinted at the fact that Chicago mobster Sam Giancana had aided the Kennedy campaign during the 1960 election. It seemed that members of organized crime were content in having John F. Kennedy elected as President of the United States. [fn]

The reasons for their support of Kennedy soon became apparent to me. Kennedy had taken a hard stand against communism during his years in politics that preceded his Presidency. It had included the decision by the American government to assassinate Cuban leader Fidel Castro in September, 1960. Both John and Robert Kennedy shared the same goal where it concerned the overthrow of the Castro regime in Cuba. As I soon discovered, neither were aware of the Mafia's direct involvement in the U.S government's plan to assassinate Castro until well after a year upon taking office. The failure of the Bay of Pigs invasion months earlier had angered a number of camps, each with their own particular agenda. While this one event served to weaken Kennedy's stature with the mob, the actions taken by his brother, Attorney General Robert Kennedy only served to worsen this relationship. [fn]

The story of John F. Kennedy, it seemed had taken a turn in a totally different direction. Its scope now reached the hallowed walls of organized crime. The elements involving the life of John F. Kennedy were increasingly becoming far-reaching. The factors that surrounded the Kennedy administration were to become more and more fascinating with each subsequent piece of information I uncovered.

Robert Kennedy's all-out assault on the mob resulted in the deportation of several members of the mob. Most notable of these was the eventual deportation of reputed New Orleans mob boss Carlos Marcello. I couldn't help but feel that John and Robert Kennedy were playing a very dangerous "cat and mouse" game with segments of the underworld.

I found myself struck with a sense of concern over the direction my research was taking. The Kennedy mystique that had once characterized my original research now seemed to be threatened by the negative forces that surrounded the Kennedy administration. It was at that moment that a sudden image came to me. The image was that of a woman and three men driving together. What immediately struck me was the vehicle they were driving in. It was an older vintage car I had seen in magazines detailing older cars.

The conversation between the woman and these three men soon became heated. It continued on for several minutes and began to deteriorate quickly. Suddenly, the woman was thrown from the vehicle at full speed. She lay motionless for several moments. I held my breath as she slowly began to move. A passing police officer noticed her on the side of the road. The image soon ended as abruptly as it had begun.

I spent the next several minutes trying to figure out the significance of what I had just seen. It seemed to come out of nowhere and did not fit anything I had come across. I began to re-focus on what I had been working on. I made my way downstairs to the kitchen to get something to eat. I made myself a quick sandwich, grabbed a water bottle from the fridge and began to make my way back upstairs. As I approached the door to my room, now half open, I could hear music playing.

I entered the room and heard music playing from the media player on my computer. I hadn't recalled having left the player on prior to leaving the room earlier so I was somewhat surprised by the music now playing. The song being played was not something I immediately recognized. I reached over and grabbed my smart phone resting beside my computer. I opened up the application I had used many times before to identify songs. I picked up the phone and placed it beside the computer speaker. Within seconds it identified the song as being "Sherry", by the Four Seasons. I had never heard of this song before and I was certain I had never downloaded it nor played it before. I turned back to my computer. On a hunch I began to research the song "Sherry". The song hit number one on the billboard top 100 in October of 1962. *(fn)*

The direct correlation was not lost on me. This was the exact time the Cuban Missile Crisis was occurring. I looked down once more at my smart phone, the words "Sherry" by the Four Seasons still strewn across the screen. I made my way back and lay on my bed and simply stared at my computer. I began to think back to all the dreams I had been witnessing, with all their clarity and intricacies.

The strange newspaper originating from the early1960s having suddenly turned up in pristine condition! A song I had never heard of before, representing the exact time frame I had read about hours earlier! The strange individual I had noticed staring at me! What did it all mean? How and why had they now made their way to me? What was the connection between all these events?

Had they been introduced to me for a reason? Were they a precursor of something fascinating, or were they the prelude to a disturbing piece of history still as yet uncovered? What was clear to me was the fact that they were all linked to the ever-growing story of JFK.

CHAPTER 4

Friday came and went without incident, interestingly enough without any dreams and visions. I decided to take another trip to the library. I looked through a few books and more newspaper articles. I made notes and continued to read articles concerning the individuals and events I had read about earlier. A couple of hours soon passed and I started to pack up my things.

As I walked towards the exit doors, I passed by the magazine section and glanced at the various copies that were there. One particular copy of a magazine caught my attention. This particular edition contained a picture of JFK along with other notable individuals who were part of a group being chosen for "man of the century".

The issue seemed interesting, if only to see where JFK was ranked among the most influential people of the 20th century. I quickly put down my knapsack and sat down to read the article. As I perused the magazine, a number of prominent and important individuals had made the list; among them were some that I recognized while others were unfamiliar to me. I turned the next page and saw a large picture of John F. Kennedy. Underneath his picture read the following: "John Fitzgerald Kennedy May 29, 1917- Nov 22, 1963". My jaw dropped, my face turned white. I stared at the photo for several minutes; I then turned and slowly made my way back home.

President Kennedy had died less than three years of taking office! It consumed my every thought that night. As I would soon discover, the disturbing images I was to witness that evening would change everything. A huge crowd greeted President Kennedy upon his arrival. The President attended what appeared to be a large gala in his honor. The images were as clear as ever. The President was given a cowboy hat by one of the dignitaries present. Kennedy remarked that the individual could come to the White House and see him with the hat on. The President's comment drew laughter and applause from all those present.

A large motorcade moved slowly down a crowded street. The plaza was full of onlookers waiting to get a glimpse of the dignitaries as they drove by. The limousine that caught the attention of the huge crowds was none other than that of the President himself. The Governor of Texas sat alongside his wife directly in front of the President and the first lady. As it passed a highway underpass, the images seemed to move slower. Suddenly, without warning the angle to which I was witnessing these events seemed to change.

The Governor suddenly turned his head towards his left and looked to be concerned with events as they were beginning to unfold. A few moments passed when President Kennedy suddenly grabbed his neck. The image ended abruptly without warning.

I awoke covered in sweat. The images I had just witnessed were as vivid as any of the many dreams I had witnessed in my mind over the past few days. It was at that moment that I realized these images held the key to the JFK story. I hesitated several moments before approaching my computer, I slowly typed in the words "death of John Fitzgerald Kennedy".

The information that stood before me would change the perspective of everything I had researched up to that point. To my dismay stood the copies of newspapers dated November 22, 1963 proclaiming the death of John Fitzgerald Kennedy, by assassination! I simply stood in front of my computer staring aimlessly at it for several minutes.

This latest revelation served host to a number of burning questions that now entered my mind. Why was the President of the United States murdered? How could such a heinous crime take place in the United States? More importantly, who was responsible for concocting such a ruthless scheme while actually carrying it out?

I peered out at the window in my room. Never in my wildest dreams would I have foreseen President Kennedy's death in this fashion. A myriad of images poured into my mind, they seemed to continue from where the others had left off.

Many onlookers carried signs while others screamed with enthusiasm, others simply waved at the President as he rode by slowly. The limousine continued on its route passing several other streets until it made a sharp turn around a large building situated in the corner of the street. The images suddenly stopped. I opened my eyes; without hesitation I approached my computer and began to scour the internet for all the information I could find.

One site in particular caught my immediate attention. It included a movie dubbed "Kennedy Assassination-Zepruder film". The letters bearing the words "Zepruder Film" seemed to be in bold type as if imploring me to investigate further. I decided to make my way back to the library the very next day.

I approached the librarian and handed her the slip for my request to view the video. This was the same person that had helped me a couple of days earlier. She studied the request and replied "The Zepruder film, an interesting choice!" I acknowledged the fact that I wanted a copy of the video. "I think you will find it to be interesting viewing indeed!" she responded. Something inside me was now telling me I had discovered perhaps the most important pieces to the JFK puzzle I had been looking for.

She disappeared to the back room and returned with the video cassette in hand. I took if from her and proceeded into one of the private viewing rooms in the library. Although in color, it was clear the movie had been shot by an amateur. Its images were grainy at best. The footage began by showing the Presidential motorcade as is it approached the large waiting crowds eager to catch a glimpse of the President as he drove by. The motorcade continued its slow methodical approach towards the person taking the video.

It was at that exact moment that it became clear; the images I had dreamt about last night were now repeating themselves. The angle of the approaching vehicle matched that of the images I had seen in my dream. It seemed as if the video I was now viewing was picking up from where I had left off in my dream. President Kennedy grasped his neck in obvious pain. Mrs. Kennedy noticed her husband's discomfort and appeared to ask her husband if he was alright? Kennedy continued to hold his hands around his neck. It was abundantly clear, President Kennedy had been shot!

Seconds later, President Kennedy's head was suddenly and violently thrown back by what was clearly a bullet to his head. I flew back on my chair and quickly stopped the video. I now stood staring at the image of the motionless body of the President on the screen before me. I had to step out of the room if only to get some fresh air. I walked pass the librarian's desk and made my way outside; as I did so I glanced back and noticed her staring at me as I continued to make my way outside. I sat on a nearby curb for several minutes to gather my thoughts.

As I put my head down images suddenly came to mind. The scene was one of complete bedlam. A host of nurses now flanked the doctor as he continued to treat the patient before him. From everything that was taking place around them, it was clear that I was now witnessing events occurring in the emergency section of the hospital.

The patient being treated was a young woman in her mid 30s. Although she appeared to be in shock, she begged those around her to listen to what she was saying. The doctor in charge continued his attempts to calm her down. He then asked one of the nurses to give the woman a sedative. She now became more distressed in her attempts to tell those around her the story of the events that had taken place earlier that evening.

The sedative soon began to take effect. She began to calm down, all the while continuing in her attempts to get her message across to anyone that would listen. She then calmly grabbed the doctor's arm and slowly pulled him towards her. She began to whisper in his ear. I looked on in my mind as his demeanor soon changed. She began to fall asleep before them. As she did so the doctor pulled himself back up and simply stared forward for several moments.

His sudden blank stare did not go unnoticed by the nurses that stood by him. He asked the nurses that remained to continue to monitor the woman who had now fallen into a deep sleep. He then turned and walked down the nearby hallway. The images soon ended.

I lifted my head back up as people around me came back into focus. It was at that moment that I realized the individual I had just witnessed was the same woman I had previously dreamt. Why had I now seen this person for a second time? It was as if I was somehow tracing her steps in history.

Like others before, this sudden image appeared to have little relevance to what I had been researching up to that point. It was now getting late; I would have to finish viewing the video tomorrow. I soon made my way back home.

John F. Kennedy, one of the most revered presidents of all time had been assassinated in his own country. As I walked back home I began to think back to the many articles I had read through over the past few weeks. My most recent research pointed to an ever-growing rift between Kennedy and any number of organizations and individuals, all of whom had a personal dislike for both John and Robert Kennedy. Could it be that the net result of this was the removal of Kennedy from office in the most horrific way possible as the whole world looked on?

I made sure that night that I would be home in time to spend dinner with my family. From the looks I had received at dinner it seemed obvious that my absence from home over the past few nights had not gone unnoticed. The last thing I needed right now was to be at "odds" with my parents in any way. My family was the most important part of my life. I couldn't bear to have any kind of rift with them.

For the remainder of that evening a number of thoughts ran through my head. What had I stumbled on? I found myself trying to substantiate all that I had discovered over the past few days. Given all that I had read and witnessed in my mind, I couldn't help but wonder if I was in over my head? One thing was becoming clear. The story of John F. Kennedy had taken on a whole new dimension! What had begun as a simple search for information on President Kenney's life had now turned into a search for the answers behind his death. As had been the case so many times, more images made their way into my mind that evening that would serve only to add to the intrigue that was JFK!

I could clearly see the Presidential limousine as it approached having just passed the oncoming freeway sign. This time however, the image was no longer grainy as in previous dreams. The events that I had first seen began once more. Governor Connally turned his head around to investigate the noise he had just heard behind him.

President Kennedy clasped his hands around his neck. It was clear he had been shot and was in a considerable amount of pain. Once again, Mrs. Kennedy quickly turned to her husband. Moments later a bullet struck President Kennedy in the head. The force of the bullet was exact. Blood and brain matter flew in all directions. I could now see Jacqueline Kennedy's blood stained dress as she turned to the secret service agent that had followed the Presidential limousine.

The dream ended as abruptly as others I had seen recently. I was suddenly awoken by this last image, my face now covered in sweat. I had once again witnessed the murder of President Kennedy. The image of the President being shot kept reappearing in my mind. The clarity of this terribly disturbing image brought to life the horror that the onlookers undoubtedly experienced. More humbling was the horror that Jacqueline Kennedy must have felt having been by her husband's side as he was murdered in cold blood.

I made my way back to the library later that day and immediately entered the viewing room. The copy of the Zepruder film was still where I had left it yesterday. I picked it up and began to play it again. There before me was the image of Kennedy's head drooped over covered in blood.

I continued on where I had left off. I watched in horror as Jacqueline Kennedy frantically motioned to the Secret Service agent following her car for help. The utter chaos that followed was evident as the Secret Service agent climbed aboard the Presidential limousine in a vain attempt to help both the President and Mrs. Kennedy.

The tape captured a few final glimpses of the chaos that followed as the Presidential limousine sped off for nearby Parkland Hospital. I paused the video for a few moments and once again made my way back to the internet station. I continued to scroll down the remainder of the library's videos on the Kennedy assassination. I came across a host of documentaries on the subject and decided to investigate them further. I began to play subsequent videos until I came across a news footage video on the Kennedy assassination.

The images of the bedlam that followed the shooting of the President now were combined with the chilling narrative that described the tragedy that unfolded. As each moment passed, it became clear that my dreams were now taking on a new level of accuracy. I had indeed witnessed events that had taken place almost 50 years earlier! I couldn't help but believe that there was now a reason for my new found ability to witness these events in history. I returned to the video room and continued to watch the remainder of the video footage.

Chaos followed as the Presidential limousine sped off at a high rate of speed in an effort to get the President, now mortally wounded, to the nearest hospital as quickly as possible. Most of the onlookers hoping to get a glimpse of the President had now fallen to the ground having realized that the President had been shot.

A policeman on a motorcycle that had followed the motorcade suddenly jumped off his bike and ran towards a small wooded area adjacent to the spot where Kennedy had been shot. As he did so, a number of onlookers rushed behind him as well, seemingly convinced that at least one shot was fired at the President from that exact spot.

I turned to the VCR and proceeded to shut if off. I began to grow tired having now spent well over four hours there. Viewing the different videos on JFK in the library was now becoming a problem. I had to be able to view them when I wanted to, on my own time!

Many of the videos in question were reference videos, still in VHS format which were not allowed to leave the library. I had to somehow make copies of these videos in order to view them at home. How was I going to get another machine in order to copy each tape? I looked at the VCR in front of me; it appeared to be fairly new so my excuse would have to be a good one. I looked at the back of the unit and discovered it had a fuse. With a small yank I pulled it out only slightly to the point where the machine's power suddenly turned off.

Without looking suspicious, I slowly turned the unit around and proceeded to the librarian's desk. I told her that the VCR in my viewing room was not working. "That's funny that is a fairly new unit!" She then followed me into the room and proceeded to turn the VCR on, to no avail. She then turned to look at the back of it and checked the power cord. All seemed to be normal.

I began to get anxious as she looked at the remainder of the back portion of the unit. I prayed she would not notice the fuse I had tampered with. She turned the unit back to its front and proceeded to get another VCR. She returned a few minutes later with a newer unit. "You can pass me the old one and I'll get it out of your way". "NO"! I exclaimed.

She was startled by my insistence on leaving both units in the room. I quickly explained that I would put the new VCR on top of the old one so as to make it easier for me to use it. She stared at me for a moment and agreed to leave both of them in the room. I waited a few minutes then proceeded to slowly open the door to the room until I was able to see that she had returned back to her desk.

I quietly exited the library and ran home as fast as I could in order to pick up blank tapes I had at home. I snuck upstairs to my room without being seen. I picked up three blank VHS tapes and put them into a plastic bag sitting on my computer desk. Time was now going to be a factor.

I quickly made my way back to the library. As I approached the viewing room I noticed that the librarian had not yet returned to her desk. I quickly glanced to my right and saw that she was helping another student find books. As I entered the room I was relieved to find that everything was as I had left it moments earlier.

I proceeded to connect the cables from one VCR to the other; I re-inserted the fuse into the VCR and watched as it came back to life. I then reached into my bag and grabbed one of several blank tapes that I was going to use to copy each video. The only question was whether or not I was going to be able to finish copying what I wanted without having someone catch me. As far as I was concerned, it was worth the risk since it was the only way for me to view the tapes at home.

An hour passed and the Zepruder video was now complete. I placed the copied tape in my bag and proceeded to remove the video and copy another. I stumbled onto several more videos on the Kennedy assassination. Each subsequent video covered different aspects of the assassination. Most of the videos were a half hour to one hour in length. Two videos could be copied on each blank tape.

I now wrestled with the debate being fought in my mind. How would I be able to finish copying the movies at a later date? Failure to do so would mean missing out on crucial information at home. Doing so however, meant I might be late in getting home. I began a steady procession of previewing and recording each subsequent tape without viewing them. My cell phone began to ring. It was my home number. I quickly looked up at the clock in the room and saw it was now 6:15pm. I was already 15 minutes late! I nervously continued to finish up the copying of the remaining 3 videos.

My cell phone rang again; it was my brother's cell number. I answered and began to talk to him. My brother Ted had always looked after me and had always been the protective brother anyone would wish to have as a sibling. He told me that both my parents were now visibly upset at the fact that I had missed another dinner. I asked him to try and stall for me as long as he could. He assured me he would do his best to try and diffuse the situation. I thanked him for trying to smooth things over at home.

Moments later, the door suddenly swung open. It was Mrs. Donahue.

She slowly closed the door behind her and stared directly at the two video machines that were before her. Her facial expression left no doubt. I had more explaining to do. Having now noticed the name tag pinned onto her vest, I responded, "Mrs. Donahue, I can explain."

"Your explanation better be a good one young man. I'm sure you are aware of the fact that it is against library policy to copy videos without the consent of library staff first!" I anxiously began to explain the crux of my project, showing her the notes I had made describing everything I had come across over the past few weeks. For some inexplicable reason I felt safe in telling her all that I had experienced. It was as if I had to confide in her all of the events I had been experiencing.

I began to explain the dreams I had witnessed in my mind over the past few days. She listened intently as I described how the complexity of the dreams I was experiencing had increased with each given day. I sensed however that she wasn't totally convinced with all that I had just told her.

I reached into my bag and pulled out the newspaper I had first come across days earlier. I handed the newspaper to her and looked on as her expression changed dramatically. She had been totally caught off guard. "This can't be an actual copy of the Dallas Star!" "There's only one way to find out", I responded. We then both made our way over to the microfiche and searched the records for past newspaper articles.

Mrs. Donahue scrolled slowly as she approached the edition printed on Nov 22, 1963. I could see the light of the screen's reflection on her face; it was completely overshadowed by the perplexed look that had overtaken her. The image before her was that of the exact copy of the Dallas Star as it was written in 1963.

A man sat down in the chair beside us. He glanced at the newspaper we had brought with us. Mrs. Donahue quickly folded the newspaper before he could make out its contents. We made our way back to the viewing room and tried to collect our thoughts. "Have you told anyone else about this?" I assured her that I had not. We spoke for several more minutes.

Mrs. Donahue wanted to know all of the details of what I had seen in me dreams. It was clear that she was now convinced of the fact that I had been entirely truthful to her. "You can't tell anyone of what you know and what you have seen over the last little while." I immediately sensed there was something about what I had revealed to her that was weighing on her mind.

We were both startled by a sudden knock on the door. She opened the door slowly; it was one of her assistants indicating that it was already a half hour past library closing hours. We spoke for several minutes then left together. I watched as she made her way to her car; she took a moment to look back at me as I began to make my way back home. All the while, I kept thinking about what I was going to say to my parents. My heart began to race as I began to approach our house.

CHAPTER 5

As I turned the corner onto my street I felt the sudden feeling I was being watched. I noticed a man standing on the street directly across from my house. He leaned against the lamp post he now stood beside. I couldn't help but feel uneasy by his stare. He appeared to be in his mid 40s. He was tall and wore a long black coat. He wore dark sunglasses so as to cover a portion of his face. I slowed down almost to a full stop as I finally reached the driveway to my home.

I made my way up our front porch and proceeded to open the front door. I turned to look at the individual one more time. He did not break his stare. I made my way inside and quickly looked through the window of our living room. The individual outside hadn't yet moved and simply continued to focus on my whereabouts.

I was taken back by the sense of forthrightness this strange individual conveyed. He looked totally comfortable with what he was doing. It was as if he had done this many times before. A sense of fear now began to overwhelm me. Who was this individual? More importantly, what was his interest in me? I looked on as he slowly glanced over at me one last time and made his way down the street.

What immediately struck me was the nonchalant manner to which he conducted himself. He was totally oblivious to those around him, nor was he concerned at what others may have thought about his presence here. It seemed that his sole purpose was to make me aware of the fact that I had been noticed.

I quietly made my way in to the house without making noise. I could hear a conversation taking place in the family room. I sat down in our living room couch for a few moments in order to compose myself. It seemed that the information I had come across over the past couple of weeks had somehow raised a level of concern. Who did the strange individual represent?

I couldn't help but wonder if the man I saw had any connection to the individual I had seen days earlier in front of the library. What was becoming apparent was the fact that my research had caught the attention of others around me. What was equally as disturbing was the difference between the two strange individuals I had now come across the past couple of weeks. While the other seemed not to pose any threat to me, the man I just came across represented something totally different, and potentially dangerous.

Did the information I had come across over the past few weeks somehow pose a threat to something or someone? The fact that both these individuals had gone to great lengths to garner my attention now spoke volumes of their need to send a message to me. What was now troublesome to me was the latest message being sent. To make matters worse, I now had to face my parents. I hadn't taken more than two steps towards the other room when I heard my name being called.

I slowly made my way into the family room where both my parents were waiting for me, both were visibly upset. My father addressed me first making it clear he wasn't happy with the fact that I had been away from home for hours on end over the past several weeks. I began to explain the research I was involved with. My mother immediately cut me off and reiterated everything my father had just said. I assured them both that I would do my best to no longer let my research interfere with my family responsibilities.

I made my way back to the solace of my bedroom. Moments later, I was startled by a knock on my door. I made my way to the door and slowly opened it. I was somewhat relieved to see that it was my older brother Ted. He walked in; I proceeded to close the door behind him. "John, is there something that you need to tell me?" He continued, "I mean, I don't think you've spent this much time at the library in all the years you've been at school!" Now you have me covering for you?" Do you mind telling me what is going on?"

Having always trusted Ted with any and all secrets in the past, I began to describe all that I had stumbled across over the past few days. I told him about the information I had come across. I described the dreams I had been having, including the individuals I had recently encountered. I showed him all the evidence I had discovered.

Ted's blank stare said it all! The look on his face was one of surprised as well as concern. The concern was undoubtedly over the strange occurrences and individuals I had come across in a relatively short span of time. Did he think I was losing my mind? We spoke for several more minutes. Ted agreed to calm my parent's growing concerns in return for my promise to update him on all that I was to come across during my subsequent research.

He then reminded me of our annual family trip to the cottage that was now days away. As a family we all looked forward to this annual outing. I certainly didn't want any of the tension I had created recently jeopardizing this annual event. I reassured him I would do my best not to spoil it. As he left minutes later I felt somewhat relieved knowing I had been able to share what I had uncovered with the one person I knew I could trust.

I spent the next day at school predisposed by the images I was now witnessing on a daily basis. I tried to map out in my mind what I was going to research next. I was then interrupted by a couple of classmates who reminded me that soccer tryouts were to start that same afternoon.

I made my way onto the school soccer field later that afternoon. The practice lasted for well over an hour. Several of us made the one mile jog around the track that circled the circumference of the soccer field. I made the final turn on lap four when I noticed an individual leaning against the fence. I slowed down to discover it was the same individual I had seen days earlier in front of the library. My best friend Jim noticed I had slowed to a complete stop. "What's the matter John?"

He noticed the individual I had been staring at. "Who is he John?" I immediately responded, "I don't quite know". "Well he seems to be staring at you! Do you guys know one another? "No", I responded, "but I have a feeling I will soon." The man continued to stare at me. He then smiled and acknowledged my stare. As was the case the first time I saw him, I did not feel threatened in any way by him. It was becoming clear that he had been keeping an interest in me. What concerned me was the fact that his continuing presence confirmed to me that I was of some interest to him. As was the case with the other individual I had come across, it seemed obvious that the source of his interest in me was undoubtedly the information I had come across regarding the assassination of President Kennedy.

I made my way off the field and glanced back once more at the man who continuously stared at me. As I exited the front entrance of the school I glanced around once to see if he was still following me. I felt somewhat relieved to see that he had now left.

As I lay in bed later that evening, I thought back to all that had transpired that day. All the while I couldn't help but wonder who the strange individual was. Was he somehow associated with the other strange man I had seen in front of the library days earlier? The fact that I was completely enthralled by the many aspects that surrounded John F. Kennedy's Presidency no longer came as a surprise to me. Indeed, from everything I had read it was clear that the Kennedy assassination was viewed by many as one of the most important events of the 20th century. I was finding myself absorbed with every aspect of it.

I stared at the newspaper I had stumbled on days earlier lying on my desk. I couldn't help but to think back to the reaction of Mrs. Donahue. It was the tangible proof that left no doubt in either one of our minds that all the visions and dreams I had witnessed were occurring for a reason. I wasn't completely sure as to what the real reasons were. Something inside me suggested I was to find out sooner rather than later.

I slowly closed my eyes and watched as more images came to focus. The man was carried off in handcuffs surrounded by a bevy of police. He was clearly overwhelmed by the confusion that surrounded him. He was fingerprinted and was quickly taken in for questioning.

Reporters kept a vigil around the police department hoping to catch a glimpse of him.

He emerged and spoke to reporters as he was escorted by them, "No I have not yet been charged with that yet, in fact the first I heard of it was when the reporter told me so." The individual was once again swarmed by a host of reporters recording his every word. *(fn)*

I was immediately awoken. I got up and began to view one of the videos I had copied from the library. I fast-forwarded for several minutes until the individual I had just dreamt about appeared. I began to play the video once more. The narrator of the video described the individual as Lee Harvey Oswald, the man accused of being the lone assassin of President Kennedy.

I continued to watch the video until it reached the portion that covered Oswald's capture and subsequent questioning. I soon realized I was again viewing the exact scenes I had previously witnessed in my mind. These coincidences were now becoming increasingly commonplace.

A reporter informed Oswald that he had in fact been charged with the murder of President Kennedy. Oswald appeared visibly shaken by the information that he had now been notified of. It was clear from his facial expressions that Oswald was overwhelmed by the commotion that surrounded his arrest.

I spent the next day pouring over documents and books surrounding Oswald. From all I had read, it was clear that Lee Harvey Oswald's life could only be characterized as one full of contradictions. As I began to investigate his life further, I quickly realized that Oswald's life was as fascinating as that of President Kennedy.

Lee Harvey Oswald's life was filled with a series of anomalies that plagued him throughout his life. Oswald's father died at a young age. As a result of this Oswald and his family moved to a number of different American cities. He enlisted in the U.S. Marines on October 24, 1956, six days after his 17th birthday. During his time as a marine Oswald was cajoled by fellow marines for his bad marksmanship. Oswald was given the nickname of "Oswaldkovitch" because of his affinity towards communism.

In spite of his open support of communism, the Marine Corps provided Oswald with radar training, security clearance, and placed him at the Atsugi Air Force Base in Japan. During the remainder of his tenure in the Marines Oswald was court-martialed twice. Oswald was given a dishonorable discharge from the Marine Reserves. With every document and article I read about Lee Harvey Oswald, it became increasingly evident that Oswald fit perfectly into the JFK puzzle that was becoming more convoluted with each passing day.

In the spring of 1961 Oswald met and later married 19 year old Marina Nikolayevna Prusakova. Interestingly enough, her uncle was a top official in the Minsk MVD, the Russian equivalent of the FBI. Given his new contacts, Oswald was given passports and Visas that allowed him to return to the United States with his wife and newborn daughter. These events all happened despite the fact that Oswald had married a Soviet woman, all at the height of the Cold War between the United States and Russia.

Oswald had been given a great deal of latitude by both the Soviet and American governments. As I was about to discover, the Oswald story was soon to take on more twists and turns. Upon returning to America in 1962, Oswald moved to Dallas and took a number of low-paying jobs. Oswald worked away from his family during the week while his wife and daughter were boarders of a Quaker family in the Dallas area.

In the spring of 1963, using the alias "Alex Hidel", Oswald purchased two firearms through mail-order. He ordered a revolver and an Italian made Mannlicher-Carchano rifle. In April 1963 Oswald's story took yet another twist. Oswald traveled to New Orleans to find work. While in New Orleans, Oswald founded the Fair Play for Cuba Committee. In October of 1963 he returned to Dallas and took a low paying job at the Texas School Book Depository Building located in the heart of Dallas.

I returned home and spent the remainder of the evening in bed simply going through everything I had read about Oswald. As I dosed off to sleep, the images that I had witnessed the day previous now continued in my mind.

Oswald was asked by newsmen about his black eye, he answered "A cop hit me." He was then asked about his earlier arraignment; Oswald replied "Well I was questioned by Judge Johnston. However, I protested at that time that I was not allowed legal representation during that very short and sweet hearing. I really don't know what the situation is about. Nobody has told me anything except that I am accused of murdering a policeman. I know nothing more than that, and I do request someone to come forward to give me legal assistance." *(fn)*

A reporter shouted out "Did you kill the President" Oswald replied, "No I have not been charged with that. In fact, nobody has said that to me yet. The first thing I heard about it was when the newspaper reporters in the hall asked me that question...I did not shoot anyone." The images in my mind ended abruptly. *(fn)*

As I thought back to all I had seen that night, I couldn't help but think how the lives of Kennedy and Oswald mirrored one another. Lee Harvey Oswald's life, like that of President Kennedy, was also full of surprises. One thing was for certain, the Oswald story fit perfectly into the persona that was John F. Kennedy.

From everything I had read Lee Harvey Oswald looked like an individual completely overwhelmed by everything and everyone around him. He certainly did fit the character of the man responsible for assassinating the President of the United States.

The characters that were involved in the assassination of President Kennedy were growing, not only in number, but in significance as well. As I was soon to discover, the images that I was to witness that evening would throw everything into disarray.

CHAPTER 6

Oswald was handcuffed and being led to a waiting car by two police officers. Surrounding them on both sides was a line of reporters all clambering to get another shot of the man accused of murdering the President of the United States. He continued to walk closer towards the waiting car. Without warning, a man suddenly flung himself in front of Oswald. A single shot was fired. Oswald gasped in pain from his wound. He was subsequently put on a stretcher and transported to nearby Parkland Hospital via ambulance. Officers had quickly converged on the individual that had shot Oswald. He was quickly apprehended and taken into custody by a number of police officers present. The image disappeared as quickly as it had come.

I spent the next day combing the internet for information on the fate of Lee Harvey Oswald. I soon found myself immersed in the circumstances surrounding Oswald's death. Jack Ruby, Oswald's assassin represented yet another twist in the Kennedy assassination. As I read more about Jack Ruby it was clear that this individual served only to further complicate the details surrounding the assassination of John F. Kennedy. The information and, more importantly, the individuals that I had now stumbled upon were as fascinating as any I had initially stumbled on. They were all leading to something on a grander scale!

The strange circumstances surrounding the life of Jack Ruby were as interesting as those that characterized the life of Oswald. Still, the facts and anomalies that provided the backdrop of Jack Ruby's life were paramount if I was to determine what role Ruby played in President Kennedy's death.

Ruby was born to a home whose family life was unstable, to say the least. By the age of 10 Ruby found himself on the streets of Chicago trying to find ways to provide for himself as well as the rest of his brothers and sisters. From his teen years onward, Ruby was to have a number of "run-ins" with the law. In late 1959 Ruby helped establish the Sovereign Club, a posh, exclusive adult club. By 1963 its name had been changed to the Carousel Club. It became one of only three burlesque clubs operating in downtown Dallas. The Carousel Club was a lucrative operation that attracted a large cliental including a number of city officials and police department staff.

As was now becoming commonplace to me, I once again found myself having spent several hours piecing together information about an individual I had no previous knowledge of. What reason did Jack Ruby have to kill Lee Harvey Oswald? More importantly, where did it all fit in with respect to the assassination of President Kennedy?

Although the exact nature of his relationship to members of the Dallas Police department was not totally known, it is clear that Ruby had a keen interest in the inner workings of police work. It soon became apparent that Ruby had more than a passing relationship with a number of officers in the Dallas Police Department. A number of these police officers frequented Ruby's Carousel Club and were given special privileges afforded only to those of higher status. From all I read, it became apparent that Jack Ruby regarded many officers of the Dallas Police Department as close personal friends. *(fn)*

Like Oswald before him, Jack Ruby represented another peculiar piece of the strange puzzle now taking shape. As I tried to absorb this newfound information, more images made their way to my mind that night.

The ghostly looking airplane taxied onto the runway during the early evening hours. A number of television cameras stood by waiting for its contents to be unloaded. The cameras caught the images of the casket being lowered from the plane. Things became somber as Jacqueline Kennedy exited the plane. With his wife by his side Lyndon

Baynes Johnson spoke for the first time as President of the United States. He spoke of the great loss, and of how he would do his best during the immediate time of transition.

I awoke and immediately made my way to my computer. I began to search for any clues to the images I had just seen. I soon found the answers to what I was now looking for. As was the case with everything else I had researched, the Kennedy funeral was as grandiose as the man it honored.

Members of the Kennedy family, close friends, government officials, and other members of the diplomatic community arrived at the White House in order to pay their final respects to Kennedy whose body was lying in state. Former Presidents Harry S. Truman and Dwight D. Eisenhower spoke for the first time. An endless stream of mourners paraded the route towards the President's casket hoping to catch one last glimpse of their fallen President.

Those who made up the line numbered into the thousands. The former President's body was then placed on a caisson and was transported to a nearby church. As his father's coffin rode by him, John F. Kennedy Jr. took a step forward and saluted his slain father. As I viewed the footage before me, the images I was now seeing seemed as real as the day this event took place. I couldn't help but feel a genuine sense of loss.

The days that followed the assassination of Kennedy were mired in round the clock television coverage. All three major networks employed countless staff and reporters whose sole job was to bring the events to the homes of all Americans. Television was a relatively new medium for information; yet, during the subsequent days of coverage all three networks came to the fore. The cost to the networks for their coverage of the assassination and the days that followed was estimated to be in the neighborhood of $40 million. The images that came from television were transmitted to twenty-three countries all over the world, including the Soviet Union. In the United States alone, it was estimated that 93% of all televisions in the nation were tuned to the coverage of the assassination and funeral of President Kennedy. [fn]

These numbers were unprecedented, laying more credence to the enormity of this event; it also helped explain the effect that it had on the entire world. For over three tumultuous days, the assassination of John F. Kennedy transcended all facets of American life. I closed my eyes for a moment only to capture a glimpse of the individual I had just seen.

The tall, older-looking man handed, what appeared to be a rather thick book to President Johnson. A number of cameramen and reporters looked on and took picture after picture commemorating the event. As had been the case so many times, the image ended as quickly as it had begun.

I began to view some of the videos I had copied days earlier. As I quickly discovered, the individual I had seen was then Chief Justice Earl Warren. The event in question was the issuing of the Warren Commission Report. I had stumbled across his name several times during my research. It was clear that my passing interest in this individual was about to change in a hurry.

The next several hours were spent finding out all I could about the Warren Commission and, more importantly, its role in the JFK assassination. The information I was to come across opened up a whole different avenue that would change the direction and scope of my research into the Kennedy assassination.

Events passed swiftly following the assassination of Kennedy. Newly sworn President Lyndon Johnson immediately appointed a panel to investigate the killing of the former President. The panel was to be headed by Chief Justice Earl Warren thereby prompting its name as the Warren Commission. The panel also included John J. McCloy, former High Commissioner of the American zone of occupied Germany, congressman Gerald Ford (future President of the United Sates), and surprisingly enough, former CIA director Allan Dulles. The more I read about the Warren Commission, the more apparent its role in history became.

The Commission's sole purpose was to determine who was responsible for the assassination of President Kennedy. By the permission of then President Johnson, and through a vote in congress the commission was given the power to investigate the assassination as thoroughly as required. The commission was also granted the full co-operation of the FBI and all necessary federal agencies to conduct its investigation. It was declared to be the lone government body authorized to investigate the Kennedy assassination. In doing so the Johnson administration had given the Warren Commission full jurisdiction on everything pertaining to the Kennedy assassination. More importantly, this meant that neither the Dallas Police Department nor the state of Texas was allowed to investigate the murder of the President. All this was despite the fact the assassination had occurred in the state of Texas. *(fn)*

What became clear was the simple fact that all information and evidence collected during the initial police investigation in the hours following the assassination, would now have to be turned over to the Warren Commission and the agents it employed. The Commission was appointed by then President Johnson on November 29, 1963, just one week after the shooting of President Kennedy. Chief Justice Warren submitted the commission report to President Johnson on September 24, 1964, less than a year after it was commissioned. In reading numerous articles and papers on the Warren Commission, it soon became clear that many observers and historians had serious doubts with the many conclusions found in the hundreds of pages that made up the report.

The information contained in the Warren Commission, while fascinating, seemed "littered" with a trail of contradictions. Like everything else I had come across, it only added to the existing controversy surrounding the assassination of President Kennedy. Upon studying the report in the hours that followed I began to have my own doubts with many of its findings.

First and foremost, the Warren Commission concluded that Lee Harvey Oswald acted alone and was the sole assassin responsible for the assassination of John F. Kennedy as well as Officer J.D. Tippet, shot and killed shortly after President Kennedy. According to the Commission there had been no conspiracy involved in the death of President Kennedy; it concluded that Oswald had no accomplices. It stated that Lee Harvey Oswald had fired three shots from the sixth floor of the Texas Schoolbook Depository where he had just begun to work a short few weeks earlier. According to the Commission the gun used by Lee Harvey Oswald to kill President Kennedy was identified as a 6.5mm Mannlicher-Carcano bolt-action rifle. *(fn)*

Perhaps the most telling conclusion put forth by the Warren Commission was its assertion that the second bullet fired from Oswald's rifle changed directions several times upon entering President Kennedy's back ultimately resting on Governor Connally's left thigh. According to the Warren Commission the third and final shot fired by Oswald killed President Kennedy. It also concluded that the subsequent killing of Lee Harvey Oswald by Jack Ruby was a spontaneous act predicated by Ruby's professed need to spare Jacqueline Kennedy the ordeal of bringing Oswald to trial. *(fn)*

Among the many other conclusions put forward by the Warren Commission, its findings made it clear that Ruby had no significant ties to organized crime. According to the Warren Commission, Ruby acted alone in the assassination of Oswald. The "magic bullet", as it was later "dubbed" by historians proved to be the fatal shot that killed President Kennedy. *(fn)*

Experts questioned aloud how this one bullet could be responsible for causing so much damage to both President Kennedy and Governor Connally who were sitting in front and behind one another? I quickly shared their sentiment.

The articles covering the information I came across seemed endless. I spent the better portion of the next afternoon at the library searching for all that I could. Glancing at my watch I quickly realized that it was now almost 5:30pm. It was imperative that I be home in time for dinner. I quickly put my books into my school bag and began the short walk towards home.

I made the final turn on the street adjacent to my house. As I rounded the corner, I began to slow down. I now stopped dead in my tracks. The individual I had seen the previous day at school now stood by the fire hydrant located on the boulevard directly in front of our house.

He then began to approach me. I slowly made my way to him.

"John, my name is William Montgomery." He put out his hand to shake mine. I reached out and shook his hand. He then continued, "Do you mind if we go for a walk? It's important that we talk!"

I turned to look around me. There was no one else on our street. I looked down at my watch. The individual turned and surveyed the street just as I had moments earlier. I looked down at my watch once again. It was now 5:45pm. He had now noticed my perusal of the time. His quick perception of my actions was not lost on me. I was somewhat re assured to see that the street was empty and that he had come alone.

He then motioned towards the park. We both turned and made the short walk to the park entrance located at the other end of our street. We sat on the park bench located in the middle of the park. Mr. Montgomery began to explain the reasons why he had been following me. "John, you may not be aware of this yet, but your research and subsequent investigation into the life, and more importantly, the death of John F. Kennedy has caught the attention of a select few people". I responded to back to him. "How is that possible? The only two people I have told about my research are Mrs. Donahue, the librarian, and my brother Ted. I can assure you that neither of the two has told anyone else about what we know."

He then asked what the source had been for most of my research. I quickly responded that most of the information I had come across had come from the internet. I now hesitated for a moment. He quickly responded. "That's just it. You need to realize that every site you have visited repeatedly has been "red flagged" and monitored by the agency I work for. It is an agency not many people are aware of. But I can tell you it does exist, as do others. The individuals that run these agencies were "on to you" the moment you typed in the call words 'JFK ASSASSINATION'."

"You have stumbled onto the information regarding the Kennedy assassination for one simple reason. It is fate that you were given your current assignment in school. It started you on the journey of information you have now come across. The direction it has taken you has now brought you to the precipice of no return."

"You must now take the next step in addressing a terrible "wrong" committed in the past in order to save your own future, as well as the future of everyone around you. You have been given a special gift that allows you to see events in the past. It is a gift, however, that comes with great responsibility, one that can be dangerous if it is not handled carefully!"

He continued, "You must stay the course and continue to delve into everything involved in the assassination of President Kennedy! You don't know this yet, but it is inevitable that the course you are currently moving towards will take you to places you would never have expected to visit. You must "stay the course" and let your journey take you to where you destiny leads you!"

I quickly interrupted him. "But how will I know where to go? And how will I know what to do when I get there?" He quickly responded, "You've come this far, you now have to finish what you've started! I must, however caution you of the fact that other agencies have been monitoring you internet activity as well. Your IP address has been monitored for quite some time, both at home and at the library. It is my understanding that you have been followed by another individual as well." I acknowledged such, all the while wondering how he had been privy to my contact with the other strange individual.

"John, you must be careful where you go. You must take routes that are out in the public with others around you so as to remain safe. Ours must be the last conversation you have alone with anyone, no matter who they claim to be. I will continue to monitor your movements but I cannot guarantee my own safety, let alone yours!"

"We are probably being monitored as we speak. I would not put anything past the individuals involved in the other agencies who`s attention you have garnered as well. These are individuals who do not wish to have any new evidence "leaked" as it pertains to the Kennedy assassination. Their job is to keep this information closed to the general public, not to have anything uncovered that would run counter to the original conclusions originally put forth by history."

He stopped for several moments having realized the affect his words now had on me. I simply sat there speechless, not knowing what to say. There were so many elements that had now been thrown at me. It was at that point that he realized he had to intercede and try to quell the fear now obvious through my facial expressions.

"I realize I've introduced quite a few things to you at one time. You need to know what you're up against. I can't tell you what to do but you will realize in time what your next course of action must be. Just know that it is imperative that you finish what you have started. You have been given a special opportunity to make a real difference in the lives of many. Don't throw that opportunity away!" "Will we meet again?" I asked. He quickly responded. "I can't answer that. It will all depend on what your next actions are. Your fate is in your own hands!"

He then got up and reached out to shake my hand. I did the same and shook his hand. He turned and began to walk towards the southerly pathway that led to another exit from the park. I then began to make the slow walk back towards the entranceway to the park. I turned back once more to look at him, but he was gone.

CHAPTER 7

I tried to pay attention to the conversations that took place for the remainder of dinner that night, all the while thinking about all that Montgomery had said to me earlier that evening. On several occasions I felt my father`s stares. It was clear he was suspicious that something else had been on my mind.

I excused myself from dinner and made my way back to my room. I couldn't help but wonder what the image I had daydreamed about during dinner meant. The event had some sort of importance to events I had already come across. I was still unclear as to what its significance was but I knew it was of vital importance. What I was sure of was the fact that the isolation from my family I had been displaying over the past few days was becoming obvious to my parents.

As I lay on my bed I stared at the light from the moon that came from my bedroom window. I thought about everything Mr. Montgomery had revealed to me. I couldn't help but feel like I had opened up a Pandora's Box into everything surrounding the assassination of John F. Kennedy.

It seemed that the scope of my foray into the Kennedy assassination had far reaching ramifications. The parameters I was now dealing with had all but changed. My every move was being scrutinized. I now had to be careful with everything I was to do from hereon in. Although he pointed out the hazards my research had created, his underlying message was clear. It was imperative that I complete what I had now started.

I began to think back to everything that he and I had spoken about earlier that day. Clearly the interest my research had generated suggested that there were elements of the Kennedy assassination I hadn't yet uncovered.

Our annual family cottage weekend was now a couple days away. Knowing how special this trip was to our family, I had to do my best in the coming days to alleviate some of the tension my research was causing with my family. One thing was certain; the puzzle that made up the John F. Kennedy story was growing bigger with each piece of history I was now uncovering on a daily basis. I was now becoming totally consumed in the JFK story. There seemed to be no shortage of intrigue.

If I was going to try and find the missing piece to what I knew hadn't yet been uncovered, I would have to revisit some of the historical evidence I had unearthed previously. Though I knew that I was now immersing myself in the history of years passed, the information I had stumbled on had led me to avenues I would never have dreamed of discovering. Each one led me closer to the real truth behind the assassination of President Kennedy. More images unfolded in my mind that night, images that went much deeper in explaining the reasons for what I had witnessed over the past few weeks.

The courtroom was abuzz with an air of anticipation. The person speaking appeared to be the lead lawyer in the case and began to discuss the arguments that made up his case. Within a few moments, it became clear that the topic of discussion was the assassination of John F. Kennedy. Everyone present was riveted to what was being said. The dream ended as abruptly as it came.

I made what was now becoming a daily trek to the library in order to find out more of what I had witnessed in my mind. Mrs. Donahue was in that night. I approached her and began to describe what I had seen. She immediately became interested in what I had told her of. The one name that stood out in this latest dream was that of 'Mr. Blakey'. We both approached the internet booths and proceeded to find the significance of this individual, an individual she herself was not immediately familiar with.

Several searches later proved to be successful. I quickly called Mrs. Donahue over and turned her attention to the result on the screen. The House Select Committee on Assassinations (HSCA) was the key to everything I had seen in my latest dream. We spent the next several hours combing through the internet until we uncovered several articles on this Committee.

It seemed the never ending kaleidoscope of avenues that were strewn throughout the journey that surrounded the Kennedy assassination kept growing with each day that passed. This latest revelation I had just stumbled on served only to accentuate this point even more.

The information I had been drawn to was as compelling as any I had come across. The Warren Commission became public knowledge in 1964. From its inception, many investigators, and later many historians, questioned the conclusions that were outlined in the hundreds of pages that made up the report.

As I had now discovered, the dissention it created gained strength in the years that followed. This culminated in a public outcry for a new investigation of the events and individuals involved in the assassination of John F. Kennedy in Dallas. As a result of this The U.S. House of Representatives voted to create the House Select Committee on Assassinations (HSCA) in September 1976.

I turned the page only to discover a picture of its chief counsel G. Robert Blakey. The face and name was now immediately familiar to me, this despite having never researched or know of him before.

The HSCA was kept in place from its inception till January 1979, the year the committee issued its report. As I quickly discovered, the conclusions put forth by the HSCA were equally as startling as those first put forth by the Warren Commission more than a decade earlier.

What became apparent was the fact that the assassination of John F. Kennedy in 1963 and the interest it garnered had not waned in the years that followed his death. This was predicated on the details of his assassination that did not sit well with most Americans wanting to know the truth behind his untimely death.

Having not grown up in this era, I could only imagine the sense of lost and outcry most Americans felt. I now felt it myself, decades after his death; this despite the fact I had not lived during the time of his Presidency. It served as more proof of the effect this one man had on a nation, if not the entire world.

I soon discovered, interestingly enough, that the HSCA agreed with the Warren Commission's conclusion that the same bullet was responsible for a number of injuries suffered by both Governor Connally and President Kennedy. The HSCA made the assertion that Lee Harvey Oswald had fired this shot as well as the fatal head shot that killed President Kennedy. (fn)

Its initial conclusions were disappointing to me in that they seemed to give more credence to the factuality of the Warren Commission report. This caused me a certain level of consternation in that I had hoped that this investigation would find more answers that those originally uncovered by the Warren Commission. However, as I read further into the HSCA report the conclusions I had hoped for did eventually come to light.

Along with its initial findings, the HSCA came to a number of conclusions that differed from those found in the Warren Report of 1964. Many of these not only served to shatter the many myths put forth by the Warren commission, they also served to verify what I had quietly suspected all along. I spent the remainder of the evening searching the internet for everything I could find on the HSCA report.

Each subsequent revelation it put forth only served to quell the fire that burned inside of me. The conclusions I had hoped for were now seemingly supported by facts put forth by exports in the field. It seemed that justice was finally being served in solving the mystery behind those responsible for the assassination of President Kennedy.

Amongst its many findings, the HSCA report hinted at the possibility of the mafia involvement in the assassination of President Kennedy. Most startling was the revelation which concluded that there had been four shots fired in Dallas that day, not three as originally suggested in the Warren Report. The HSCA went a step further and concluded the probability that one shot had been fired from the grassy knoll area located in Dealy Plaza. (fn)

Indeed, the HSCA report brought forth a number of new revelations that threatened to blow the Kennedy assassination wide open. The Warren Commission's findings paled in comparison.

First and foremost was the evidence that came from a police patrolman riding adjacent to President Kennedy. He had inadvertently turned his police microphone on. A number of sounds picked up on this microphone included those of the gunshots fired during the assassination. A host of acoustical experts who studied these sounds concluded to a degree of certainty of over 95% that at least one shot had come from the grassy knoll. *(fn)*

The very notion that a shot had been fired from another area proved beyond a shadow of a doubt that Lee Harvey Oswald had an accomplice in the assassination of Kennedy. I sat back and contemplated all that I had read. If what the HSCA had concluded was in fact true, it clearly pointed to the fact that the assassination of John F. Kennedy involved more than one individual. If this were indeed the case, this clearly pointed to a conspiracy to assassinate President Kennedy.

Amongst its many other conclusions, the HSCA concluded that the security measures taken in Dallas with respects to the motorcade route were substandard. It also concluded that the autopsy performed on Kennedy following his death was equally inadequate. I couldn't help but think about the many mistakes made during the initial investigation into the death of John F. Kennedy. *(fn)*

As I read on, I discovered that the HSCA report covered a number of other aspects of the Kennedy assassination, including Jack Ruby. Among other things the commission concluded that Ruby was involved in a number of dealings with organized crime. The commission based this on, amongst other things, an increasing number of phone calls made by Ruby to members of organized crime. The HSCA also concluded that Ruby's murder of Lee Harvey Oswald was not a random killing done to spare Mrs. Kennedy the horror of a murder trial. It suggested that the subsequent assassination of Lee Harvey Oswald was part of a pre-arranged plot to silence Oswald! *(fn)*

The HSCA's conclusions did not stop there. Investigators surmised that the FBI and the CIA had not divulged all the information it had on the Kennedy assassination to the Warren Commission. Interestingly enough, it's most scathing criticism was left for the Warren Commission itself. It also concluded that the Warren Commission failed to properly investigate the possibility of a conspiracy that may have been involved in the assassination of President Kennedy. [fn]

I sat in class the next day, my mind totally consumed by the findings of the HSCA I had now become privy to. The assassination of John F. Kennedy had taken on a whole new meaning for me. What first appeared to be a crime committed by one lone crazed individual was clearly the work of many individuals. Even more disturbing to me was the realization that these same individuals had both motive and the means to carry out the most heinous of crimes.

CHAPTER 8

Walking home that afternoon I couldn't help but feel that the research I found myself thrown into had created a whole different level of stress for me. It reached a level I had never experienced before during my academic career. I took solace in the fact that our annual family cottage weekend had finally arrived. Given all that I had come across over the past few weeks, it couldn't have come at better time.

Our cottage was located on a secluded portion of cottage country; the only way of getting to it was by boat. Our particular section contained only two other cottages nearby. I had always found this one weekend to be the one "outlet" I could rely on to get away from the stress of everyday life.

There seemed to be an added "air" of enthusiasm as we all arrived together as a family this time. As was normally the case it didn't take long for the family boat to make its way into the water. Several of us spent the entire afternoon fishing. What followed was the usual inaugural family weekend diner. This was in turn followed by the nighttime roasting of marshmallows by the fire pit.

As was always the case, my brother Robert and I were the last ones to leave. This time, perhaps by design, my older brother Ted and I were the last ones left. Having realized that this might be the only time him and I would have alone, he immediately asked how things had gone with my research. I shared with him the information I had come across earlier that day. As was the case before, he was understandably taken back with everything I disclosed. He asked what I would research next.

I indicated that I would continue to take a closer look at the latest bit of information I had come across earlier that day.

It was now almost 2am in the morning and we decided to get some sleep. Saturday mornings at the cottage always called for our family breakfast. Given everything that had transpired with my parents, I wanted to have some normalcy. Our second day began early with breakfast followed by a day of fishing on the nearby lake. My father had decided to try a more secluded section of our lake this time around. He had been told of this spot by nearby anglers so we decided to try it out.

As was always the case, we all caught a number of fish that afternoon. This was just what I needed to clear my mind of all that had consumed it lately. As we approached 5pm in the late afternoon, my father declared that it was time to head back to the cottage to be with the rest of the family for the remainder of that evening.

As we made the turn around the first inlet towards our cottage I was struck once again with the overriding feeling that I was being watched. I turned to look towards the cottage now adjacent to our boat. A man stood at the edge of the dock of the cottage now situated directly in front of us. I couldn't help but notice that he was staring straight at me. It was customary that all cottagers wave at all boats that passed by their cottage.

I stared back at him, all the while waiting for him to break his stare and give the obligatory wave. To my dismay, it immediately became apparent this was not going to be the case. We continued to stare at one another. Many seconds now passed and he refused to break his stare at me. A few more moments passed when my sister caught the blank expression on my face. She glanced over to now catch the rather serious stare the strange individual continued to put forth, aimed squarely at me. His stare had now turned to a glare. Her initial curiosity had turned to one of concern. "I wonder what his problem is?" she asked. I hesitated for a moment and then responded back, "I don't know!"

I did not break my stare, almost in defiance of his. She continued. "Well it sure looks like he has it in for you!" A couple of minutes had transpired; my father took notice of the man staring at me. He now matched the strange individual's stare. No sooner had my father done so, the man suddenly turned and began to walk back towards the cottage behind him. In a very slow and calculated fashion he continued to walk methodically back towards his cottage. I watched as he slowly disappeared towards the front of his cottage and out of view. We made the slow drive back to our cottage where my mother and sisters waited. I found myself once again having to now figure out the significance of the individual I had seen that day.

The serenity I had enjoyed for most of the day had all but been replaced by the apprehension I now felt. My father, having sensed the concern I was feeling, asked if I had any idea as to the identification of the individual we had seen that afternoon. I responded that I was unaware of the individual's identity. My mother interceded and asked who we were speaking of. My sister described to her the events that had taken place an hour or so earlier that afternoon.

"That was one weird individual at the Fitzgerald's cottage this afternoon. I have never seen him at that cottage before. For some reason he was staring at us the whole time we drove by." My mother was somewhat surprised by my sister's account of what had transpired that afternoon. "The Fitzgerald's cottage? From what I've been told, that cottage has been left vacant from the balance of last summer, ever since Robert Fitzgerald had his stroke back in June of last year!"

We all looked at one another. My mother's declaration only served to fuel the fear that I was now feeling. Was this strange individual somehow connected to the other person I had seen days earlier. While they looked to be quite similar in height and stature, given the distance between him and our boat I couldn't verify if these two men were one in the same.

Our cottage was not easily found, nor accessible. One had to travel by boat to get to any of the cottages in our area. For this individual to have had the where with all, and more importantly, the means to get so close to my family was of immediate concern to me. If this was the same individual I had seen before, or even an associate somehow involved with the same organization, then my research now posed a direct threat to my family. It was a threat that meant the people involved were now able to gain access to my family virtually anywhere!

I spent the remainder of that evening in my bedroom. I began to recant the individual I had encountered that day. The images of his stares were disconcerting to me. The methodical way in which he turned and walked away suggested a feeling of infallibility that did not sit well with me.

While the remainder of the weekend continued without incident, the events that had transpired that Saturday afternoon put "a damper" on the remainder of the weekend. The one burning question stayed with me the remainder of that weekend. Had my research, and all the variables it involved, now begun to plague my family life as well?

I sat in my room late that Sunday night upon our return from the cottage. A whole new concern entered into all that encompassed my research into the life and death of John F. Kennedy. I tried to get my mind off all the thoughts that had hampered me over the last day and a half. I picked up some of the articles I had put aside prior to our cottage weekend and began to read through a myriad of pages that made up part of the HSCA report I had photocopied earlier that day.

Everything I was reading left no doubt that a number of aspects of the Kennedy assassination were plagued with crucial mistakes, strange occurrences, and events that could not be explained. I thought back to the aspect of the report that had concluded the fourth shot fired from the grassy knoll. The very notion of a second shooter in the grassy knoll could only mean that Oswald was not the sole assassin of John F. Kennedy.

Oswald professed his innocence throughout his arrest and subsequent interrogations. Oswald's death only added to the number of unanswered questions that characterized the assassination of President Kennedy.

I began to retrace the steps of all that I had read and seen of the Kennedy assassination. Looking back, a great many things just didn't make sense. I spent the remainder of the evening combing through everything I had collected on the HSCA report. The information I was coming across began to take on a life of its own.

There were still aspects of the report that troubled me just as the Warren Commission had. The one portion of the HSCA report that didn't make sense was its acceptance of the Warren Commission Report's theory that the same bullet was able to inflict damage to both Kennedy and Governor Connally. In my mind the "magic bullet" theory seemed implausible. This disturbed me somewhat in that it served to undermine my initial view of the HSCA's report. However, looking at it closer it was understandable that the HSCA did not wish to totally dismiss a previous report that had been commissioned by its own country a mere 10 years earlier.

The HSCA concluded that there were four shots fired in Dallas on the day of the assassination. Given all the new evidence it had uncovered, its investigators failed to overturn many of the conclusions first put forth by the Warren Commission some ten years earlier. It also supported the Warren Commission report's conclusions with respect to the fatal head shot that ultimately killed President Kennedy. Despite the contradictory description of the damage to the President's brain, the HSCA stuck to the original conclusion put forth by the Warren Commission.

In the end, whatever credibility the HSCA had built during its initial investigation seemed lost in its own contradictions as well as the failure of state bodies to investigate further any of the leads it had uncovered in its investigation. I couldn't help but wonder why more was not done by the Washington to follow up on some of the assertions put forth by the report. The very suggestion of a fourth shot provided the basis for a probable second shooter responsible for the fourth, and possibly more shots.

The panel of pathologists had the opportunity to study x-rays and photographs allegedly taken at the time of the autopsy; this was a luxury the pathologists at the time of assassination did not have. In my mind, these same pathologists also had an opportunity to review testimony by the doctors who had performed the autopsy. More importantly, they had the opportunity to study all the evidence before them without the duress that the original pathologists were under at the time of the Warren Commission.

Given all this, I found it disappointing that they ultimately agreed with many of the findings that the Warren Commission had concluded. Rather than challenging the assertions of the Warren Commission outright, the HSCA report refrained from totally dismissing the original conclusions put for by the Warren Commission.

What I found most disturbing of all was that this report came to light a decade after the assassination itself. The HSCA had been created due to the pressure and demand from the American public to find the truth behind the assassination of President Kennedy. Unlike the Warren Commission, it had the means, evidence, and the technology at its disposal to help discover the truth behind the assassination.

In the end, two federal bodies had been commissioned in different times, presumably with the same goal in mind; to find the truth. In my mind both failed to force their government to take the steps required to prosecute those involved in the assassination of President Kennedy.

The final epitaph of what I had read concerning the HSCA was the suggestion put forward that John F. Kennedy may have in fact been murdered as part of a larger conspiracy. The members of the Warren Commission seemed to go out of their way to dissuade the public from believing that the murder of President Kennedy was part of a much bigger picture. Yet the HSCA suggestion regarding the possibility of a conspiracy to assassinate President Kennedy had far-reaching implications in many ways.

One question remained; "who was the architect of such a conspiracy"? This lingered in my mind for hours. I fell asleep with a countless thoughts running through my mind. As I was soon to discover, my questions were to be answered beyond a shadow of a doubt. The images I observed in my thoughts that evening would lead me to the answers I was searching for.

CHAPTER 9

The Presidential Limousine approached the large crowds of people hoping to catch a glimpse of President Kennedy as he rode by. The number of people forming the crowds that had lined the streets of Dealy Plaza that day numbered in the thousands. I immediately awoke.

Upon awaking, the first thought that came to mind was simply this: with all the potential witnesses that had strewn the motorcade route, it seemed strange that their names never showed up in any of the papers and books I had read. I thought back to what I had read about in the HSCS report. A number of people directly or indirectly involved with the Kennedy assassination hadn't been interviewed by the investigators in 1978.

I got up and logged onto my computer just as I had done in the wee hours of the morning so many times before. I spent the next couple of hours reading through a number of articles covering eyewitness accounts during and after the assassination.

I sat in class the next day reading alongside my classmates. Our teacher had given us class time in class to work on the paper that was now due in two weeks. While everyone else was busy studying their notes, I continued to sift through articles I had photocopied and hidden underneath my school papers.

The public address system sounded. Calls into the classroom were seldom allowed unless it was an emergency. To my total disbelief the person being paged was none other than myself. A phone call awaited me at the office. I anxiously made my way to the microphone. I picked up the receiver only to discover it was Mrs. Donahue. She spoke in a low voice and explained that she had uncovered a vital piece of information that she thought was important. She asked if I could come to the library right after school. I agreed to do so without hesitation.

Throughout the remainder of the day I wondered what information Mrs. Donahue had found. As I approached the entrance to the library later at afternoon, I could see inside that she had been waiting for me to arrive. She immediately told her assistant that we would be pre-disposed for a couple of hours. We walked towards the viewing room. Mrs. Donahue turned on the light inside. The table was covered with a host of books and articles.

As I would soon find out, the information she had uncovered was as compelling as anything I had come across. As she had now discovered, there was a very good reason why a number of witnesses had not been interviewed by the HSCA during their subsequent investigation into the assassination of President Kennedy.

In the years that followed the submission of the Warren Commission in 1964 a number of witnesses with information pertinent to the Kennedy assassination had mysteriously died. In fact, many died under circumstances that could only be viewed as suspicious.

As I read through the documents that Mrs. Donahue had set aside, a number of specific cases came to the fore. Gary Underhill, a CIA agent and Hue Ward, the Mayor of New Orleans at the time of the assassination were both killed when their plane crashed suddenly in May of 1964. Perhaps the most telling death was that of David Ferrie. He was a suspect in the Kennedy assassination with links to the mob. In February of 1967 Ferrie suffered an untimely death caused by a blow to the neck that at the time was ruled accidental. [fn]

The one similarity associated with all these deaths was immediately apparent to me. These people all had information pertaining to the assassination of John F. Kennedy yet they were all dead within a very short period following the submission of the Warren Commission. We spent the next couple of hours reading through more. As we were soon to discover, a number of mysterious deaths followed the assassination of President Kennedy.

Johnny Roselli was a well known mobster. Together with Sam Giancanna, he worked with the CIA in its attempts to murder Fidel Castro in the early 1960s. Roselli testified in front of the HSCA during its hearings and was slated to testify again at later hearings. His body was found in July 1976 stuffed inside a steel drum, the victim of yet another untimely death in the hands of those that did not want him to divulge any further information to the HSCA. Sam Giancana, the mob boss of Chicago was also slated to testify before the HSCA during its investigation in late 1975. In June of that year Giancana was murdered before he had the chance to do so. *(fn)*

It was now obvious that these deaths were more than mere coincidence. They were all eerily similar in that many were of the suspicious variety and all occurred within a short time following the assassination of Kennedy. These witnesses all had a number of things in common that made their deaths all the more telling. Each of these witnesses was not given the opportunity to testify as to what they knew about the Kennedy assassination. Many of their deaths all had the earmarks of a mob style hit.

It seemed inconceivable to me that these people could all meet their deaths in the manner they did in such a short time following Kennedy's death. A whole host of new questions haunted me that night. Who had the means to carry out these deaths? More importantly, who orchestrated their completion?

One thing was certain, these victims each carried the information they knew to their graves. Had the HSCA been able to interview these individuals under different circumstances, it seemed quite conceivable to me that the conclusions found in its report might have been different had the personal testimony of these witnesses been taken in account.

In my mind, there was no longer any denying the fact that the murder of John F. Kennedy involved more players than simply Lee Harvey Oswald. It was inconceivable to me that Oswald could have acted alone in the assassination of President Kennedy.

I spent the next day revisiting the information regarding Oswald's role in the Kennedy assassination. I now concentrated my efforts on the Oswald's actions before and after the assassination. As I soon discovered, the Warren Commission's initial beliefs were thrown into disarray by the testimony of several witnesses, none more important than that of James Tague.

Tague stood near the Triple Underpass slightly ahead of the motorcade. He made it clear to investigators that he had been wounded by a passing bullet, a bullet that had allegedly missed the presidential motorcade.

The actions taken by Oswald in the Texas Schoolbook Depository building where he worked on the day of the assassination were themselves strange. Oswald, throughout his capture and subsequent interrogation stuck to his claim that he was on the 2nd floor lunchroom when the assassination of President Kennedy took place. His assertion was never taken seriously by the Warren Commission's investigation. His claim however, was substantiated by eyewitness accounts.

The timeline of events as suggested by the Warren Commission, based on eyewitness accounts, seemed to be implausible. In my mind it did not seem possible that a normal person under such "trying" conditions could have done what the Warren Commission suggested Oswald was able to do.

Oswald's own arrest was suspect. Having read eyewitness accounts of that fateful day in Dallas many described having witnessed snipers at the Schoolbook Depository building. Other witnesses present that day also described smoke emanating from the grassy knoll.

Dallas police quickly focused their attention on the Schoolbook depository building where they later found a rifle and "spent" bullet shells. They then turned their attention to a man who had entered a nearby movie theatre without paying. In a short period of time, Oswald became the prime suspect.

I loaded one of the videos I had made copies of at the library and viewed the excerpts of Oswald's assertions to reporters. It was at that moment that I came to the chilling realization that flew in the face of everything I had previously come across. In my mind Oswald did not fill the description of the kind of person responsible for the death of President Kennedy. Yet, if Oswald was not the man responsible, who then was the mastermind behind such a sinister and intricate operation?

I was beginning to struggle with the fact that the assassination of John F. Kennedy was much more complex involving many more players than I could have ever imagined. I fell asleep with these thoughts in mind.

I spent the next day sitting in the library viewing room I had used so many times before. I spent the better of three hours studying the same books and articles I had used before to investigate the life of Jack Ruby. I re-acquainted myself with Ruby's biography including his ties to organized crime. As was the case throughout my research, instances of sheer coincidence simply seemed too improbable to be real. What was Ruby doing in, of all places, a police station on the day before he was to assassinate Oswald? More importantly, why did Ruby find it so important to correct reporters in their questioning?

As I delved deeper into the events that took place prior to the assassination, I stumbled onto a conversation that took place over the phone between then Dallas police officer Billy Grammer and an individual who called him at police headquarters on the night before Oswald was murdered. Although the caller did not identify himself, Grammer later told investigators that he was certain the voice on the phone was none other than that of Jack Ruby. Grammer had spoken to Ruby on a number of occasions in the past and was familiar with his voice. During the phone conversation Grammer stated that the caller warned of Oswald's impending death the next day. Grammer found the threat to be credible. The caller was aware of the details surrounding the transfer of Oswald from police headquarters to the Dallas County jail including the exact time the transfer was to take place. [fn]

I sat back in my chair and was taken back by everything I was reading. This latest piece of evidence pointed to the fact that many events that preceded the assassination of Kennedy might possibly have been pre-determined.

Why was Ruby trying to warn a Dallas Police officer of the impending death of Oswald? By doing so, was he not taking the chance of having himself identified by someone who had spoken to him in the past? Another thought then came to me. Was it possible that Ruby was in fact attempting to sabotage the killing of Oswald? If Grammer had been tipped off on the imminent shooting of Oswald within the next 24 hours, why hadn't arrangements been made to change the date, time, or location of the transfer so as to avoid the possible threat that he had been made aware of?

Indeed, Jack Ruby proved to be as much of an anomaly as Lee Harvey Oswald himself. Both men had a strange place in history and seemed "tailor" made for the roles that they played in the Kennedy assassination. This became even more apparent by the images I would witness later that evening.

The group of men entered the cell and began to approach the man. From my vantage point I could clearly see that they were in the jail cell of Jack Ruby. Ruby began to speak to them. One of the men he spoke to was none other than Chief Justice Earl Warren.

Ruby began to speak "Is there any way to get me to Washington?" Chief Justice Warren replied, "I beg your pardon!" Ruby repeated his request to be taken back to Washington. Warren replied back "I don't know of any. I will be glad to talk to your counsel about what the situation is, Mr. Ruby, when we get an opportunity to talk." Several minutes passed and Ruby continued, "Gentlemen my life is in danger here". He continued, "I may not live tomorrow to give any further testimony." (fn)

I suddenly awoke and proceeded to view a few of videos I had copied from the library weeks earlier until I found the footage I was looking for. The video footage seemed to corroborate what I had witnessed earlier that night. Several members of the Warren Commission, including Chief Justice Earl Warren had in fact visited Ruby in jail.

I navigated through the video and came to the portion of it I had skimmed through before. The importance of it became all to clear to me. Flanked by his lawyers Ruby told reporters back then what I now knew to be true. Ruby proclaimed, "I'm the only one in the background that knows the truth. Everything pertaining to what's happening has never come to the surface. The world will never know the true facts of what occurred, my motive. The people who had so much to gain and had such an ulterior motive for putting me in the position I'm in, will never let the true facts come above board to the world." (fn)

Ruby's assertion was a telling reminder of the parties that were privy to information surrounding the assassination of President Kennedy. They seemed to mirror the images that I kept witnessing. He was asked whether the people he spoke of were in very high positions. Ruby immediately responded with the answer "yes". During his subsequent trial for the murder of Lee Harvey Oswald, Ruby again reiterated his theory by proclaiming to the media…'It's a complete conspiracy what…if you knew the true facts you'd be amazed at it." (fn)

Jack Ruby would later be found guilty of the murder of Lee Harvey Oswald. Plagued with a declining state of mind, Jack Ruby died in jail. As was the case with the man he killed, Ruby died before he could divulge all that he knew regarding those responsible for the assassination of President Kennedy. As for the question of those responsible for Ruby carrying out what he was seemingly instructed to do, the answer to that question was to become evident later that evening.

CHAPTER 10

The two men stood alone at a table. The conversation centered on Robert Kennedy. The heavier set of the two was visibly upset at the Kennedy administration and made his view quite clear. When asked about the Kennedy brothers, the man replied "If you cut off a dog's tail, the dog will only keep biting. But if you cut of its head, the dog will die." [fn]

The other man seemed somewhat surprised at the statement the other had made. I awoke soon after. There was something about the man making the statement that seemed familiar to me. A thought suddenly came to mind. I quickly began to sift through some of the articles I had previously read. Within moments, there before me stood the photo of Carlos Marcello, reputed mob boss of New Orleans, the same man Robert Kennedy would later have deported. I couldn't sleep the rest of that evening and was determined to find out the role, if any that the mob played in the assassination of President Kennedy.

I approached Mrs. Donahue the next day and described to her all that I had uncovered since our last conversation. Although my dreams now were commonplace to her, this particular dream seemed to open up a host of avenues that threatened to change the course of my investigation into the Kennedy assassination.

Upon reading a host of articles and documents, more revelations came to light that provided the backdrop for a host of future events. As had been the case before, I soon discovered that I had only skimmed the surface of the many factors that provided the backdrop of events surrounding the Kennedy assassination. Their relevance however, was crucial in providing an explanation of the reasons behind the series of actions that ultimately led to the assassination of John F. Kennedy. The information I came across proved to be as riveting as any I had come across thus far.

The relationship between the Kennedys and the mob had become strained as early as 1959. Both Kennedy brothers were involved in the McClelland Committee hearings that took place that year. A number of mob leaders were forced to testify and never forgave the Kennedys for the humiliation they suffered throughout the hearings. As I had read previously, Kennedy's assault against organized crime did not stop with these men; his efforts were also concentrated on Teamsters Union President Jimmy Hoffa. Hoffa was forced to testify and also felt humiliated by Kennedy's questioning and brash arrogance towards him. [fn]

In the minds of mob leaders, the Kennedy's had betrayed them in every aspect. The President and Attorney General had not only undermined their interests abroad, it now attacked mob interests at home as well.

Mrs. Donahue walked into the viewing area and noticed the blank stare on my face. The pieces of the rather large puzzle that made up the Kennedy assassination were now beginning to take shape. The picture they began to paint became more and more disturbing with every piece of information I uncovered. There was no doubting the fact that the mob had the motive to oust Kennedy from power. The question I now asked myself was simply this; did they have the means to eliminate Kennedy?

The most disturbing aspect of the information I had now amassed was the realization that there was now an ever-growing number of individuals in place with the willingness to erode President Kennedy's hold on power. It all made sense to me now.

Jack Ruby had correctly prophesized that the "players" involved in the assassination of President Kennedy would not let the truth come out. Ruby referred to these individuals as "the people" who had put him in the position he was in. There was no doubt in my mind that the individuals Ruby spoke of were in fact members of the American underworld.

Indeed, all pieces to the Kennedy assassination were now fitting into place. It was now conceivable to me that Jack Ruby might have been ordered by the mafia to silence Lee Harvey Oswald for good. The mob leaders personally attacked by Robert Kennedy had contacts in the Dallas area. In Ruby, they had an individual with contacts and access to members of the Dallas Police department. The key factors involved in the assassination of President Kennedy had the venue and the players in place to help ensure that the "fallout" that followed the assassination was kept at a minimum.

The story that was unfolding was becoming more disturbing with every bit of evidence I now uncovered. Although my research was becoming more and more complex with each passing day, the information I was coming across made the Kennedy assassination that much more intriguing. Every added element led to the next, linked by the fact that it ultimately led to the death of John F Kennedy. The events I was to witness in my sleep hours later only served to provide further proof that my suspicions were in fact correct. They would prove to be as startling as any I had witnessed before.

The room I now found myself in was empty and dark. From just outside the hall I could hear a commotion of sorts, it was loud and appeared to be serious in nature. I opened the door in front of me slowly. As I peered through the small crack I had opened I was able to see several individuals involved in a conversation that clearly grew tenser with each passing moment. The individual leading the conversation appeared to be a doctor. I pushed the door open a little wider. It was at that moment that I realized I was in a hospital.

The doctor was involved in a heated argument with two other men dressed in suits. To his right lay a casket. The casket was nestled in between the three men, it appeared to be open but I couldn't see who the individual was in the casket. Suddenly, and without warning, Jacqueline Kennedy appeared and approached the casket. It was at that moment that I realized that the body inside the casket was that of the now deceased President Kennedy. She reached for her late husband's hand in despair.

I looked on for several minutes as the argument between them continued. It centered on the body of the now deceased President. It was at that point that I realized that the men wearing the suits were undoubtedly FBI agents. The doctor then tried to leave the nurses station but was deliberately blocked by the agents in charge.

"My friend, this is the body of the President of the United States, and we are going to take it back to Washington". The head doctor snapped back "No, that's not the way things are done. When there's a homicide, we must have an autopsy". The casket was then closed; Mrs. Kennedy reappeared though she did not join the fray that was now becoming more and more "heated" with each passing moment. The FBI agent exclaimed in an even louder voice "We are taking the President back to the capital". The doctor responded once again by proclaiming "You are not taking the body anywhere. There's a law here. We're going to enforce it!" (fn)

I continued to peer outside from behind the door I stood behind. The chaos that had gone on for several minutes continued on for several more. As more and more individuals appeared, I began to become increasingly uncomfortable.

A few minutes passed and the casket suddenly disappeared from my view. It seemed the body of the President had been moved from the hallway. I suddenly began to feel like I was being watched. I peered back once more and suddenly caught a glimpse of an agent that appeared to be looking directly at me. His attention was now fixated on the small opening I had been peeking through all along.

He motioned to the person standing beside him, moments later he began to point right at me. Panic set in and I quickly closed the door entirely; I ran towards the bed nearby me and crouched behind it. I felt a bead of sweat run down my forehead. The door then flung open!

I opened my eyes and quickly reached for my night table. Thankfully, I could feel the clock radio that had always stood within arm's reach from my bed. I was back in my room! I found myself covered in sweat. As I stood up, the images I had just witnessed left an immediate mark on me. This latest dream was different from any other

I had experienced over the past few weeks. All the images in previous instances appeared to be events that had taken place in history. This time I felt like I had actually been part of the actual events. For a few crucial moments I felt as if I had been part of history itself!

How was this possible? Was I just imagining having been there in person? It seemed there was absolutely no doubt in my mind that one of the agents I had been spying on had actually seen me! It was at that moment I realized I had to corroborate what I had witnessed. I spent the next day trying to find all the information I could to support what I now suspected to be true.

I made my way to the library after school and looked for Mrs. Donahue. As fate would have it, she was not scheduled in that day. I decided to sift through the video I had looked at so many times before. I soon reached the portion of video I had skimmed through in past viewings. This particular portion of the video lasted about 8 minutes. I viewed it a couple of times trying not to miss any portion of it. It didn't take long for me to realize I was now viewing images on the video that were identical to those I had witnessed the previous evening.

I walked over to the computer section and searched the internet for any information I could find. I soon discovered several more articles that covered the events I had witnessed just mere hours earlier. There was no doubting the significance of my visions.

The events that followed the attempts by Parkland Hospital emergency staff to save the President were as crazy as the bedlam and confusion that followed the assassination of the President itself. Dallas County Medical Examiner Earl Rose rightly insisted that an autopsy should have been performed in Dallas since it was the place in which the death of the President occurred. Rose's attempts to have President Kennedy's body remain in Dallas for the official autopsy were thwarted each time by the Secret Service in Dallas. A shoving match ensued that went on for several minutes. From all that I read, eye witness accounts verified that Mrs. Kennedy did appear twice during the mêlée thereby corroborating what I had witnessed in my dream. [fn]

Earl Rose was well within his realm of authority in his insisting that the autopsy be performed in his State of authority. The United

States government apparently had other plans. For a few moments the images as I had seen hours earlier began to filter through my mind, thereby allowing me a further glimpse of the chaos that actually took place that night.

The scene at the hospital ended in the same abrupt manner it was handled with at Parkland Hospital. The Secret Service actually commandeered the O'Neal hearse and drove the body of the President to the Airport to an awaiting airplane set to fly President Kennedy's body back to Washington.

Why did Washington not allow the autopsy of the President of the United States to be performed in the State to which federal law dictated? As I would soon discover, the answer to this question lay with, what many would dub, "the autopsy of the century"

The autopsy of President Kennedy was itself filled with anomalies and contradictions from start to finish. The three doctors assigned to perform the autopsy were James J Humes, Thomas Boswell, and Pierre Finck of the US Army. Of the three doctors assigned to perform the "autopsy of the century", only one was actually a forensic pathologist. All three doctors were inexperienced in the type of autopsy being performed on President Kennedy. [fn]

Why were these relatively inexperienced men chosen to perform the autopsy of the century? Recollections from some of those present during the autopsy described chaotic and often tense moments during the autopsy. They described a situation whereby it seemed as though the doctors performing the autopsy actually appeared to feel as though they were being lead by those watching them during each phase of the autopsy. [fn]

The circumstances surrounding the autopsy of John F. Kennedy were strange, to say the least. The findings of the autopsy were themselves bizarre creating more questions than answers. The conclusions that arose from the autopsy bore distinct discrepancies between the observations made by the doctors at Parkland Hospital.

The events that surrounded the aftermath of the Kennedy assassination disturbed me a great deal that night as I thought about all that I had read. Like the assassination itself, there were so many things that just didn't make sense, especially given the fact that it involved the President of the United States!

The observations made by the doctors who tried to save President Kennedy in Dallas were totally different than those made by the doctors in Washington. The wound to the back of Kennedy's head, though significant was not described in the same manner by the doctors performing the autopsy as it had first been described by the doctors who tried to save President Kennedy at Parkland hospital. [fn]

If the events prior to the assassination of President Kennedy suggested that there was a conspiracy involved in the murder the President, the events that followed the assassination suggested a subsequent effort to cover it up. The Secret Service agents present at Parklands hospital defied all laws and codes of ethics. They were determined not to leave the hospital without the President's body in tow. The decision to take Kennedy's body back to Washington was done in haste.

More telling was the "gag order" placed on these individuals assuring that the truth behind the autopsy would be kept secret for some time. It was only after these men retired from active service that they were then allowed to discuss what had occurred during the autopsy. In the end, the autopsy of President Kennedy was flawed from beginning to end. It seemed that the powers in Washington appeared to only be interested in supporting a theory that fit the official story as first prescribed by the Warren Commission. The Warren Commission accepted the autopsy's conclusion that the wound to the President's neck was not one of entry, but rather an exit wound. According to the official autopsy, the bullet entered the lower back portion of President Kennedy's neck and exited from the front. This was consistent with its assertion that Kennedy had been shot from behind by Lee Harvey Oswald. [fn]

CHAPTER 11

That evening's dinner was unlike most I was normally accustomed to. It was one of the few nights that all my brothers and sisters were home thereby allowing us to eat as one large family. I sat there listening to conversation everyone was having as they all spoke about the day they had experienced. Moments later, I was totally consumed by sudden thoughts that now began to pour into my mind.

I was witnessing a conversation between two individuals. They were in the process of listening to a taped recording. While I could not hear what they were listening to, the looks on their faces were ones of total disbelief. It was clear to me that the contents of the tape had a far-reaching effect on both of them. The image stopped and I began to become aware of those around me once again.

My older brother Ted noticed the fact that I had been totally oblivious to the conversation that had just been taking place. He asked me if everything was okay. Startled by his question I immediately snapped back that all was fine. Having realized my abrupt response to his concern for me, I quickly apologized to him. He immediately acknowledged and accepted my apology.

My father immediately interceded. "No John, I don't think everything is fine. In fact I don't appreciate your response to your older brother's concern!" There was now complete silence as my father finished speaking. Knowing I had to respond to my father's concern, I calmly and quietly responded. "I'm sorry that I have been predisposed of lately. It's just that the essay I'm working on has become quite complex and has simply gotten the better of me. I apologize if I have seemed distant and abrupt."

Having sensed my sincerity, my mother addressed the situation in her customary calm demeanor. "Your dedication to your work is to be commended, but you cannot forget what is really important. Your family takes precedence over everything and everyone. Never lose sight of that!" I acknowledged her advice and soon after excused myself from the dinner table.

As I lay in bed that night, I thought back to my brother's questioning of my recent behavior. Perhaps he was right. I had never been this withdrawn before. I was normally the one to initiate the interactions at home. I was totally withdrawn from everything and everyone around me. Was the assassination of President Kennedy overtaking everything in my life? Were my family and friends now becoming the victims of my obsession?

As I sat in class the next day, my mind was clearly elsewhere. I felt trapped in a daily struggle to try and make sense of everything that was now unfolding. Everything about the death of President Kennedy now had a disturbing "air" to it, and was affecting every facet of my life.

I arrived home that afternoon, my mind consumed with all that I had thought about that day at school. I made my way to my room to change out of my school clothes. As I walked out of my room towards the staircase, I could hear that the television in the family room had been turned on. I was certain that it hadn't been turned on when I first arrived. I immediately called out to my brothers and sisters to see who had arrived home. I waited several moments for a response.

It seemed strange that no one answered. Without warning, the volume of the television began to increase. I called out once more but there was no response. I made my way towards the family room. There was no one in the room. I was immediately struck by the programming currently showing on the television. Having always been an avid television viewer, I was somewhat surprised of the fact that I had never seen this commercial before.

The commercial was being shown in black and white. The items being advertised were unlike any I had ever seen before. A second commercial soon followed. It too advertised items I had never seen before. I felt somewhat confused with the images before me. The unfamiliar commercial soon ended. "Now back to Bonanza!" proclaimed the announcer. The episode, also in black in white now continued, seemingly where it had left off before.

I looked on as the episode continued. I stared aimlessly at the television in front of me. The picture was grainy at best, a far cry from the high definition broadcast I was accustomed to watching. I immediately grabbed the cable remote and pushed the "guide" button to see the programming for the channel I was currently on.

The information on the guide, now in color, clearly stated that the channel I was viewing should have been ESPN. The current programming called for the broadcast of the afternoon baseball game between the Boston Red Sox and the New York Yankees.

I was at a lost to explain the programming I had been watching which was clearly not the programming that was supposed to be on at this time. I quickly released the guide button to bring me back to the channel I had been watching. To my utter dismay, the Red Sox/Yankee game was now on my television screen in full HD color. To say I was perplexed at what had just occurred would have been an understatement. However, with all that I had witnessed and come across over the past few weeks, it didn't come as a total shock either.

A thought immediately came to mind. On a hunch, I made my way back to my room and began to search the events that were taking place in the months that preceded President Kennedy's untimely death. My first order of business was to search the pop culture and events that took place during this time. As I soon discovered, the year 1963 was to be the pre cursor to the British Invasion that was to grip America for years, culminating in the dominance of the Beatles a year later in 1964.

The top rated television shows for 1962 included the Dick Van Dyke Show, the Beverly Hillbillies, and fittingly enough, Bonanza! Despite the wholesomeness this period in history seemed to have engrained in it, the underlying chain of events happening behind the scenes only served to dampen my memory of what took place during that time.

In keeping with this, civil rights continued to be the most contentious issue facing America in what would be President Kennedy's final year in office. On April 3, 1963 civil rights activist Marin Luther King Jr. led a civil rights drive in Birmingham, Alabama. The peaceful demonstration was met with strict resistance by state police.

On June 11, 1963, in a televised address to the nation, President Kennedy proposed the enactment of civil rights legislation. It marked the first time an American President called on all Americans to recognize civil rights as a crucial issue inherent in the rights of all Americans. On Aug 28, 1963, the march on Washington attracted 250,000 demonstrators to the nation's capital in support of civil rights. Those involved in the demonstration included such Hollywood icons as Marlon Brando, Charlton Heston, Sidney Poiter, as well as singers Sammy Davis Jr. and Bob Dylan. [fn]

At the Lincoln Memorial Martin Luther King Jr. delivered his now famous "I have a Dream" speech that would serve as the symbol for the call of civil rights and civil equality in America. On an international level, the United States and the Soviet Union signed the Limited Nuclear Test Ban Treaty that same month. This treaty called for a cessation of nuclear testing in air, space, and water.

Finally, in October, 1963, President Kennedy signed a limited nuclear test-ban treaty between the Soviet Union and the United States. What immediately struck me upon reading all this was the fact that President Kennedy had come farther than any other President before him. Kennedy championed for the cause of civil rights as well as the end to the Cold War that had once brought the world to the brink of destruction.

These causes that President Kennedy fought so hard for, along with his quest for the moon enamored him to all Americans. I sat back in my chair and tried to disseminate the message being given to me by the events I had been led to by the black and white images I had seen that night.

Given all that I had come across, the one underlying message I drew from all that I had seen became clear. What started out as a promise, as witnessed by the steps taken during Kennedy's Presidency, ultimately never reached their conclusion! I closed my eyes and quickly fell asleep.

The man sat on his desk and listened to the contents of a taped recording. It soon became apparent from the look of concern on his face that the contents on the tape proved quite disturbing to him. He rewound the tape and invited another individual to listen to the contents on the tape. His response was swift. The images in my mind ended abruptly. I realized that these were the exact images I had day dreamed about during dinner last night. I couldn't help but wonder as why I had now witnessed these same images in successive nights.

There still remained the unfinished business of the images I had seen. Upon entering the library the next day, I walked straight to the video section. I proceeded to sign out the video I knew could shed more light my dream. Mrs. Donahue noticed that I had walked right past her into the viewing room.

She quickly proceeded to enter the room. I explained to her details of my latest dream and proceeded to play the tape. I then told her about the individual I had seen at school. "John, it's becoming clear that the information you've come across has somehow caught the attention of others. How, I'm not quite sure as of yet!"

We began to view portions of the tape I knew would help explain what I had recently seen. I began to skip past other sections of it for well over an hour until we reached the part of the tape I had been looking for. The images before us produced the most startling revelations to date.

The conversation took place a month before Kennedy's trip to Dallas and involved a Miami Police dept informant and a 1960s extremist Joseph Milteer. The conversation that took place between them was unlike anything else I had come across during my research into the Kennedy assassination. The conversation went as follows:

Milteer- The more bodyguards he has, the easier it is to get him."
Informant- "Well, how in the hell do you figure would be the best way to get him?"

Milteer- From an office building, with a high-powered rifle."

Informant- "He knows he's a marked man..."They are really going to try to kill him?"

Milteer- "Oh, yeah, it is in the working."

Informant- "Boy, if that Kennedy gets shot, we have got to know where we are at. Because you know that will be a real shake if they do that."

Milteer- "They wouldn't leave any stone unturned there, no way. They will pick up somebody within hours afterwards, if anything like that would happen. Just to throw the public off" *(fn)*

I stopped the tape. We both simply stared blankly at the screen before us for several moments not knowing what to say. The eerie recording was a warning sign. It served as a prophecy of what was to happen less than a month after the recording was originally made. More importantly, the images I had just seen were the same as those I had witnessed hours earlier!

Thoughts began to swirl in my mind as Mrs. Donahue continued to stare blankly at the screen before her. There was no longer and doubt in my mind that my dreams were now becoming the lifeblood of my research. They now served as a guiding point to what I would have to research next. What immediately struck me with this latest revelation was the tape's degree of accuracy in predicting the manner in which President Kennedy was to be assassinated? We spent the entire afternoon searching recently declassified documents. The information we came across was as shocking as any we had come across before.

The events leading up to the President's trip to Dallas were noteworthy, to say the least. President Kennedy was scheduled to attend a college football game on November 2, 1963. The visit was cancelled at the last minute. Interestingly enough, this was the same day Diem, the leader of South Vietnam was assassinated. Many people felt that the President had cancelled the trip due to the sudden crisis in Vietnam. However, information that I had come across pointed to something far more serious! Secret Service agents in Chicago had been alerted of a threat against the President. The threat involved a team of sharp shooter assassins. President Kennedy's visit to Chicago was subsequently cancelled. [fn]

As I soon discovered, the trail of events did not end there. In early November Miami police had received the tape between Milteer and the police informant. Upon hearing the tape, Miami police officials informed the FBI of the tape and the warnings it foretold. One would have assumed that the FBI would have acted promptly to the notification given to them by Miami police. Surprisingly enough, the action taken by the FBI given the threat that the tape presented was minimal at best. [fn]

The Secret Service did check on Milteer's whereabouts, but he was never arrested nor was he ever questioned about his conversation on the tape. Those responsible for President Kennedy's visit to Miami changed the itinerary for the trip drastically so as to avoid a catastrophe there. A planned Presidential motorcade was immediately cancelled. Upon arriving in Miami on November 12 President Kennedy was flown by helicopter to a planned dinner at a Miami hotel. Once finished his speech, the President was flown back to the airport by helicopter then back to Washington on Air Force One. [fn]

I took the slow walk back home and simply thought about the events I had read about that day. As was the case for many of the details surrounding the Kennedy assassination, there were so many things about the days leading up to the assassination that just didn't make sense. Given the fact that President Kennedy's trip to Chicago had been cancelled so abruptly, it seemed inconceivable to me that the authorities missed warning the Miami Police department of the possible threat to the President.

If the Secret Service was lax in warning Miami Police of the threat to President Kennedy, its failure to warn the authorities in Dallas was inexcusable. The Miami Police department was fortunate enough to have been given ample warning. In my mind, it seemed that they made the most of it and took the proper security steps required to ensure that the President was safe during his trip.

The President abruptly cancelled his trip to Chicago in early November. His itinerary had been drastically changed for his trip to

Miami a week later, so much so that the planned motorcade had been scrapped altogether. Had these changes been made several months prior to Kennedy's trip to Dallas, one could expect a relaxation of security measures upon his arrival in Dallas. However, the events that transpired in both Chicago and Miami preceded President Kennedy's visit to Dallas by a mere three weeks.

It now seemed inconceivable to me that members of the Secret Service were somehow totally unaware of the possible threat to President Kennedy. If this were the case why wouldn't the authorities in Dallas have taken every step to ensure the safety of the President? I lay on my bed and simply digested all that I had read and seen that day.

CHAPTER 12

I woke up the next morning for the first time in a long while without having experienced any dreams. Given all that I had discovered the day before, I couldn't understand why I hadn't foreseen the possibility of these events in my visions.

I spent a good portion of that afternoon at the library looking through a host of sites, searching for anything I had not yet come across that could help shed more light on everything I had learned. I later made the usual trek back home earlier in order to make it home in time for dinner.

I finished dinner as quickly as I could as I was eager to continue my research. I made my way back to my room and gathered my thoughts as I lay on my bed. I looked up at my computer and something immediately caught my eye; a set of pages I had photocopied earlier on the Warren Commission now seamed to stand out.

A thought then came to mind. I got up and began to sift through the set of articles strewn on my desk. I spent the better part of the next hour combing through the information before me. I soon realized I had uncovered one of those untapped elements I had suspected earlier that day. It would introduce yet another variable involved in the Kennedy assassination.

According to the Warren Commission, the formal decision for a Presidential trip to Dallas was made on June 5, 1963 during a meeting between Governor Connally and President Kennedy. During this meeting it was agreed to that the President would visit Dallas in late November of that same year. The Commission's report made it clear that the planning of events was to be left to Governor Connally to take care of. The notion of a Presidential motorcade became the centerpiece of Kennedy's visit to Dallas. An important part of the President's visit to Dallas included a speech to be given by President Kennedy at a luncheon to be held by business and civic leaders. According to the Warren Commission it was decided that President Kennedy would arrive at Dallas' Love Field airport. *(fn)*

Organizers of the trip felt that the route chosen provided the safest path to the Stemmons Freeway while at the same time providing good vantage points for those wishing to catch a glimpse of President Kennedy. The chosen motorcade route was reported by several Dallas newspapers in the days preceding the President's arrival in Dallas. The Warren Commission was quite clear and specific about the steps taken to select the final motorcade route. It also was quite adamant in its assertion that the parade route had been public knowledge for several days. *(fn)*

As was the case before, there was something peculiar about the great lengths the Warren Commission had taken to describe the steps in organizing President Kennedy's trip to Dallas. Given all the inadequacies the Warren Commission had exhibited in its report, I now found it odd that the report had been so thorough in outlining the steps taken in organizing the trip to Dallas. The Warren Commission report painstakingly described the history behind the trip, the selection process for the route taken by the motorcade route, as well as the efforts made to advertise the route decided upon through the local newspapers.

It was beginning to all make sense now. By outlining these factors in such detail, the Warren Commission attempted to justify the routes taken once Kennedy arrived in Dallas. Many historians had questioned the choice of the President's motorcade route. The Warren Commission when out of its way to justify the route taken, this despite the fact that many believed this particular route left the President totally vulnerable to what eventually occurred in Dallas that fateful day.

In my mind, there was one aspect that was never considered by the Warren Commission. In pointing out that the motorcade route was public knowledge by Nov 19, 1963 this meant that everyone was made aware of the exact route the Presidential motorcade was to take. This included the very enemies that were now becoming united in their desire to see the President removed from office.

I was left to contemplate one simple question. Were the actions taken simply mistakes made or were they by design? The images I was about to witness would shake the entire the foundation of everything I had witnessed before.

Air Force one touched down on the tarmac and taxied down the runway. Soon after, its doors opened with a limousine awaiting its occupants. They included President Kennedy, Jacqueline Kennedy, Governor Connally, along with his wife.

President Kennedy was on the last stop of his whirlwind tour of Texas; previous stops had included San Antonio, Houston and Fort Worth. Moments later the Presidential limousine was met by Vice President Lyndon Johnson and his wife riding in another limousine. They were part of a large motorcade that began to drive off.

I awoke for a brief few moments having realized that I was now viewing images in Dallas on the day of the assassination. I had never dreamt about this before but the clarity and detail of this particular dream was incredible; it was as if I was actually there.

I soon found myself looking down at the triple underpass that overlooked Dealy Plaza. Over to my right I could clearly see all the trademarks that characterized the crime scene of President Kennedy's assassination, including the Texas Schoolbook Depository building with its many open windows. I witnessed hundreds of cheering spectators that adorned the streets in anticipation of the President's arrival. I then caught a glimpse of the infamous grassy knoll area.

A blue pickup truck had pulled alongside this grassy area parked partially on the sidewalk adjacent to it. Out of this vehicle walked an individual who then approached the bed of the truck, from it he removed an object that was wrapped so as not to conceal its contents. The man then approached the white picket fence at the edge of the grassy knoll and disappeared from view.

I suddenly awoke from my dream; a bead of sweat began to flow down my forehead. As I closed my eyes again, the images continued. I looked up at the Texas School Depository building again and concentrated my attention on the sixth floor. I then focused my attention on the white picket fence behind the grassy knoll area again.

The crowds in the street began to cheer loudly. To my right I could see the motorcade as it slowly made its way towards the awaiting crowds. I counted the cars as they slowly came closer. There were a host of cars, buses, along with a number of Dallas police motorcycle officers that made up the motorcade. I could now see John and Jacqueline Kennedy along with Governor Connally and his wife waving to the crowds that lined the streets beside them. President Kennedy sat in the rear right seat alongside Jacqueline Kennedy. Directly in front of the President sat Governor Connally with his wife seated to his left. Two Secret Service agents sat in the front.

As the motorcade made the slow sharp turn on to Elm St from Houston St., Mrs. Connally turned to President Kennedy. "Mr. President, you can't say Dallas doesn't love you." "That's very obvious" responded President Kennedy. The images in my mind were as clear as the day they occurred. [fn]

It was at that precise moment that I realized I had just witnessed the last words spoken by President Kennedy. Suddenly, the sound of what appeared to be a firecracker rang out and startled everyone in the Presidential limousine. Although I had seen portions of these images before, the angle and scope to which I now witnessed them were unlike anything I had experienced before.

The Presidential limousine was now parallel to the Stemmons Freeway Sign when a second shot rang out. I immediately looked to President Kennedy as he immediately clutched his throat in reaction to the wound in his neck. Kennedy could not speak. Jacqueline Kennedy had heard the second shot as well and noticed her husband clutching his throat. Another shot was fired but it missed the Presidential limousine entirely.

As events continued to unfold, Jacqueline Kennedy reached for her husband and began to console him not yet realizing the nature of the injuries to him. Governor Connally, in an effort to determine what had happened to President Kennedy was immediately hit by another bullet from behind. I could see the Governor's cheeks blow out as he reacted to being shot; he then slumped into his wife's lap as she sat beside him.

The Presidential limousine continued on slowly. I looked on in horror as the final fatal shot hit the President in the head. The impact of the bullet had created a large wound effectively blowing out the back portion of President Kennedy's head.

It was at that point that I awoke again. The clarity and detail of what I had just witnessed gave credence to what had transpired during the fateful few seconds that made up the last moments of John F. Kennedy's life. I dozed off once again as the images continued.

Portions of President Kennedy's brain were strewn out in all directions. Jacqueline Kennedy reacted immediately and began to climb up the back of the limousine in a desperate attempt to save a portion of her husband's brain. The two Dallas Police motorcycle officers riding to the left rear of the car were now reacting to events that were occurring in front of them.

A Secret Service officer attempted to climb onto the car as it suddenly accelerated. He almost fell off the vehicle as it began to accelerate; both he and Mrs. Kennedy hung off the back of the car as she attempted to help him onto the car. The Presidential limousine then sped off following the lead cars to Parkland Hospital.

CHAPTER 13

Two men looked out the window of the Texas Schoolbook Depository building as the Presidential limousine sped off. They both began to quickly disassemble their rifles and put them away in the compact cases they fit into. They were quite serious in their demeanor and were in a hurry to vacate the area they were in. Given their methodical and calculated calm demeanor, it was quite clear that they were proficient in what they were doing. They carefully and methodically exited the building in an abrupt manner.

I awoke and suddenly felt my stomach drop as the reality of what I had just envisioned hit me. It was that moment that I realized I had just seen visions of those responsible for assassinating President Kennedy?

The two men looked down at the Presidential limousine as it sped off in an attempt to save the President. This particular dream seemed to take on a life of its own. The images continued.

Two more men stood behind a wooden fence. I could hear the commotion coming from all around them. One man was clearly dressed as a police officer; the other man was dressed in a suit. Both men were completely oblivious to all that was happening around them. The one man disassembled a rifle and quickly carried it off. The two men left in opposite directions so as to conceal their relationship to one another. Moments later the dream ended.

I sat up on my bed now covered in sweat and simply stared ahead. I felt like I was reliving history as it unfolded. I had witnessed first-hand those truly responsible for the assassination of John F. Kennedy. My heart was beating intensely. I could feel the adrenalin piercing through my entire body.

Objects suddenly came to focus; the silence that I had left in my room had been replaced with the ever-increasing noise of cheering crowds that were all around me. I looked around in stunned silence. I was no longer in my room; inexplicably I found myself in different surroundings.

I continued to pan the area I now found myself in, hoping to identify exactly where I was. As I turned to my left, I was immediately overwhelmed. Unaccountably, there before me stood the Texas Schoolbook Depository building.

I began to rub my eyes in an attempt to wake myself out of whatever strange dream I was having. Opening my eyes once more, I quickly realized that I was not dreaming. As had been the case in the hospital room, I realized I had once again transcended time. I now found myself in the heart of Dealy Plaza. Before I could attempt to make sense of what was happening to me, the sounds I had heard so many previous times before, now began to match the images that had already come to focus.

The cheer from the crowd of people on both sides of the street was enthusiastic and loud. Many people were holding up signs welcoming the President who was seemingly on his way. I rubbed my eyes one last time as if to reassure myself that I wasn't in-fact dreaming.

Without any warning, my journey into the past had now been taken to a whole new level, one that I could never have imagined. Yet before me lay the proof in the form of the many buildings and individuals that now surrounded me. I looked over to a person standing beside me and glanced down at his watch. I could clearly see that it was now 12:20pm in the afternoon.

If everything I had read about and seen in videos was in fact correct, President Kennedy was due to arrive in less that 10 minutes. I walked around and simply stared at the many onlookers around me. All the while I wondered how this was all possible.

The noise level of the crowd then began to rise dramatically. I looked to my left and felt a sudden sense of apprehension as the Presidential motorcade now came into view. It had made the sharp turn around Elm St. and slowly made its way towards the area where I stood. The noise and cheers grew even louder as more and more members of the crowd began to see the Presidential limousine slowly approaching them.

If history was correct, the time of the first shot fired was mere minutes away. I once again panned the area and stared at everyone around me. I then slowly began to walk towards the grassy knoll area and looked on intently. While I couldn't be certain, in the area behind the picket fence I could make out a figure of what appeared to be at least one individual behind the fence. I then looked up at the depository building across the street. I concentrated my efforts on the sixth floor window that was now open. History, it seemed was indeed repeating itself; all the players involved in one of the darkest days in American history were now in place.

I looked up, there before me was the figure in history I had seen only in photos and in film. Chills ran through my entire body as President Kennedy now approached me. He was indeed larger than life with all the pageantry that film footage and photos could not do justice to.

Beside President Kennedy sat Jacqueline Kennedy waving to the crowds of people who had lined up to catch a glimpse of their President. An innumerable set of emotions swept through my mind knowing full well that the scene of excitement was soon to be replaced by one of sheer horror.

It was at that very moment that I then heard what appeared to be the sound of a firecracker going off. I looked up at the Presidential limousine that was now almost parallel to me. Kennedy reacted to the first shot fired at him. Another sound rang out as he grabbed for his neck with both hands.

What was transpiring around me was simply incredible. Every sequence and event that I had read about and seen on film was now happening before my very eyes. Jacqueline Kennedy began to speak to her husband showing a great deal of concern. Governor Connally had heard the initial shots fired and started to turn towards President Kennedy.

Without warning, another shot rang out hitting him directly from behind. The Governor immediately collapsed onto his wife sitting beside him. More shots rang out immediately thereafter, one put a hole in the Presidential limousine, and the other seemed to have missed the car totally.

The final few moments of John F. Kennedy's life were now happening right in front of me once again. I looked in horror as the fatal shot hit the President, snapping his head back with tremendous force; the entire left side of his head was blown off. Blood and brain matter were strewn in all directions. Jacqueline Kennedy reacted immediately in horror; she stood on her knees on the trunk of the limousine trying in vain to retrieve what little of her husband's brain was left. The windshields of the police motorcycles accompanying the Presidential limousine were splattered with blood.

A Secret Service agent tried to climb on board the Presidential limousine. As he finally did so, he helped Mrs. Kennedy back into the vehicle. I was now witnessing in real life what I had seen so vividly in my mind earlier that day. I had momentarily lost all concepts of those around me as everything took place. The chaos, confusion, and screaming became louder as the Presidential motorcade sped away at a high rate of speed towards nearby Parkland Hospital.

Everyone around me was in total shock. Many of the onlookers had hit the ground immediately following the last fatal shot fired at President Kennedy. If there was any doubt that the noises heard were in fact gunfire, the fatal headshot had all but removed that doubt. Entire families now lay on the ground, many people were crying still in shock as to what happened.

There was a sudden rush to the grassy knoll as many onlookers spotted puffs of smoke from behind it. A member of the Dallas Police dept quickly followed the crowd and searched the area. He returned a few moments later only to search elsewhere.

I walked slowly amongst everyone. Although I had viewed these scenes many times before, the shock of what had just taken place before me began to overtake me. The entire scene remained chaotic. Members of the Dallas Police department scoured the area.

Within a few minutes, police officers centered their search on the Texas Schoolbook depository building. A couple of officers pointed to open windows of the building while others entered inside. Once again, every image I had seen over the past few weeks was now happening before my very eyes.

I sat down on a nearby curb and simply looked around as onlookers began to console one another. As I sat and continued to stare at the bedlam before me, I tried to come to grips with the fact that I had been a part of perhaps the darkest moment in American history. I put my head down for a few seconds; on the ground beside me was a U.S. quarter. Ironically enough it had been minted in 1963 and was in pristine condition. I reached down and took the quarter in my hand. I then closed my eyes all the while wishing everything around me was not real.

As I opened my eyes, everything slowly came back into focus. After rubbing my eyes a few times I realized I was back in the present and in the confines of my room. I looked down to find that the quarter I had picked up earlier had fallen onto the floor. I reached down, picked up the coin and stared at it for several moments. The coin served as a memento of what I had just experienced. More importantly, it was proof of the fact that I had actually somehow traveled back in time.

My foray into the assassination of President Kennedy had come full circle. As I lay in bed that evening, I began to piece together everything I had been through in the hours that had just followed. I tried to make sense of the fact that I had somehow transcended time and witnessed first-hand the assassination of President Kennedy. Surely there had to be a reason for my presence there!

CHAPTER 14

Unable to sleep for the remainder of that evening, I felt the need to talk to the only person who was aware of the information I had come across over the past few weeks. As I entered the library the next day, Mrs. Donahue quickly noticed me, she quickly followed me into the viewing room.

I immediately told her of what I experienced hours earlier. The events that I subsequently described to her had the most profound event on her yet. We spoke at length; Mrs. Donahue wanted to know as many details as possible. I was immediately struck by her penchant for wanting to know more about this latest incident. It was obvious that this particular event had much more significance than any of the previous ones I had described to her in the past.

I wasn't sure whether it was this particular event in itself or whether it was the culmination of images I had described to her over the past few weeks. Yet her reaction to what I had told her was far different this time around. I was sensing there was something she hadn't yet disclosed to me.

"John, I haven't told you as of yet but I have kept a former colleague of mine abreast of your research. I've also informed him of the images you have encountered over the past few weeks. He has been interested, to say the least, in all that you have seen and heard!" She continued on. "He is currently a Professor of modern history and is an expert of 20th century history. He considers himself an expert on the Kennedy assassination. He is eagerly awaiting an opportunity to meet with you in person to discuss everything that you have experienced. Given what has now transpired over the past couple of days I don't think we should wait any longer!"

Mrs. Donahue pulled out her cell phone and began to make a phone call. She walked away a few feet and began to speak to him. They spoke for a couple of minutes. She then put the phone down for a moment. "John is there any way that you can take the time to meet with him tonight? He is of the belief that it is imperative we meet immediately." I asked her to wait a few minutes while I called home. I walked over to the other corner of the viewing room we were in and immediately called home. My father answered the phone. I began to tell my father that I would have to skip dinner and would be home late.

I could tell he was not impressed with the fact that I was going to be away from family for yet another evening. I promised him I would explain all that was happening afterwards. He reluctantly accepted my explanation. I turned back to Mrs. Donahue and indicated that I could meet with them that evening. She immediately continued her conversation with him once more indicating we would be at his house within the hour. We agreed to pick up something to eat and then proceed to the Professor's house.

I had spent countless hours with Mrs. Donahue over the past few weeks. She was somewhat reserved as we ate. I sensed that something was bothering her. What it was, I wasn't sure of, but I had a feeling I was soon to find out.

We drove for about 20 minutes until we arrived at a part of town I had never been to before. I had always heard of the upscale Thompson Creek area. The opulence of the surrounding homes was not lost on me. It was matched by the house we now drove up to. Upon reaching the driveway to the home, the sensors that surrounded the outside periphery of the house engaged a host of lights that lit up the outer perimeter of the house. The light of the inside foyer to the home turned out and the door opened.

Professor Osborne immediately acknowledged Mrs. Donahue. He then held out his hand to shake mine and introduced himself to me. I shook his hand and introduced myself as well. He proceeded to walk with us down the large foyer of his house that led to his study. Judging from the large number of books that surrounded its walls, it was obvious that he was a well-educated man that had a penchant for reading. What immediately caught my attention was a copy of the Warren Commission that stood almost in the centre of the wall that stood behind his desk.

Professor Osborne noticed me starring at the book. "I see you have noticed the copy of the Warren Commission Report!" "Yes" I quickly replied. He responded back. "It is the cornerstone of my whole collection. If you look around, you'll quickly realize the interest I have had for many years regarding John Fitzgerald Kennedy, including unfortunately, his assassination in 1963!"

He continued on. "Having been 12 years old, and living in America at the time of the assassination I can still remember to this day the pain and despair we all felt that day. I remember the affect President Kennedy's death had on my parents. I can still picture, to this day the image of my father crying upon hearing of his death. It was perhaps the one and only time I had ever seen my father cry!"

Professor Osborne stood and simply stared ahead for several seconds, as if to take a moment and think back to what he had just described. He seemed to compose himself quickly and turned to face us once again. "John, Judith had told me a great deal of what has occurred over the past few weeks, including the information and individuals you have encountered during this time." Before he could further continue, Mrs. Donahue interrupted him and informed him of the fact that new events had taken place.

Somewhat shocked by the information she had indicated to him, he asked me to describe what had occurred. I began to tell him about the vivid images I had seen earlier in the day. I then proceeded to describe my second foray into the past. I described in great detail all that I had seen, including my witnessing of the assassination itself.

I continued by describing the individuals I had seen behind the grassy knoll as well as in the Texas Schoolbook Depository building. I described the chaos and mayhem that followed. He looked on with great interest. He then spoke. "John, I don't think you realize the position you now find yourself in. I am a true believer in fate and I believe that everything you have discovered, everyone you have come across has all been pre-ordained."

He explained that my journey began with the initial visions I had seen in my sleep. What started out as visions, turned into dreams and now evolved into the ability to witness and actually become part of past events as they originally occurred. Everything he said all made sense. The manner at which I had experienced everything had changed with each day that passed.

I had indeed gone back in time to witness events as they occurred 50 years earlier. However, it was now clear that a definite pattern had emerged throughout all of my most recent dreams. In their infancy they acted as a guide to information that I was to uncover as my investigation into the Kennedy assassination evolved. They now began to take on an even greater importance.

I was now able to transcend time. My most recent experiences led me to the truth behind the assassination of President Kennedy. I came to the realization as to why I was now somehow able to travel back in time to the exact moment in which the assassination occurred.

There was pause for several moments. Professor Osborne then broke the silence. "John, you may have been sent back in time for many possible reasons. Perhaps to alter the events of the past. You may also have been brought back in time so as to confirm that events as first set out in history are NOT meant to be changed. Your actions COULD possibly do more harm than good!"

There was now a defining silence in the room. I looked up at Mrs. Donahue. Not a word was exchanged between us. We both knew everything he said was right. I turned to face Professor Osborne once more. "How will I know what to change what occurred in Dallas almost 50 years ago? There are so many variables, so many individuals involved!"

"I mean, I'm just a teenager, I barely know how to drive a car, let alone prevent the assassination of a President!" Osborne sat up from his chair and leaned towards me. "It is hard to image that you'd be able to travel back in time. Yet, here we are and as far as we know, anything and everything is possible."

"The information was given to you for a reason. None of us can be sure as to the reason for all of this, but the truth will be uncovered in due time. That I am sure of; my instincts tell me so. Once again, I caution you to be wary of any actions you take, especially in the past; the results could be disastrous!"

The three of us spoke for several more minutes. Mrs. Donahue and I assured Professor Osborne that we would keep him updated on everything that happened. As was the case with Mr. Montgomery, Professor Osborne was adamant that we discuss our conversation with no one else, including my family so as to ensure the safety of everyone involved. I asked for his number at home.

He immediately indicated how very few people were aware of his home phone number. He then reached into his pocket and gave me his cell phone number where he instructed he could be reached at all times. Mrs. Donahue and I left shortly thereafter.

Upon returning home that night, I thought back about the conversation the three of us had that evening. Still, a number of questions remained. Would I actually be able to change the course of history? If so, how would I "pull off" such a feat? More importantly, if I were able to actually change the course of history, would it be right to do so? Professor Osborne's warnings quickly came to mind. They represented the first warning sign of the possible adverse effects my actions in the past could have on the future.

The fact still remained; I had somehow been given the opportunity through the gift of hindsight to help change the course of history. It was a course riddled with lies, deceit, and contempt, all of which created a recipe for disaster. As far as I was concerned, the benefits far outweighed any negative repercussions.

Everything was now fitting in place. I had witnessed previous events that led me to the truth so as to leave no doubt as to the people and circumstances involved in the assassination of President Kennedy. My arrival in Dallas prior to the assassination of Kennedy had somehow been pre-determined by some twist of fate.

I had been given the means and the opportunity to "right" a terrible "wrong" in history. It was an opportunity and I wasn't about to waste. The burning question still remained. How would I be able to prevent this terrible event from happening? In my mind, the same factors that convinced me of the probability of a conspiracy in President Kennedy's assassination would be the most effective method of proof. Who would I have to convince regarding the real truth behind President Kennedy's death? One thought, however kept me awake for most of the night. What was it that had peaked Mrs. Donahue's interest in my research and subsequent foray into the past? More importantly, what was her stake in all that I had made her aware of over the past number of weeks?

CHAPTER 15

I made my way back to see her the next day. As if awaiting my arrival, Mrs. Donahue immediately followed me into the viewing room we met numerous times over the past week. She was somewhat subdued and stared at me for several moments, not uttering one word. From the look on her face it seemed obvious she had been up most of the night thinking about what she was going to say to me. She turned away and slowly lowered her head. For the first time, I felt rather uneasy in her presence. She stepped out for a few minutes. I sat on my chair waiting nervously for her return all the while wondering what she was up to.

A few minutes passed and the door finally opened. She walked in now holding a DVD in her hand. She loaded the disc into a DVD player that had already been setup in the room. She fast forwarded through the contents of the video until it reached the focal point of her concern. The footage Mrs. Donahue now reached covered the events that took place immediately following the fatal shot fired during the assassination. She anxiously looked on as the video continued to play. This particular copy was much clearer than the tapes her and I had previously viewed.

I looked on as it began to show footage documenting the reactions of the many individuals and families who had just witnessed the assassination of President Kennedy. I turned to look at Mrs. Donahue. Her facial expression made it clear that she had viewed the footage a number of times before. She now focused her attention on me. "John, I want you to pay particular attention to what is coming up."

I continued to view the footage on the DVD intently, concentrating on the events that were taking place. I quickly glanced back at Mrs. Donahue for a moment; her expression now seemed to have turned to one of total apprehension, seemingly aware of what was to come.

The video now concentrated on the grassed area near the grassy knoll. A host of families had dropped to the ground well aware of the fact that shots had been fired at the Presidential motorcade which had begun to speed away. The children in the video were visibly and understandably inconsolable given the events that had just taken place around them. Many of the children chronicled were in tears while others seemed confused as to what they had just witnessed.

As the film continued, my thoughts began to digress. Throughout my forray into the Kennedy assassination, my intuition had never failed me. Something now told me that there was a reason why she had gone out of her way to have me see the footage we had before us. I glanced back at her once more and proceeded to rewind the video. I viewed the events for a second time, concentrating more intently on the images before me. Mrs. Donahue then got up; she rewound the video and paused it. She stared at the image now frozen for several more seconds, not saying a word. Her face was now expressionless.

The image on the screen was that of two sisters, both of which couldn't have been more than 10 years old; yet old enough to understand the horror that took place a few feet away. The look on their faces was one of shock and bewilderment. Mrs. Donahue began to speak, all the while continuing to stare ahead at the image still frozen in front on the screen.

In an almost hypnotic fashion, she began to speak. "I can still remember the horror of that day. The sound the bullets made as they hit President Kennedy. I remember hearing Mrs. Kennedy scream as she realized what had happened to her husband. It is as painful now as it was then. Those are the sounds I will remember for the rest of my life. It is a painful reminder of the world we live in."

As she continued to speak, teardrops flowed from both her eyes; the memories still too painful to recant 50 years later. "My father said it was the saddest day in American history. He said it marked the end of America's innocence. Years later, his comments would come true once more with the assassinations of Martin Luther King Jr. and Robert Kennedy!"

I didn't know what to do, let alone what to say. What do you say to a person who had lived through such a harrowing experience? From the expression on her face, it was clear that the memory of what had occurred that day had caused her pain for so many years.

I got up from my chair and put my hand on her shoulder. In an almost apologetic fashion, I asked if she was okay. She put her hand on my hand and acknowledged that she would be fine. She finally turned to face me now seemingly having gained her composure once again. I turned back to look at the screen. The frozen image now before me was none other than a young Mrs. Donahue along with her family having just witnessed the assassination of President Kennedy. The same chills I had felt after having first discovered the truth of the Kennedy assassination enveloped me.

Unbeknownst to me, I had been in the presence of an eyewitness to the Kennedy assassination, someone who had witnessed, first-hand, the terror of that one day that would live on forever in the memories of those present. I glanced over once more to the image still frozen on the screen.

Mrs. Donahue continued to talk about her place in Dealy Plaza that fatefull day. "My father was a huge fan of President Kennedy. He had promised to take us to Dealy Plaza the moment President Kennedy's visit to Dallas had been announced. He took the day off work so as to ensure that we could arrive early enough to get a good view of the motorcade. My sister and I were so excited to be there amongst the many that had all turned up that day to catch a glimpse of President Kennedy. It was a beautiful sunny day, everything seemed perfect."

I simply looked on and listened as Mrs. Donahue continued to chronicle what happened that afternoon. "I could feel my adrenaline as the Presidential motorcade drove directly in front of us. I remember hearing the initial shots fired, there were at least three. At first I thought they were fireworks. It was only after I looked up at the others around me that I realized something was wrong."

"My father had been stationed in the army for three years; from the first shot fired he knew right away that the Presidential motorcade was being fired on. He yelled for my mother to get down and then proceeded to grab both my sister and I. As I fell to the ground, my momentum threw to me to the side facing the grassy knoll. It was at that precise moment that I turned to see the fatal shot that killed President Kennedy. I'll never forget the distinct odour that emanated from the area in and around the knoll."

I sat there totally perplexed by what I was now hearing. To have seen the footage of the events that took place in Dealy Plaza was one thing, to actually hear an eyewitness account in person was quite another!

She then turned to face me once more. "I will never forget the effect the assassination of President Kennedy had on my family. My father, in particular was devistated for weeks. He died five years ago but swore to his dying days that Oswald was not the man responsible for the death of the President. In my own mind, there is no doubt that the fatal shot came from behind me!"

Mrs. Donahue's unbelievable story only served to create new revelations in my own mind. Her admission now explained her interest in my research. The most telling revelation of her past was that it provided an explanation as to why I had been the one chosen to stumble onto the information regarding the Kennedy assassination.

It was more than mere coincidence that I had entrusted someone who had not only witnessed the assassination first hand, but was now in a position to guide me towards the evidence that would help me uncover the truth behind the assassination. Everything was beginning to fit into place.

She walked over to the DVD player and proceeded to play the remainder of what was left to view. She hesitated, clearly having realized something in her mind. She then turned and walked out of the room making sure she closed the door behind her. I continued to stare in awe towards the screen. The images of Mrs. Donahue with her family having witnessed the assassination of a President would remain ingrained in my mind forever.

Mrs. Donahue's return then startled me for a moment. She held a magazine in her hand. She slowly placed it down on the desk with its cover face up. She indicated that the copy had just come in that same morning. I began to read the cover story. It included the now infamous photo of JFK just before he was shot.

The caption was in bold letter: "Fify years ago, when the shots ran out in Dallas, Nov 22, 1963". She then drew my attention to the date of the issue, Nov 20, 2013. It was at that moment that I realized the importance of the timing of my research into the Kennedy assassination. Everything had all come together exactly 50 years following the assassination of President Kennedy. We were literally days away from the anniversary of Kennedy's death half a century earlier.

Mrs. Donahue then spoke, "It is more that shere coincidence that you would see the images that has made us cross paths exactly 50 years after having witnessed it personally. You and I are two of perhaps a handful of individuals who can say they were at Dealy Plaza to witness the events that took place that day."

She continued, "You and I have been brought together having both witnessed this event first-hand in order to prevent the horror that has haunted all who were there to see it." Everything I had seen and the people I had come across, were a testament to the fact that the time had come for me to correct a terrible injustice that occurred half a century earlier.

The discovery of Mrs. Donahue's connection to the assassination of President Kennedy only served as the final motivation to right the wrongs in Dallas. Suddenly it mattered even more! She returned minutes later having "gathered" herself. The only thing left was to decide what our next course of action would be.

CHAPTER 16

We spent the next couple of hours formulating a plan of action. The very fact that I had arrived just prior to the assassination itself meant I would not have a great deal of time if I were to attempt to change the course of events. Last-minute arrangements would undoubtedly take up a great deal of President Kennedy's time. Even if I were to somehow gain access to those close to the President and convince them to view the evidence I was to prepare, time would undoubtedly be a factor in trying to get this information directly to him.

The solution we came up with involved the creation of an edited video encompassing different excerpts from all the footage I had collected throughout my research into the assassination. The video proof that we were to prepare had to be supported by hard evidence. We both realized that I was privy to information only a handful of individuals knew even existed. We also knew that this information would be instrumental in convincing those close to President Kennedy that the information presented was in fact credible.

The next couple of hours were spent reviewing all the tapes I had amassed over the past few weeks in an attempt to determine which video footage would be used in conjunction with the articles and papers I would present to support the video evidence.

A thought then came to Mrs. Donahue's mind that would prove crucial. She correctly pointed out the fact that I was going back to the year 1963, a time when the video equipment currently being used was far away from becoming reality. While the most important piece of the puzzle, television, did exist, film technology was still years behind its current form.

An idea then came to mind as well. I had seen advertisements regarding the transfer of Video into DVD just as Mrs. Donahue had done with the video footage she had shown me today. The same method could now be used to transfer the video footage I had compiled to the Super 8 film format that was available at the time of the assassination! This video transfer would be crucial if I was to be successful in showing those of importance the evidence that would make up the genesis of my entire case.

She accompanied me to the video store a couple blocks away in order to find out if the transfer could be done. The owner of the store informed us that, while he himself could not transfer the video to 8mm, he knew of an associate who could. He agreed to transfer the video and indicated that it would take a couple of days to complete.

All the pieces were now in place. What now remained was the process of preparing the video itself. Mrs. Donahue agreed to take the next couple of days off work so as help to prepare the video evidence in a timely fashion.

As I made the slow walk home again that evening, a host of thoughts ran through my mind. I tried to piece together everything that had transpired over the past few weeks. One thing was for certain, Judith Donahue was the missing link to the Kennedy assassination, and the last piece of the puzzle I knew had been forthcoming.

I spent the majority of that evening thinking about what was to be included in the evidence I was to bring with me. Hundreds of images ran through my mind as I struggled to determine which images were to be included in the footage I would bring to the past.

There were so many excerpts, so many documentaries that were available to us; all of which were equally effective and equally important in their ability to convey the message that was so crucial. A thought immediately came to mind. Walter Cronkite was the first to inform Americans that Kennedy had been shot in Dallas. Who better than Cronkite, the one person every American would be familiar with, to provide the introduction to the video evidence we were now preparing.

The next day Mrs. Donahue and I began to view the footage that we would use to create the version which would make up the final copy. We spent hours viewing each subsequent video. There were well over 20 hours of video at our disposal. We had to somehow select only those portions that best described each element of the Kennedy assassination.

Each subsequent portion of video I viewed as part of this latest process served to stir up "demons" from the past that made me look at things differently. They served as a rallying point that fueled my desire to change the terrible hand that had been dealt to President Kennedy half a millennium earlier.

The entire process of creating the condensed video copy took the better of two days. There was so much material that was deemed "necessary", a good portion of a second tape was needed to cover everything. We viewed the final copy of both tapes convinced we had created a summary that covered every aspect of the Kennedy assassination.

We then began sifting through the many articles and pieces of written information we were convinced would serve to further corroborate and support the video evidence we had prepared. The documents and video evidence we had compiled left no doubt as to the facts and individuals responsible for the assassination of the century. I was now ready for my most important trip back in time.

I once again made the short trek back home with my evidence in tow. As I approached our house this time, I noticed my father sitting on the front steps with a paper in his hand. He was visibly upset. He immediately insisted that I follow him into the study. He then proceeded to tell me he had received a letter from school indicating that I had missed a number of days at school over the past month. The letter went on to say that steps would be taken if I was unable to explain the reason for my recent absences. I made no attempt to challenge the letter in any way. My school attendance had always been the least of his worries.

My father began to speak. In a stern voice he explained, "John, time spent on your own is one thing, not showing up for school is quite another!" A myriad of thoughts ran through my head. Should I lie and come up with an excuse for my sudden absence in school?

It immediately became apparent that it made absolutely no sense for me to lie to him. My father and I had built a special bond based on trust, I wasn't about to break that trust now. I asked him to sit down; I then proceeded to explain all that I had witnessed over the past several weeks.

I began to outline the visions I had experienced and described how they developed into complex dreams that eventually led to my travel back in time. By the look on his face, it became immediately apparent that my father was having trouble accepting my explanation. Given all I had just told him, I couldn't blame him for not initially believing me. It was at that point that I realized I needed help in convincing him that my story was indeed the truth.

I suggested to him that we meet with Mrs. Donahue. He reluctantly agreed to do so; we soon made our way to the library. As we walked into the library I could see that she was preparing to go home. I quickly walked over to her and explained the reason for my visit with my father.

The three of us proceeded towards the viewing room which was becoming a second home to us. Mrs. Donahue explained everything that had transpired over the past few weeks thereby corroborating my story. The look on my father's face was one of resignation. It was clear that her submission was proof of what I had tried to explain earlier.

We then began to show him the video we had prepared over the past couple of days. My father had always been fascinated with the assassination of President Kennedy. He was visibly surprised by the complexity and nature of information we had compiled together. Mrs. Donahue then rose from her chair and proceeded to pick up her cell phone to make a call. Moments later she pulled the phone from her ear and suggested in a loud voice "John, I think your dad should meet Professor Osborne!"

While my father was somewhat surprised by her suggestion, she felt that the Professor would provide the final piece of credibility needed to secure my father's support for what I was about to do. The three of us soon arrived at Professor Osborne's estate. We were once again greeted at the front door by Professor Osborne. He shook my father's hand, introduced himself and escorted us to the same large study we first met in days earlier. I began to describe events that had had taken place since our last encounter. Mrs. Donahue and I updated the Professor on the video footage and evidence we had accumulated over the past couple of days. He was impressed with the choices we made. He asked if I still planned to travel back to the past. Somewhat surprised by his question, I reiterated to him that I remained determined to present the evidence to those readily able to brief the President on the events that had transpired prior to his upcoming trip to Dallas.

My father interceded and asked if I had told anyone else of what I had experienced and seen over the past few weeks. I informed him of the very few individuals who were aware of what I had stumbled across. I sensed his uneasiness at the fact that I had confided in my brother Ted some of the details of what had occurred. I then turned to both Mrs. Donahue and Professor Osborne for a moment before concentrating my attention once again to my father. I proceeded to describe the two individuals whom I had recently encountered.

Professor Osborne quickly interceded. "John, the two men you have come in contact with recently; have you spoken to either one of them? I informed him of the fact that agent Montgomery and I had spoken in person. Professor Osborne interrupted me once again. "Montgomery? Robert Montgomery? I quickly acknowledge such. He continued. "John, I have known Robert Montgomery for a number of years. It is no secret that he was fired from the Secret Service due to behavior that breached protocol. I wouldn't pay much credence to what he may have told you!"

"While he is privy to classified information, I can assure you that his intentions are "suspect" at best." I glanced over to Mrs. Donahue. Professor Osborne quickly followed my stare and glanced over to her as well. I turned back to respond to Professor Osborne. "While I appreciate your advice, I actually found him to be an honest and credible person."

Professor Osborne continued, "John, you must always be cognizant of the fact that people aren't always as they first appear!" I acknowledged his advice one again and simply nodded in agreement. Professor Osborne then turned his attention and addressed my father. "Sir, I understand your concern as a parent. However, the truth still remains. None of us can truly understand the reasons why your son is the one person that has been chosen for this task!"

He continued, "What I do know for certain is this. There is something none of us are yet aware of. I believe it is the only reason why fate has chosen your son for such a monumental task. Whether your son's actions in the past can be successful remains to be seen. As I have indicated previously, no one can be sure if his actions in the past will have a positive effect in the future!"

I looked at Mrs. Donahue for a few moments. As if to read my mind, she then turned to address Professor Osborne. "Robert, while we cannot be totally sure as to what effect John's actions will have in the future, I think we can all agree to the fact that he has been given the gift of seeing and being part of the past for a reason. We all know the terrible effect President Kennedy's assassination had not only in America, but the world at large. I was there to witness it in person!

"President Kennedy was prepared to do wonderful things. He headed man's quest to reach the moon. He was at the forefront of civil rights. One can only imagine the progress that would have occurred had he lived to serve the remainder of his first time and possibly a second!"

She continued, "I for one am of the belief that the information that has literally been "handed" to John as well as his ability to transcend time has been set in place for a purpose. I don't think we can waste the opportunity we are all a part of now. I for one most certainly don't believe we should be discouraging John from doing what he feels in his heart is necessary!'

Mrs. Donahue's diatribe left the rest of us speechless for several moments. It was clearly a direct challenge to the Professor Osborne's previous warnings. From the look on his face, it was evident her message did not go unnoticed by the Professor. They seemed, for several moments, almost at "odds" with one another.

Sensing the tension between the two of them, my father quickly interceded before it worsened. "I think we should all take a step back and simply look at the facts. I see the value in what both of you are saying. I do believe that John has been given an incredible opportunity we dare not waste! However, Professor Osborne is equally correct in pointing out the fact that you must be cognizant at all times of the effects your actions may have in both the past and the future. I shudder to think of what would happen if your attempt to save the President proved to be unsuccessful. Your actions could change the course of history to follow and make any subsequent cover up of the assassination worse!"

As if to continue the momentum of my father's warning, Professor Osborne continued, "Correct", he exclaimed. I am not trying to undermine your plans; I am merely stating the dangerous repercussions your actions could have."

Mrs. Donahue responded by describing how she herself was initially skeptical at first of my revelations. She then spent the next several minutes explaining her place in history as it pertained to the assassination. My father looked on, totally perplexed at what she had just disclosed to us. It also became evident that Professor Osborne was also unaware of her place in history.

I turned to address my father one again. "Dad I understand your concern, but history had already been changed on November 22, 1963! John Kennedy should not have died that day. We have the chance to change history in so many ways. We can stop this terrible injustice from happening and save President Kennedy's life. We have the ability to show President Kennedy the effects that the Vietnam War had on his country for years to come! A chance to show him the permanent scars it left behind"

My father simply stood speechless having listened intently to everything I had just described to him. There seemed no doubt in his mind that I had knowledge and the means to make good on everything I so passionately spoke of. Suddenly, my reasoning made all the sense in the world. I felt as if I was being drawn ever so closely to the past.

If there had been any doubt as to the legitimacy of the revelations I had brought forward, they had all been erased. He turned to address everyone in the room and asked what he could to help us. Mrs. Donahue indicated all that was left to do was to prepare the written evidence that was to support the video proof we had compiled.

Just as she had finished speaking, her cell phone rang. She recognized the phone number on her display as having been the video shop owner that had transferred the video into Super 8 form. "That's strange; I picked up the films yesterday and paid him in full. What could he possibly want?"

My father and I looked at one another immediately sensing something was wrong. My dad asked Mrs. Donahue to switch her phone to speaker mode. She proceeded to do so and began to speak to the person on the other end. "I forgot to tell you that the second copy of your film footage was picked up yesterday shortly after you had picked up your copies".

Mrs. Donahue's face turned completely white. "What do you mean the SECOND COPY? He responded back to her. "Oh I'm sorry, I thought you knew. I received a call from your associate directing me to make two copies of your video films. He called minutes after you and I spoke. He told me he was working on this project with you and he therefore required a copy as well. I didn't think anything of it so I went ahead and made two copies. He came to pick up his copy early this morning, minutes after I opened my store for the day!"

Before Mrs. Donahue could respond to him, Professor Osborne interrupted, "tell me, how would you describe her associate? The shop owner responded, "he was quite tall and really serious; a man of few words. Come to think of it, I found it strange that he wore gloves when he picked up the video! Gee, I hope there wasn't a problem with him asking for a copy as well?" Professor Osborne quickly responded. "No, don't worry about it. I am an associate of Mrs. Donahue as well. Should this man contact you again, please contact Mrs. Donahue at once." He agreed to do so and hung up.

"Well, I don't think there is any doubt that our every move is being monitored. What is clear is the fact that they are now monitoring your cell phone calls! What is equally true is the fact that these individuals have undoubtedly already begun the process of studying the video evidence you have compiled and know a great portion of what you have concentrated your research on."

Professor Osborne continued on. "What's troubling is their ability to monitor Judith's cell phone call to the store owner. The fact that they were able to setup surveillance so quickly and efficiently suggests a high level of sophistication and resource! If there was any doubting the fact that we need to move quick on our next actions, this has all but been rendered academic. We need to prepare the written information as quickly as possible so that you may start your journey to the past immediately."

"I would also suggest that you keep all the information you have compiled with me. I have a large safe in my study that I use to store any pertinent information that is vital to my research. You can bring all your research and videos to me and I will store them for you. Rest assured that this valuable information will be kept safe. Keeping this information at home puts your family in danger!"

My dad and I looked at each other; each of us now reading each other's thoughts. I tried hard not to convey the fear I felt, aware of everything that was happening around me. I couldn't help but feel that I was in the same position John F. Kennedy found himself years earlier; our lives seemed to mirror one another. Like JFK himself, I felt the growing number of enemies that were now coming to the fore.

From their facial expressions, it was obvious that my father and Mrs. Donahue had come to the same realization. Mrs. Donahue seemed particularly shaken by the fact that her conversations were now being monitored. It was obvious she feared for the safety of both her and her husband.

The three of us then got up and were escorted by Professor Osborne. As he opened the front door to let us out he turned back to me and put his hand on my shoulder. "John, I wish you all the luck in the world. I will be praying for you. For the sake of many I hope that you are successful in what you have now committed yourself to". He turned and shook my father's hand as a sign of support for the concerns he was certain my father was undoubtedly feeling. He then turned to Mrs. Donahue, almost as a gesture of faith. "Judith, we will keep in touch on a daily basis; please be careful!" Mrs. Donahue acknowledged his concern.

My father and I drove Mrs. Donahue back to her house. As we pulled out of her driveway, I noticed a car parked across the street. The car was not there when we first picked her up. I noticed that Mrs. Donahue had glanced over to take a look at the car; she seemed unfazed by its sudden presence there.

CHAPTER 17

Upon arriving home, my father and I spent the next several hours in his study preparing the written evidence I was going to bring back to the past. My father typed out all of my written notes; he then bound it together with the remainder of supporting documentation in a binder. The written portion of my evidence was now ready to be presented.

He opened the closet door behind his desk and reached in. He grabbed a thick duffle bag which he used for presentations at work. It was made of a thicker plastic with reinforced handles thereby making it easily able to carry heavier items. We put the two film reels along with the two bound books encompassing my typed evidence in the bag.

My dad reached over and gave me a hug. It was the kind of hug a father would give to a son leaving on a long trip far away. It also acted as reassurance to the both of us that everything was going to turn out fine. "Good luck son. I will be praying for you and I'll see you when you get back. Please be careful!" On the corner of his eye I could see a teardrop stream down the side of his eye down his cheek. I acknowledged him, all the while doing my best to conceal the fact that I had seen my father cry for the first time in my life.

I made the slow walk towards my room. I felt a sudden sense of relief knowing that I had his blessing for the task that now lay ahead of me. Everything was now in place for the journey I was about to embark on. As I sat in bed that night, I found my mind consumed with a host of thoughts; not least of which was the newest revelation involving the second copy of my video evidence that had undoubtedly been scrutinized by the very people agent Montgomery had warned me of.

What now concerned me was Professor Osborne's suggestion that we keep all my research with him in his safe. This in itself suggested a level of danger for anyone involved in the journey back to the past; it included my family! While my father's acceptance of what I had committed myself to was important to me, I felt a sense of uneasiness knowing he was now involved in my plan to revisit the past. Still, Professor Osborne's reservations about my impending foray into the past seemed to momentarily dampen my initial enthusiasm towards it. Mrs. Donahue's impassioned response to his initial reservations easily outweighed his concerns.

I glanced over at the magazine containing the front page picture of John F. Kennedy. The promise and hope his pose represented seemed to get the better of me. It was at that moment that I came to the same realization Judith Donahue had arrived at. Fate had now given me one shot to make the impossible POSSIBLE!

I began to turn my attention towards all the things I might do once returning to the past. I had no way of knowing where I would end up. All the while, I wondered how much time I would have to warn those closest to President Kennedy of the events that were to occur. My biggest challenge would be for me to somehow find a way to get my evidence to them. I was convinced the proof would speak for itself.

I stared down at the bag that contained the 8mm film and the binder with all the written evidence I was to bring with me. A thought then came to mind. I reached over to grab the loose change that always lay on my nightstand. Sifting through the coins, I managed to find a 2013 minted quarter. I put the quarter into my jean pocket. I opened the drawer of my nightstand and pulled out the quarter I had brought with me from the past. The quarter I was to bring back would also serve as something tangible that could later prove my own place in time.

I turned to face the light now emanating from the closet in my room. The door that had previously been closed was now slightly opened allowing more bright light to shine through. The first thought that immediately came to mind was the fact that this was more than mere coincidence.

The time had come for me to travel back in time and attempt to do what now had to be done. I took a deep breath and stared at the light that now shone brighter than ever. It was the final sign telling me there was no turning back now. I closed my eyes in anticipation of what was to occur next.

I awoke moments later unsure if I was dreaming. I found myself standing behind the desk of a large office. I slowly took a couple of steps to my right trying not to get the attention of the individual near me. I soon realized my efforts to elude attention were in vain. It was at that precise moment that John Fitzgerald Kennedy turned to face me.

I was totally speechless for several moments having realized I was now standing in front of President Kennedy himself. If there was any doubt as to whether or not I was going to be able to reach the President, those fears had been rendered academic. I was immediately awestruck by his very presence.

He sat up in his chair and in stern and somewhat loud voice demanded. "Who are you and how did you get in here?" I immediately remembered the sound of his voice, with that distinctive New England accent I had heard in videos some many times during my research.

I tried to muster the same courage that had brought me back to the past. "Mr. President Sir, I have information that is vital to your safety!" No sooner had I finished speaking two Secret Service agents, having overheard the President's initial response, burst in and asked if he was okay. President Kennedy quickly collected himself and responded that he was fine.

The two Secret Service agents immediately approached me. One of them grabbed me tightly by the arm. Within minutes, the other, having noticed the bag I had brought with me, began to empty it of all its contents. Both the videos and binder fell out.

The door to the President's office opened wide again as several more agents entered the room followed by a host of advisors to the President. For the first time, I found myself overwhelmed with the reaction of those around me. One of the advisors immediately asked President Kennedy if he was okay.

He once again assured everyone present that he was fine. The one agent continued to hang onto my arm. I looked down at the contents that had been removed from my bag and now lay on the floor for all to see. My whole reason for returning to the past hinged upon these same items that now lay on the floor in front of me. I then looked up at President Kennedy. He looked down and the items on the floor with some semblance of surprise. He could see from the look on my face the importance attached to them.

The second of the original two agents reached down to pick up the items that had dropped on the floor. The Presidential aide in charge immediately instructed him to take the items with them so as to have their contents investigated further. In a last ditch effort to prevent their removal, I shouted out "you can't take my things, the safety of the President depends on them!" The agent completely ignored my plea and grabbed the bag from me. He began to place the films and binder back in the bag.

I put my head down, seemingly accepting the fact that I was not going to be able to keep my belongings. Just as the agent turned to hand the bag over to the aide in charge President Kennedy interceded. "Officer, please hand me back the bag." He was totally surprised by Kennedy's request. The officer replied, "Sir, normal protocol requires us to investigate any packages deemed suspicious. We don't know where it came from or what its contents are. We don't even know where this young man came from, for that matter!" Kennedy responded to him. "I understand your concern, but I want to give this young man a chance to explain his reason for being here before we do what we have to do." The door then opened as two more individuals walked in.

These two men seemed to immediately command the respect of the agents that had entered earlier. I stared at one of them for several moments. This particular individual looked familiar to me. I remembered him from several of the videos I had seen during my initial research. President Kennedy immediately called the two men over to the other side of the room and spoke to them for several minutes. Both men took turns looking back at me as the other spoke to the President.

President Kennedy turned back to the others standing in the room and informed them that he wanted a few moments alone with me. He then instructed the agent holding onto the bag to leave it on his desk. The agent hesitantly did as he was instructed to do. Everyone left the room leaving me alone with the President. He immediately turned to me. "Son, I don't know who you are or how you got in here but all I'll say is this, you damn well better have a good explanation as to how you got here. You've got two minutes to explain how and why you are here!"

I realized I had to convince him of the gravity of the situation he was to soon face. "Mr. President I have evidence with me that can save your life if you allow me to show it to you." President Kennedy responded back, "Son how old are you?" I replied that I was 17 years old. Before he could respond I continued, "Mr. President, I totally understand how this can seem kind of crazy to you but I assure you that your life is in danger. I have information that may be instrumental in saving your life."

He walked over to his desk and made a phone call. He spoke to the individual on the other line in a low voice for a few moments and then put the phone back down. He looked squarely at me as he spoke on the phone. He then instructed me to sit on a chair that stood nearby. The next several minutes that passed were by far the longest and most awkward few minutes I had ever felt.

A host of thoughts began to flood my mind. I hadn't even begun to skim the surface of revealing to the President the reasons why I had arrived. He had seemingly taken the bold step of having at least given me the opportunity to talk to him alone.

An overwhelming sense of fear began to take over my whole thought process. What if he were to dismiss what I was soon to tell him? Would I be stuck in the past as a prisoner? I sat and began to go through everything I was going to say next. All the while, I tried to formulate how I was to start explaining the contents on my films so as to make my evidence as credible as possible.

The doors to the President's office suddenly swung open. I could see that there were now several Secret Service agents stationed outside his office, each of them trying to catch a glimpse of me. Just as I took my attention off them it was at that moment that I suddenly realized that Robert Kennedy had just walked into the room. I could not help but feel the same sense of astonishment I felt upon initially being in the presence of President Kennedy.

As was the case with his brother before him, Robert Kennedy was totally caught off guard by my sudden presence. With a look of concern, he now began to stare at me for several moments. He walked to get a closer look at me. "Son, do I know you from somewhere?" I responded, "No sir, you and I have never met" I replied. He continued to stare at me in an effort to try and determine where he had seen me before. I felt somewhat uncomfortable with his repeated stare. I now turned to look at President Kennedy.

As if to read his mind, President Kennedy indicated to him that he himself was still trying to determine how I had appeared out of nowhere. Sensing the need to break the tension that had now transpired, I immediately reached in and removed the 8mm film still in its case from my bag.

President Kennedy rose from his chair, clearly surprised by my sudden actions. I quickly explained, "I need to have access to a projector so as to show you the contents found in this video. My whole purpose for being here will be explained through its contents." John and Robert Kennedy looked at one another; both were equally caught off guard by my request. They spoke to one another in a low voice; President Kennedy proceeded to pick up the phone and began to speak for several minutes. All the while, Robert continued to stare at me seemingly convinced he had seen me elsewhere.

We were interrupted by a knock on the door. A man walked in wearing glasses. I sensed his uneasiness towards my presence there as he stared at me. I recognized him from several of the videos I had viewed during my initial research into the assassination. I particularly remembered the glasses he wore in all the footage I saw of him. Given the commotion that was now taking place, I couldn't pin point his exact identity but I knew it would come to me in time given the complexity of the research I had immersed myself in recently.

He was a serious looking man who looked at me in a concerned manner. It was clear that my very presence there posed a threat to national security. Although the three of them spoke softly in front of President Kennedy's desk, I was able to make out a portion of their conversation.

I could hear them both reassuring the individual that I did not pose an immediate threat to them. The fact that I was so young had presumably minimized the threat I may have presented at first glance. President Kennedy then instructed me to follow him and Robert. I followed them both down a hallway in the White House. I had seen photographs of this magnificent building; I was now in awe of both its size and beauty.

As the three of us walked down its long hallway I found myself being stared at by several members of the Secret Service as well as other staff members present. He led us to a smaller room. An aide setup up a screen and projector and proceeded to leave the room as per the President's request.

"By the way", responded President Kennedy "You haven't told us your name yet" I hesitated for a moment. I immediately replied that my name was John. They both looked at one another. The fact that the President and I shared the same first name was somewhat ironic. "Well John, you definitely have our attention and I can assure you that it is safe for you to show us this important material you so urgently speak of."

I felt somewhat uneasy about what I was about to show the both of them; still I had accomplished more than even I could have hoped to at this point. I had, at the very least been given the opportunity to present them the evidence I had so desperately wanted to share.

"Mr. President, I don't know how to tell you this, but if history plays itself out as it is destined to, you will die in less than three days!" From the expressions on their faces it was clear that I had certainly caught the attention of both men. I continued, "Mr. President, what I am about to show you is going to be disturbing to you as it was for me when I saw if for the first time. It is the very reason that I am here today. I don't know how or even why I was chosen to be the one that stumbled upon this information. The images I am about to show you are excerpts from a number of films and documentaries that I have edited into two films which will show all the events surrounding your imminent death."

President Kennedy immediately cut me off before I could say anything more. "Let me see if I have this correct. Are you telling us that what you are about to display represents events that have not yet happened?" He continued, "With all due respect son, you'll have to excuse us if we find what you are now saying unbelievable?"

I knew at that moment I had now reached the point of no return. I had to prove my credibility to them. I quickly responded, "Mr. President, I know that what I have just told you seems crazy and hard to believe but I swear to you both that I am telling the truth. If anything else, how do you explain my being here? How is it possible that a seventeen year-old kid can suddenly show up at the most heavily guarded building in America without any member of your security spotting me?"

I then pulled out one of the two quarters I had brought back with me. I handed it to President Kennedy. He looked down and began to peruse the quarter I had just handed him. "This is a 1963 quarter minted this year. I don't quite understand its significance!" I then reached back into my pocket. "How do you then explain this?" I handed the newly minted 2013 quarter to him that I had purposely brought with me as well. Within moments, his facial expression turned deadly serious. Robert Kennedy noticed change in his brother's demeanor.

President Kennedy then handed the quarter to Robert Kennedy who, in turn studied it closely. Like his brother, the Attorney General's look quickly turned stoic as he realized the quarter he now held had been minted 50 years into the future. The two of them stared at one another for several more moments, clearly at a loss to explain what was now before them.

I reached down into my bag and nervously loaded the first of two films onto the projector. I hesitated for a couple of seconds then proceeded to turn the projector on. Both brothers now turned to face the screen before them, still baffled by the quarter I had handed them moments earlier.

The film began with Kennedy's arrival in Dallas and showed President Kennedy as he stepped off Air Force One along with his wife Jacqueline. As the narrative continued, the documentary followed the Kennedys as they were greeted by Governor Connally and several others including Vice President Johnson.

I had remembered to put all the poignant moments of the trip that served to show the enthusiasm and vigor that John F. Kennedy exuded upon his arrival in Dallas, Texas. Although I followed portions of his film as it played, my attention centered on the reactions of both John and Robert. The film continued as the narrator described the President's acceptance of a Stetson hat offered to him by those who greeted him.

As I watched President Kennedy's reactions, I could only imagine the thoughts that were running through his mind. The film continued with crowds of people who adorned the streets waiting for the arrival of their President. Many carried signs and all were enthusiastic. The tone of the film changed dramatically as its focus turned to the Zepruder film. I now turned my attention to President Kennedy; his face had turned white, Robert Kennedy looked on in stunned silence; not one word was said.

The segment of video now being played recalled the final seconds of President Kennedy's life culminating in the fatal shot that ultimately killed him. They both shrugged as the film showed the President's head thrown violently back in reaction to the fatal shot that ultimately killed him.

"This must be some kind of a joke!" cried President Kennedy. "How and where did you get this film?" He was visibly upset by what he had just seen. Robert Kennedy put his hand on his brother's shoulder as he turned to me. "Son, I don't know how you got hold of this footage but you had better tell us what this all means!"

I turned to address the both of them. "Gentlemen, as crazy as this may seem the truth is I have come back from the future having myself stumbled onto the information you are now watching. I have come back for the sole purpose of trying to somehow prevent all that you are about to see from happening!"

The film continued to play as I spoke. On the screen was none other than Walter Cronkite, proclaiming to the world that President Kennedy had in fact died of the injuries suffered in Dallas. My usage of Cronkite's speech had the desired effect I had hoped for. He was the one individual all Americans living during the 1960s were familiar with.

Robert Kennedy's stoic facial expression caught the attention of President Kennedy as well. He continued to stare at the screen in front of him seemingly unaware of anyone around him. President Kennedy asked his brother what he was fixated on.

Robert approached the projector and proceeded to rewind the film back to the portion showing Walter Cronkite's announcement which confirmed the death of the President. He immediately stopped the film. It was at that moment that I realized the significance of what was now transpiring before me.

It was clear he was witnessing something he felt he had seen before, even though it hadn't happened yet. He turned back to face his brother. "John, I don't know how, but everything we have just witnessed somehow seems familiar to me, it's as if I remember it to be true."

President Kennedy was clearly stunned by his brother's admission. In my mind it was apparent that John and Robert trusted each other like no other. To hear his brother proclaim his belief in the validity of the contents now being shown, gave my film instant credibility. It seemed that something inside of Robert now told him he was going to somehow witness Walter Cronkite as the person who was to first personify the proclamation of the events that were soon to occur in Dallas.

The somber images of Cronkite later taking off his glasses, his eyes clearly watery showed the sadness of someone visibly distraught with the news of the passing of a President. I looked over to the President; he too now stared aimlessly in sadness at the screen in front of him.

As Cronkite announced the time of death, President Kennedy picked up the phone, all the while not taking his eyes off the screen. He called his secretary and asked her to bring him a copy of that day's newspaper along with three glasses of water. He did not break his stare at the film in front of him, as if not to miss a moment of its content. The narrative continued back to the moment following the fatal head shot and showed it in slow motion. It then played the events that followed at regular speed showing Jacqueline Kennedy's immediate reaction to the last fatal shot.

I continued to watch President Kennedy, his eyes fixated on the screen watching the images of his wife climbing onto the back of the Presidential limousine in a vain attempt to get help for her husband now mortally wounded. The film followed the actions of a Secret Service agent as he climbed onto the back of the limousine just as it sped towards the hospital. President Kennedy asked me to stop the film; I did so immediately. It was clear the information on the film had begun to takes its toll on him.

He put his head down, brushed his hair back with his hands, and simply gathered his thoughts. Robert Kennedy stared blankly at me for moments as if to elicit a response. I felt a sudden uneasiness. I knew, however that what I was doing was the right thing. It was the only way possible if I was to have any hope of convincing both men of the fate that was to await the President.

The three of us then took a break from the film and walked back to President Kennedy's office. As we walked down the same long corridor we had walked past previously, I was struck by the increased presence of Secret Service personnel. More importantly, it became apparent to me that the curiosity these same individuals had shown towards me had now turned into animosity.

President Kennedy's top advisors and staff were clearly not happy with the fact that I had simply "turned up" out of nowhere and suddenly commanded the full attention of both the President and the Attorney General. The three of us were halfway down the hall when I suddenly realized that we had left my film as well as my binders back in the room we had just vacated.

What if something were to happen to either bit of evidence? What if someone were to view the film, even for a few moments! Robert Kennedy immediately ran alongside me down the hallway, having realized that we had left the evidence behind unguarded. It was only a couple of minutes away but it seemed like an eternity as we arrived back.

A number of Secret Service agents ran behind us, having not seen Robert's initial reaction. Upon re-entering the room we were relieved to find both the film and binder still present and untouched. I immediately took the film from the projector and put it along with my written evidence back into my bag. My concern over the contents did not go unnoticed by the Secret Service agents that had followed us back to the room. They looked on as I removed the film reel from the projector and placed it alongside the other documents left in my bag. We proceeded to make our way back to the President.

Moments after returning, both the President and Attorney General were summoned outside of his office by several members of their staff. I sat and waited for, what turned out to be several minutes.

CHAPTER 18

It was obvious that my sudden appearance had now created quite a stir amongst the President's key advisors. The Texas trip was quickly approaching. His advisors were undoubtedly upset and curious as to why both the President and the Attorney were committing so much time to a complete stranger rather than preparing for an important political trip that was just days away.

Upon their return several minutes later, President Kennedy turned to me and asked how I had come across the information I had shown them thus far. It was clear he had been briefed in the short time spent with his advisors. I began to describe how my foray into Kennedy's life began as an assignment for school. I continued by describing how it manifested itself into an obsession as my dreams became more and more complex with each passing day.

Both Kennedy brothers sat and listened as I continued to describe how I finally became convinced of the legitimacy of my dreams having later realized that I had actually ventured back into the past. I was careful not to stray too deeply into what was to be presented next. Not the least of which was the explanation of the World Wide Web, the main source of my research which ultimately led me to the many documents that made up the crux of my research. I spent several minutes explaining how it worked and the many intricacies involved with its use.

It was at that point that I began to believe that my age was becoming less of a factor that played any part in hindering my credibility. The information I had now revealed to both men began to break the walls of doubt both of them may have initially felt.

As we prepared to move back to the viewing room, the man I had seen before knocked and entered the room. Having seen him for a second time in person, I now realized he was none other than Robert McNamara, President Kennedy's Secretary of Defense. McNamara had been one of President Kennedy's closest advisors. He was visibly concerned with my presence there and asked me where I was from. Before I could answer the question, President Kennedy interceded and indicated that I was the son of a family friend. Stunned by the President's assertion, I did not say a word. He immediately motioned for McNamara to talk to them in the room next door; he asked me to wait as the three of them now made their way to the room next door.

I walked towards the wall that separated the two rooms and began to listen as much as possible to what was being said between them. It became evident that the President and Attorney General were engaged in a heated exchange with a number of their advisors. While understanding the frustration that his advisors must have been feeling with the Texas trip so close, I couldn't help but wonder if any of them were involved with the hidden agenda that surrounded it.

If this were in fact the case, it suddenly dawned on me that I now represented a legitimate threat to any plan already in place. My trip back in time suddenly took on a whole new meaning. The more time I spent with the President and the Attorney General, the greater my threat to the Texas trip became.

The arguing then stopped as I heard the door to the room open. The discussion and activity I heard next door had now moved into the hallway outside. I walked quickly back to the chair I had been sitting in previously. Just as I sat down the door quickly opened; John and Robert entered the room and informed me we were going back to the viewing room.

As the three of us walked down the hallway, I quickly realized that I now drew more stares by advisors that were strewn along the long hallways of the White House. We entered the viewing room we had vacated earlier. I reloaded the film onto the projector and proceeded to resume play. I took out the binder that contained the written notes I had brought with me as well.

The film continued with the narrative on the events that surrounded the arrest and detainment of Lee Harvey Oswald. It captured the numerous attempts by Oswald to request legal representation throughout his detainment by Dallas police. It then began to outline the events involving Oswald in the months that preceded the assassination of President Kennedy. These images were still fresh in my mind but were new to both the President and Attorney General.

The film narration now turned its focus to the television coverage of Oswald's jail transfer. I hadn't seen this film footage for some time. I too found myself fixated to the images that soon followed. We looked on as Oswald, flanked on both sides by members of the Dallas Police Department walked towards an awaiting police car. I drew my attention to the reactions of both Kennedys as Jack Ruby lunged forward and shot Oswald at point blank range!

John and Robert Kennedy now stood perplexed as they listened to the bedlam as described by those covering the events that day. They both looked on as members of the Dallas Police Department successfully dispossessed Ruby of the gun he had used to shoot Oswald. The moans of pain that Oswald let out as he was shot served to further accentuate the enormity of what had just occurred.

I shut off the projector. President Kennedy immediately called for more water as he attempted to compose himself. Within a few moments, the door opened and someone brought the three of us the water that the President had requested. He immediately asked me to restart the projector.

The focus of my film now turned to Jack Ruby and his role in the Kennedy assassination. I had chosen the portion of video that described Ruby's past. It described Ruby's Carousel Club and its possible ties to Dallas police. Both John and Robert listened intently to Ruby's comments. President Kennedy immediately asked me what Ruby's ultimate fate was. I informed him of the fact that Ruby was sentenced to jail only to die a few short years into his sentence.

It was at that moment I realized that President Kennedy had moved passed the notion of any doubt regarding the evidence I was presenting him with. I wondered all the while if Robert Kennedy had done so as well. I approached the projector and stopped it for a moment. I opened my binder and began to read off the many notes made on Oswald and Ruby. I spent the next several minutes explaining everything I had uncovered about both men.

While describing the events surrounding Oswald on the day of the assassination, I outlined the evidence of those present in the Texas Schoolbook depository the morning of the assassination. I couldn't help but wonder how strange it must have seemed to both of them having me refer to events that had not yet taken place in history.

I continued by explaining Ruby's role in the assassination. I then turned the projector back on and watched as the narration on the film described the numerous phone calls that were made by Ruby to various members of the mob. The movie outlined how the frequency of these calls increased dramatically following the announcement of President Kennedy's trip to Dallas.

The most compelling portion of this section of film that covered Ruby's role in the Kennedy assassination began to play. Both Kennedys looked on in utter dismay as Ruby, flanked on both sides, proclaimed to all who would listen that the world would never know the true motives behinds his actions.

President Kennedy put his head down and began to brush his hair back with both hands; he then drew his head back up. In a sign of obvious frustration he asked loudly "What the hell is going on? Has everyone gone insane? If what you say is in fact true, I am going to be assassinated in cold blood, in my own country! How is that possible?" Robert Kennedy put his head down, having now sensed the helplessness in his brother's voice. For a few fleeting moments, I didn't quite know how to respond to the President's plea.

There was a sudden knock on the door. An individual I hadn't seen before asked to speak to both John and Robert. I quickly turned off the projector. A conversation between him and President Kennedy quickly ensued. I did my best to be as discreet as possible. It soon became clear

their conversation once again centered on the time being spent with me.

I was suddenly startled as President Kennedy, in a raised voice exclaimed "As President and Attorney General, WE'LL decide who we talk to and for how long! As for the Texas trip, that's what we have YOU PEOPLE here for; now do your jobs and take care of things!"

I did my best not to look up at the exchange that was taking place. I could see that the individual had been caught totally off guard by the President's heated response. Robert did not respond; however, from the look on his face it was clear he supported his brother's outburst. As the man left the room, he stared at me with the same cold stare I had received from the others. He took one last glance at the film projector and the image now frozen on the screen.

What was becoming evident was the simple fact that the film I had brought back with me had garnered a great deal of attention. Its presence there was now becoming common knowledge to many of President Kennedy's most senior advisors.

As the door to the room opened once more, it was clear President Kennedy grew increasingly upset with each subsequent interruption. I had bent down to get more sheets of paper out of my bag. As I turned around, I now faced the back of a woman that was speaking to the President.

To my utter dismay, the woman was none other than Jacqueline Kennedy. I was immediately awestruck by the presence she conveyed. I found myself captivated by the combination of beauty and respect she exuded. Though she hadn't totally turned around to face me, I was sure it was her. As she spoke to her husband, it was clear from her expression that she had been informed by her husband's staff about my sudden arrival. They spoke for several minutes. Robert soon joined in on their conversation. They spoke quietly. I could make out only a very small portion of their conversation.

Jacqueline and the President turned and proceeded to approach me. I felt incredibly nervous, more so than when I had first met the President himself. "John, I'd like to introduce to you my wife Jacqueline". I nervously acknowledged her. Her immediate reaction upon seeing me was one of surprise. President Kennedy quickly noticed her response. He then responded, "Jacqueline is everything okay?" She hesitated for several more seconds. I put my hand out to shake hers.

"Pleased to meet you Mrs. Kennedy" I responded. She immediately reciprocated. "Have I met you before" she asked. "No, that wouldn't be possible given where I've come from", I responded. She seemed confused at first. She then spoke briefly to her husband for a few moments. She turned to face me. "Please to meet you John." I acknowledged her response once again and simply smiled back. I was immediately captivated by her charm and grace mirrored through the soft spoken manner to which she conducted herself. She exited the room with such poise.

I walked towards the projector and looked at both John and Robert Kennedy. I took a deep breath and slowly proceeded to start the projector. My film continued by showing images of the President's body lying in state; the lineup to view his body numbered in the thousands. It showed images of the many dignitaries that waited in line to catch a glimpse of the deceased President. Included in the long lineups were ordinary people from all walks of life. The narrator commented on how profound an effect the President's death had on the American people.

I stared at President Kennedy; once again he was totally speechless and simply stared at the images as they came across the screen. The film continued with images of the TV coverage of the funeral which showed the President's body being transported by cartage towards the church where his funeral was to take place.

The initial images were of Jacqueline Kennedy walking beside both her brother in-laws in the front of the procession. She was dressed in black, her face covered by a dark veil. I now glanced over at Robert Kennedy. He was clearly moved by the film footage he was watching. His eyes began to water as he watched images of himself walking beside Mrs. Kennedy dressed in black looking somber and despondent.

The film reached the portion of coverage that showed the image of Jacqueline Kennedy standing beside her children. As the casket of the late President slowly passed by them John F. Kennedy Jr. took his now famous step forward and saluted his deceased father as he passed by.

I turned around and saw a visibly despondent President Kennedy wiping a number of tears from his eyes. Robert Kennedy did the same as he rested one hand on his brother's shoulder. I walked up to President Kennedy and asked him softly "Mr. President, are you okay?" He acknowledged my question and seemed to be "moved" by my gesture of concern. He then left the room for a few moments.

Robert Kennedy had seen enough. Recognizing his brother had left the room, he now echoed what President Kennedy had asked earlier. "Given everything that you have uncovered, how in god's name does this happen? It just doesn't make any sense! I can't help but feel that I am viewing these images as if I have seen them before. I know it doesn't make sense but I know how I feel. What I do know however, is this; I believe them to be real. Something inside of me is telling me that these events are going to happen!"

Robert Kennedy's assertion affected me to my very core. It was clear I was the only person he could divulge the emotions and fears he now felt. His very belief in the validity of the events I had shown him served to reinforce the fact that my decision to show them these future events was indeed the correct one!

He continued, "There has got to be a way for us to prevent this from happening!" There was a mixture of both desperation and urgency in his voice as he tried to come to grips with everything I had shown him. There was no doubting the importance John F. Kennedy had on Robert Kennedy's life. Indeed, the two brothers were as close as siblings could be. It immediately reminded me of the relationship I had with my own brother Ted. I turned to address him. "Mr. Kennedy, as difficult as this is to see and accept it is imperative that I convey to you all that I know. Both your lives depend on it!"

His facial expression changed dramatically. It was clear the message I had just conveyed was not lost on him. He was speechless for several moments now trying to determine exactly what I was trying to convey to him. Before he could respond further, President Kennedy returned carrying a folder; he quickly sensed that his brother and I had conferred during his absence but he chose not to press for any information as to what we had conversed about.

I looked down at my watch and saw that it was now 4pm in the afternoon. The President was due to leave for the Texas in less than 48 hours. Time was starting to become a factor! I proceeded to re-start the projector. It continued by showing the images of reporters crowded inside a small room as another man spoke. He declared that the President had died as a result of a bullet to the head. The man gestured that the shot entered from the front.

The film then turned to the events that took place at Parkland Hospital. As I watched the film I closed my eyes for a few moments. The events in the hospital that I had witnessed first-hand in my dreams suddenly came back to me. I could once again picture the arguing and fighting that occurred between medical staff and members of the Secret Service intent on transporting the President's body back to Washington immediately.

The film then began discussing the differences in the findings that were noted by the hospital physicians and the official autopsy performed at the Bethesda Naval Hospital hours later. It continued by providing the many startling revelations concerning the autopsy of President Kennedy. Perhaps the most startling of these were the autopsy photographs. President Kennedy's jaw simply dropped as each photo came up on the screen. Robert Kennedy had a look of total dismay on his face.

John and Robert were now clearly "spent". President Kennedy asked me to shut off the projector. It was now 6:00 pm; they decided to break for dinner. He immediately called down to have the room locked. We made the now familiar walk to Kennedy's office. Moments later, several people brought in food for the three of us to eat. As we sat and began to talk President Kennedy began to ask more details about where I came from and the events that surrounded my ability to travel back to time.

I began by telling them all about my family in Boston and how I missed them. Both men were clearly amazed at the story of my first foray into the past and the circumstances that surrounded it. A half hour passed when we decided to continue viewing the evidence. It was at that moment that I realized I had once again left my items behind a half hour earlier. Both John and Robert had picked up on my concern. We quickly rushed back to gather my belongings.

Upon arriving I immediately noticed that, unlike the previous times we had left, the film projector had been moved from its original spot in front of the viewing screen. It was now placed at the extreme corner of the room and was unplugged. We simply looked at one another without making a sound. President Kennedy immediately called for one of his aides. As he entered, the President berated him, asking why the projector had been moved from its original spot. The individual did not have an answer.

President Kennedy picked up the phone in the room and began a short conversation. Within a couple of minutes a man walked in. The President was again quite livid and demanded to know why anyone would have had any reason to enter the viewing room. He demanded that the projector be moved to a different room. There seemed to be a feeling of urgency in the President's insistence that we immediately transfer to a safer and secure room. It was clear he began to trust no one. Within minutes we were situated in our new viewing room along with the projector and screen.

President Kennedy immediately asked me to continue with my presentation. Given the ever-growing suspicions by his staff he too was becoming increasingly aware of the fact that time was now becoming a factor.

CHAPTER 19

My film evidence now centered on the Warren Commission. The documentary I had chosen began with a narrative account of the members of the commission. Both John and Robert's faces were once again fixated on the screen as they discovered the individuals who made up the Warren Commission.

The President's face in particular, became expressionless upon seeing that Allan Dulles was part of the team chosen to investigate those who were responsible for his assassination. The irony of the situation was soon apparent to all of us. As fate would have it, the man President Kennedy has fired earlier was now the same man chosen to uncover the truth regarding his assassination!

The film's documentary on the Warren Commission continued by detailing the commission's findings and recommendations including its assertion that Lee Harvey Oswald had acted alone in assassinating President Kennedy

I reached into my bag and removed my binder from it. I began to delve further into the Warren Commission controversy by covering details that I had uncovered during my research. I handed them both a list of names indicating their relevance to the assassination as well as the dates and causes of their deaths. Both John and Robert Kennedy perused the list with a great deal of interest. I explained how a number of witnesses close to the investigation had all died a short time following the assassination.

I then concentrated on the Warren Commission, on its assertion to the fact that it relied on the improbable "magic bullet" theory and the conundrum it presented. There was a sudden silence and uneasiness in the air. President Kennedy put his head down for a few seconds; Robert Kennedy stared straight ahead. It was clear that everything I had shown them began to weigh heavily on them. In a low voice he then asked, "Do you know who was responsible for my impending assassination?"

I didn't know how to respond to the President's question. It was the ONE question I had been consumed by for so many sleepless nights. I chose not to answer his question for the moment.

I now had the undivided attention of both men. In an effort to further curtail his question, I began to detail the events that directly led to his assassination. Once again, both men were completely caught off guard as I began to outline the series of events that preceded President Kennedy's assassination.

The in-depth information I presented on such events as Operation Mongoose and the Bay of Pigs invasion once again left no doubt of the fact that I had been privy to information only a select few were aware of. The specific details regarding the events surrounding America's involvement in the Vietnam War introduced revelations neither one of them could have ever dreamed of, nor anticipated.

I began to describe the events that occurred throughout history that ultimately led to America's full-scale involvement in Vietnam. As was that case with all the other information I had previously presented to them, the scope and detail of my research left no doubt as to the credibility of the information I now possessed.

These latest revelations caught the attention of both men. President Kennedy sat up in his chair and walked over to the window nearby. Moments later, as he peered out the window with his arms folded, Robert Kennedy joined him. The two now began to speak softly seemingly debating the information that had now been brought to their attention.

I began to remove the second binder from my bag along with the second of the two 8mm films I had brought with me. I loaded the projector and walked back to my seat. It was now almost 10 pm. I knew I had to finish presenting all my information to them before it was too late.

Robert Kennedy returned to his chair and asked me to outline the events in Vietnam as they transpired in time. It was clear that my assessment of Vietnam had "peaked" the interests of both men. The events I began to describe proved to be even more disturbing.

Both men sat and listened intently to everything I now described to them. I opened my binder and pulled out copies of NSM 263, the document that many scholars felt offered proof that President Kennedy had every intention of "scaling back" American involvement in Vietnam. (fn)

I handed Robert the copy of the document. He immediately handed the copy to his brother. From the look on their faces it was clear that both men were shocked at the fact that I had somehow come across this top secrete document. It was at that moment that I paused for a few moments and simply read my notes. As I did so I could hear them conversing with one another about the information that I had now brought before them. It wasn't every day that a complete stranger came to you and divulged classified information about the future outcome of a war your country had just entered in. Yet this was the reality they now faced.

I then began to describe how events in Vietnam changed drastically following the death of President Kennedy. I was now presenting my facts with an efficiency of flow and order that kept both men enthralled. I paused for a moment and began to reflect on how truly amazing it was that I was showing the two most important men in America pieces of history that no one else could have been aware of.

I could read it in both their minds. It was clear from their facial expressions that they both felt that our country had thrown itself into another war fought on foreign soil that meant the loss of many American lives. President Kennedy lifted his head up slightly and in a soft voice proclaimed "we entered ourselves into a war we had no business being a part of!" I acknowledged his concern and proceeded to turn the projector back on.

The film continued on as it chronicled the events of the Vietnam

War including the many protests throughout the United Sates by those who opposed the war in Vietnam. I stopped the film with the images still fresh in their minds. I delivered the final epitaph of the Vietnam War by describing to both men the effects the Vietnam War had on America. John and Robert both held their heads down as I described the emotional scars the war had on those who fought in it.

I got up from my chair and walked up to both of them, all the while trying to muster up the courage that now burned inside of me. I concluded my own final assessment of all that we had now seen. "The Vietnam War was a war that the United Sates should never have been involved in. It was a war we could not win."

President Kennedy rose from his chair and once again walked towards the window nearby. He looked out for several moments. "From everything I've seen it is clear that we have miscalculated our role in many things." He spoke in a soft low voice as if resigned to the fact that history was to go ahead as originally set out.

I paused for several moments then responded to the President's comment. "Mr. President, in order to stop this war from happening you must live past November 22, 1963 or history will continue as it was first destined to happen. You WILL NOT be here to prevent all that I have shown you from happening!"

I then turned my attention to Robert. I immediately asked him if he recalled all the speeches made by President Nixon concerning America's withdraw from Vietnam. Robert acknowledged that he did not recall the speeches at all. "How could I? It hasn't even happened yet!" He then stopped suddenly. I did not utter a word. President Kennedy looked on as well, having picked up on the fact that his brother was suddenly at a loss for words. Having now come to a certain realization, Robert quickly composed himself and now stared aimlessly as he began to speak once again.

"For many of the events you have spoken of that are to take place in time I have been able to acknowledge in my mind a sense of familiarity for each and every one of them. For some inexplicable reason, I have no semblance of familiarity with any of these events you have just shown us." Having quickly realized what his brother had now surmised, President Kennedy immediately began to realize the relevance of what he had just spoken of. He then turned to me, almost in a complete daze. "John, you do know why this is the case, don't you!"

For several moments I found myself unable to respond to them. My sole purpose in returning to the past was to inform President Kennedy of his impending death. Doing so meant I would have to describe the details of his assassination. To now have to inform Robert Kennedy of HIS own assassination was not something I had prepared myself for. I hadn't anticipated the fact that the information regarding his brother's assassination would spell out so clearly the reality of his death as well.

As was the case for President Kennedy, I now found myself burdened with the unenviable task of informing Robert Kennedy that he too would suffer the same fate as his brother less than a decade later. In his case however, Robert had already surmised what I was now about to confirm!

I then turned to address both men. I began to describe the events surrounding Robert Kennedy's assassination. Once again, they were totally fixated on me as I revealed to them details neither was yet aware of. I described the events that took place at the Ambassador Hotel on the night that Robert Kennedy was himself assassinated. I explained how Kennedy was celebrating having just won the Presidential primary for California.

I approached the projector and turned it on. I fast-forwarded the film to a portion of my film that I had first added as an afterthought. Within a few moments images of Robert Kennedy filled the screen. Upon arriving Robert raised his arms in victory, thanked his supporters for their hard work during his campaign. The film continued on as Kennedy's speech then turned to a serious note. He called for the nation to overcome the racial divisions that continued to plague America; he also called for an end to the war in Vietnam.

Like his brother before him Robert watched in stunned silence as the images of what took place on the night of his assassination continued. Robert Kennedy ended his speech with the sign of victory. "Now on to Chicago, and let's win there!" [fn]

They were the last words he would speak. The three of us looked on at the film footage. There was now a defining silence between us, broken only by the images before us. The film footage now followed Robert as he walked towards a side door of the ballroom that would lead him through a short cut to a waiting throng of press reporters. In the midst of all the chaos that followed, he had collapsed onto the ground having been shot several times.

I glanced at Robert Kennedy. He was fixated at the images that emanated from the screen; his face was expressionless. It was the same reaction I had seen from President Kennedy when he saw the initial footage of his own death. I immediately turned off the projector and continued to describe the events that followed.

I tried to compose myself as I turned back towards them. Both men simply stared at the empty screen in front of them. Robert hung his head down and simply stared at the floor below him. I turned the projector off in order to give them time to collect their thoughts.

I walked up to Robert. "Mr. Kennedy, I know that this must be hard for you to accept." He replied back, "You are sitting there trying to tell us that we are both going to be the victims of the most heinous of crimes. A death neither one of us knows for certain is going to happen!" I looked down, once again not knowing what to say. The guilt I felt in describing their untimely deaths began to take its toll on me.

I made my way to the door in our room and walked outside. The Secret Service agents that were stationed around me now seemed irrelevant. Their stares felt insignificant given all that I was feeling. For the first time I began to question the information I was showing the Kennedys. Was I wrong in disclosing to them the information regarding their future fate in life? Was Osborne correct in his warning that my actions could cause more harm than good! All the while something inside of me did not sit well. There had to be some other piece of concrete evidence that would leave no doubt as to the probability of these events happening!

CHAPTER 20

Dr. Mellings made his way down the long corridor that led to his office in the hospital. The images that appeared in my mind were that of a traumatized and now weak Rose Cheramie. She spoke in his ear, trying in vain to get a message to him; this permeated in his mind as he made his way back to his office.

He pulled his sleeve back and checked the time on his wrist watch. It was 2pm. Somewhat relieved he picked up the phone and began to dial the number on the sheet of paper that lay on his desk. He made several more inquires and phone calls until he reached his desired location, the Governor's office! "This is Dr. Jeremy Mellings, I am the head of Emergency at Parkland Hospital in Dallas. I need to speak to the Governor at once. I have pertinent information regarding President Kennedy's upcoming visit to Texas!

As my premonition continued, I could see the increased apprehension he felt as he was put on hold. He continued to hold for the secretary he had been speaking to for several moments. Minutes later she came back on the line. He quickly began to raise his voice as it became increasingly clear that his concerns were not being taken seriously.

"Look, I don't care if the Governor is busy at the moment. The information I have is a matter of national security! It may very well save President Kennedy's life!" He now continued in an almost frenzied state. "No, I can't pass the information on to you. It is classified and needs to be told to the Governor himself! Listen, doesn't anyone there care about the President's well being. Do you want something tragic to happen in your own backyard?" Now exasperated with her lack of urgency, he simply slammed the phone back onto its receiver.

He pulled his head up and brushed his hair back. Beads of sweat now poured down his face as he realized his efforts were clearly going to be in vain. The images soon dissipated in my mind as the dream soon ended. A thought suddenly came to me. It was at that moment that I knew I had to return home in order to bring back the crucial bit of information that I would need to piece everything together. Without warning and hesitation I closed my eyes. As I slowly re-opened them, I suddenly found myself staring at the bright light that greeted me each time I came back home from my journey to the past.

I walked over to my computer and searched through a number of sites I had looked through a few weeks earlier. Within a few minutes I found what I had been so desperately seeking. The key to everything now lay with the story involving Rose Charamie. The source was an article I had found during my initial research into the mob "angle" of the Kennedy assassination. The article concentrated on the story that was told to hospital doctors by Rose Cheramie; it detailed her warnings that the President was going to be shot in Dallas.

Another thought then came to mind. I walked to the back door that led to the laneway behind our house. I quickly made my way back to the library to talk to Mrs. Donahue. She immediately noticed me as I walked in and followed me into the viewing room we had deliberated in so many times before. I spent the next several minutes explaining all that had happened during my incredible journey back into time.

She was enthralled by everything that had transpired, including my time with everyone I had come into contact with. I then explained to her why I had returned. We spent the next few minutes photocopying the latest information I was going to take back with me to the past. A library staff person walked in and reminded her that the library was soon to close. I continued to photocopy scores of notes while she escorted the remaining library staff out and proceeded to lock the doors to the library.

Mrs. Donahue returned and insisted she would drive me back home. She turned off her computer and the two of us made our way downstairs to her car. She unlocked the passenger door for me and began to walk around to the driver's side. I began to open my door when I noticed a car across the street. It was the same car I had seen previously and was now parked on the roadway directly across from us. While I could not make out their faces, I was close enough to see that there were two men sitting in the car.

Mrs. Donahue had made the same connection as well. She proceeded to start her car and immediately began to drive ahead slowly. I looked behind me; to my utter dismay the car quickly made a u-turn and began to follow us. I now began to worry. Mrs. Donahue followed the movements of the strange car through her rear view mirror. We arrived and drove past my house. As we passed the house I looked at my side mirror being careful not to turn my head, thereby arousing the suspicions of the men in the car trailing us.

"What are we going to do?" I asked. "I'm thinking" she replied. "It's not safe for me to go back home by myself with my husband out of town for the next several days. Can I come back home with you and call an associate of mine so as to arrange for her to sleep over my house tonight?" I immediately replied to her that it would be okay for her to do so. We then proceeded to drive cautiously back to my house. As we arrived, neither of us made any attempt to look at the vehicle that had now parked itself along the roadway across the street.

My mother walked into the hallway as I entered with Mrs. Donahue; my father followed shortly. She had an angered look to her that she tried to conceal. It was obvious that she was caught off guard by Mrs. Donahue's sudden entrance. I introduced Mrs. Donahue to her; moments later my father entered the kitchen as well. She immediately asked me if she could use our telephone. I brought her the phone and she proceeded to make her call. My parents and I then made our way into the family room to give her some privacy.

Mrs. Donahue soon returned and stood by the entranceway to the family room. I immediately got up and followed her out to her car, all the while avoiding any eye contact with the vehicle that had now moved to another portion of the roadway across from my home. I turned and walked back towards the front door; in the corner of my eye I could see that the vehicle turned around and began to follow her once again. I tried to make out the license plate of the car as it slowly drove off. I walked quickly into the kitchen and wrote the license plate number down on a piece of paper. I quickly folded the paper and put it in my pocket for safe- keeping.

I nervously made my way back to the family room where my parents anxiously waited. I thought about what excuse I was going to tell my mother regarding my repeated absences from home in recent weeks. As I entered the room I began to speak, not wanting to give my mother the opportunity to take over the conversation. I totally disregarded everything I had planned to say earlier.

My father and I proceeded to explain all the events surrounding my initial research in JFK and the subsequent events that followed over the past few weeks including my contact with John and Robert Kennedy. My mother was in absolute disarray. I began to describe the events that had occurred that evening involving the strange vehicle that had followed me home. My father became noticeably concerned when told of the events that had unfolded that evening. We decided to drive to Mrs. Donahue's house to ensure that she was safe.

My older brother Ted then walked into the kitchen. He looked at me and immediately asked, "Where have you been?" "Busy", I responded. "Well that's pretty obvious", he returned. He then sensed that something had transpired. "You guys all look like you've seen a ghost or something; is everything okay?" My father immediately responded that everything was fine. As we both got up from our chairs to leave, my brother motioned to me as if to verify that all was indeed fine. I indicated to him that everything was under control.

My father and I made the short drive towards Mrs. Donahue's house. As we approached her street he immediately told me to put my head down so as not to be seen. He was careful not to turn his head towards me. My father continued to drive down towards her house. As we arrived, he confirmed the same black car with two men was parked across the street.

I indicated to him that this was indeed the same vehicle that had followed us earlier that evening. My father took a slight glance over at the vehicle as we drove by, being careful not to be conspicuous to the passengers in the car. As he pulled out his cellular phone I could sense his anxiousness as he began to dial her number. Her phone rang several times before she finally answered. He put the cellular phone in speaker mode so that we could both hear and talk to her at the same time.

I immediately asked her if she was okay. From the sound of her voice it was clear she was quite nervous. She informed us of the fact that the vehicle had followed her immediately after she had left our home. My father asked her if there was any way of gaining access to her back entranceway without being seen. She indicated that there was a laneway behind her house that allowed for access to her backyard.

My father began to drive towards the laneway. He pulled up slowly to it and parked across the street so as to attract as little attention as possible. Mrs. Donahue quickly opened the back door for us, she was visibly shaken. Her fears were magnified given the fact that her husband was away.

My father assured her that she was going to be okay. He immediately called the police and informed them of the suspicious car that had been parked outside her home for quite some time. No sooner had he hung up the phone, the headlights of the car outside suddenly turned on. The vehicle quickly sped off. Within minutes two patrol cars showed up and approached Mrs. Donahue's house. Moments later the doorbell rang; two police officers now stood on her front porch. Mrs. Donahue opened the door and let both officers in.

The lead officer immediately asked a number of questions including the description of the car. Mrs. Donahue and I explained to them that neither of us were able to get a close enough look required to describe either of the mysterious men in detail. I had, however taken down the license plate and handed the information to his partner. The officer asked several more questions in order to finish his report. A few minutes later his partner returned with a piece of paper in hand. He informed us that the plate number I had given him was untraceable.

Mrs. Donahue then escorted the two officers to the door; she now appeared to be even more frightened. It was at that moment that we all realized the degree of danger we were all facing. Given the fact that the strange vehicle could not be traced, I began to worry about the safety of everyone I had implicated through my research. It was obvious that the Kennedy assassination and my subsequent fascination with it had now led to a chain of events that were having negative repercussions in the present, as well as the past!

Mrs. Donahue then picked up her phone and proceeded to call Professor Osborne. He told her that he was to arrive at her home within the hour. Her demeanor changed immediately knowing that he had now agreed to stay with her for the next several hours. My father assured her that he would drive by her house on a regular basis for the next few days should the strange vehicle reappear. We then made our way back home; my father was visibly quiet during the short drive back. I asked him what he was thinking of. He hesitantly reminded me of the speed at which the mysterious car fled immediately after we had called the police.

A sense of fear now consumed me as I began to understand the relevance of what he had surmised. The two individuals left immediately after the police had been called, it was as if they had advance warning of the impending arrival of the police.

We arrived back home, I quickly made my way back to my room and immediately noticed the bright light that now emitted from it. It was brighter than ever. I felt a feeling of urgency as if something was telling me that I had to return back to the past before it was too late. I focused on the bright light as I lay on my bed. I slowly closed my eyes. Moments later I found myself back in the President's office.

President Kennedy sat behind his desk. He was somewhat startled having realized I had reappeared before him. He immediately got up and walked towards me. "John, we looked up and you were suddenly gone!" He walked back to his desk and called for his brother. As I followed his movements I noticed that my bag containing all my information and films now lay beside his desk.

Robert soon returned and acknowledged my presence. I approached both men and told them that the information I was about to tell them would remove any doubts as to how history was to unfold. I began to detail the circumstances behind the Rose Charemie incident. I described how she was originally on her way to Jackson, Louisiana but was forced to ride instead to Dallas, Texas. I described how Ms. Charamie had been told by the individuals she rode with that arrangements were now in place for an assassination attempt during President Kennedy's upcoming trip to Dallas.

Robert Kennedy suddenly stopped me before I could continue. "Wait a minute, if what you say is true then this event occurred yesterday!" I nodded to him acknowledging that he was correct in his assertion. President Kennedy was clearly entrenched in knowing what was to transpire next. I continued by explaining that Ms. Cheramie was one of the many witnesses that died mysteriously shortly after the assassination of the President.

He then rose from his chair. "Assuming this was even the case, why would underworld figures divulge the information about a plot that had supposedly been in planning for several months? Why would they be careless enough to take such a chance?" A thought then entered my mind.

I continued, "It is my contention that the mob figures who freely offered this information to Ms. Cheramie thought better of what they had told this woman. Once they realized the information they had made her privy to, they were intent on making it clear to her that her life depended on her ability to keep the information to herself."

I described how Rose Cheramie was admitted to a Dallas hospital after being beaten and left for dead. John and Robert looked squarely at one another. It was clear at that precise moment that they had come to the same conclusion; it was one I had never thought of. They had both surmised that the circumstances surrounding this incident were so recent, they could actually be verified. My information was no longer based solely on circumstantial evidence!

CHAPTER 21

President Kennedy sat back down on his chair. He then called down to his secretary and asked for a telephone book to be delivered to him. The door opened and an aide handed the President the telephone book he had requested. President Kennedy looked up the numbers of the hospitals in the Dallas area. Calls into the first two hospitals proved fruitless. A subsequent call to the third hospital finally produced the result he had been hoping for.

The secretary in the emergency department confirmed that a woman by the name of Rose Cheramie had in fact been treated the previous night. John and Robert looked at one another knowing full well that they were indeed going to be able to test the validity of my evidence. President Kennedy then asked for the name of the attending physician on duty during the evening in question. I looked on as he continued to write more information down on the pad of paper in front of him.

Minutes later a Presidential advisor I had not seen before walked in and began to openly question why the President had asked to be driven on the eve of his trip to Texas. He then looked at Robert Kennedy asking him to explain the importance of such an impromptu trip. Robert made it clear to him that he supported his brother's decision and assured him that he and I were to accompany the President. The advisor then insisted that the President be escorted by Secret Service agents. President Kennedy nodded to his brother, having agreed to his advisor's counsel.

Jacqueline Kennedy walked in and approached her husband. She glanced over to me for a moment, the expression on her face made it clear she was concerned with her husband's hasty request. It was evident that the President's latest request had spread like "wildfire" throughout the White House. He took her aside and spoke quietly to her for several minutes in an attempt to convince her that what he was doing was of vital importance. He reassured her of the fact that he would be escorted by several Secret Service staff for the duration of his trip.

The door to our room opened as a Presidential aide informed us that a car was ready and waiting for us outside. I grabbed the bag with my belongings. The three of us then took the long walk towards the awaiting car. As we approached the limousine I could see that our vehicle was to be escorted by three other vehicles, one in front and two more behind. Little was spoken between the three of us throughout the ride there. It seemed that both John and Robert were careful not to say much so as not divulge the purpose of our trip.

President Kennedy held the sheet of paper he had written notes on tightly in his hand. I moved closer to him in an attempt to read part of what had been written. It contained the address of Dr. Melling's home. Within a few minutes our small motorcade pulled up to the driveway of the house. Three Secret Service agents waited in the two cars that trailed behind us while three other agents scouted the area. The front lights to the house suddenly came on.

A knock on the front window of the car seemed to indicate to the Secret Service agents seated in front that the area had been secured. The agent gave the three of us the sign that it was safe for us to exit our vehicle. As we approached the house I could see that Dr. Mellings had opened his front door to see who had arrived.

We soon made our way up the steps to the front porch. Dr. Mellings initial reaction was one of total shock as he immediately recognized who he was now in the presence of. President Kennedy shook his hand and requested permission for the three of us to enter his home. The door closed, two Secret Service agents were now stationed outside the front entrance. I peered through the side window beside the front door and could clearly make out at least six agents stationed outside at various locations surrounding the house.

Dr. Mellings tried to keep his composure as he led the three of us to a large table in his kitchen. I could only imagine the thoughts that now ran through his mind. Having the President of the United States enter your home was not an everyday occurrence!

President Kennedy began to describe the nature of our impromptu visit. Moments later Dr. Melling's wife walked into the kitchen, all the while indicating to her husband that the men were still stationed in front of their home. He quickly stood up from his chair and escorted his wife to the table we were all sitting around. I introduced myself to her; my presence was not nearly as shocking as that of the President and Attorney General.

Dr. Mellings finally mustered up the courage to speak, "Mr. President it is an honor to have you here before my wife and I." He immediately asked what the purpose of our being there was. President Kennedy then spoke, "Dr. Mellings you worked the Emergency room shift last night, did you not?" Mellings responded by confirming that he had in fact worked on the evening in question.

President Kennedy continued, "Sir, you saw a patient last night that may have spoken to you. The information she may have divulged to you is of vital importance to me, as well as our country." Mellings and his wife now looked at one another; it was obvious that the two had spoken about the events that had transpired on the previous evening.

Mellings nervously responded by reminding the President of the patient/doctor confidentiality oath he would now compromise were he to divulge what was said between him and his patient. I was somewhat surprised by his reluctance to share the information he had previously been so adamant to share. He now glanced back his wife. They both stared awkwardly at one another. It was clear to me that there was something important they were holding back.

Mellings then turned to address the rest of us. He gave his wife a quick glance so as to reassure her that he was he was doing the right thing. What he was about to disclose would prove to be crucial. He began to describe what took place after having completed the call to the Governor's office.

He was met by two individuals who identified themselves as agents of the FBI. They indicated their interest in a woman that had been brought to the hospital earlier that evening. He described in detail how he knew right away the individual they were referring to was Rose Cheramie.

He continued by recounting how he described to them the fact that she was clearly in a state of shock. He indicated that the one agent immediately asked what it was that she had said to staff that evening. He continued, "I remember distinctly how the one agent in particular wanted to know every detail as to what Rose Cheramie had said to anyone present that night! I told them that I was the doctor in charge and had been present with her throughout her stay in the hospital. Given his demeanor it was clear that these men were not fooling around. I decided to tell them nothing of what she told me. As I did so, the second of the two agents left the room for a few minutes."

He continued, "I spoke with the other agent for several more minutes and described to him my recollection of what had taken place earlier. He joined his partner shortly thereafter and they spoke in private; all the while, the agent I had spoken with kept glancing over at me several times. He proceeded to speak to me again. The expression on his face was one I will never forget. He disclosed how one of the nurses on duty had witnessed the fact that Ms. Cheramie had whispered something to me. He demanded to know what had been said between us!"

"As scared as I was at that moment, I mustered all the courage I had and simply told him that she wanted me to ease the pain she was experiencing. I described to him how I told her that I would do what I could to control her pain. Judging by the look on his face I knew he wasn't totally convinced of my story. I asked him to check my medical notes from that evening which I knew would show that I had given her a very small dose of morphine following her arrival. All the other sedatives I had given to her had not been effective in minimizing her pain. I remembered that I had made the decision to give her the dose of morphine so as to calm her down given the mental state she was in."

He continued, "Sure enough, the second of the two agents left only to return moments later having checked my log and verified such with the nurses present at the time. He promptly relayed the message to the agent I was being interviewed by. Two things were made abundantly clear to me at that very moment. My story was credible enough to have saved me for the time being. More importantly, I realized that these men were quite serious and would go to great lengths to get to whatever it was they were searching for!"

A thought immediately crossed my mind. "Dr. Mellings, can you describe these men?' He responded quickly, "How can I forget! They were both very tall, menacing men. They both wore dark black overcoats with gloves. They weren't your "typical" agents; especially the one that led my interview. I myself have been known to be an intimidating person to those around me. The individual who interviewed me was every bit as intimidating as I've always been. I knew seconds into our conversation that this was a man not to be fooled with."

I tried desperately not to divulge the fear that now consumed me inside. There was no doubt in my mind; the two men Mellings had just described were the exact two men that were now following me in the future! The lead agent he had just described definitely matched the description of the individual I had most recently come across! If this were in fact the case, it was now evident that these men had transcended time just as I had done. They had themselves traveled into the future to do what I was now attempting to do in the past. The difference however was the fact that these men were intent on doing whatever it took to circumvent any attempt to get to the bottom of the Kennedy assassination, let alone try to stop it!

President Kennedy moved forward in his chair; "Sir, the information you have been made privy to us could hold the key to saving my life, as well as that of the Attorney General. It is vital you tell us everything that was said between you and Ms. Cheramie! He then sat back in his chair waiting for a response from the doctor. There was a dead silence for several moments. Mellings looked at his wife as if to once again gain her approval for what he was about to divulge to us.

He hesitantly acknowledged that an incident had in fact occurred during his last shift. He began to describe the events that had unfolded that night. "She came into emergency last night in a way that could only be described as a state of shock and panic. It was immediately evident to me that this woman had been physically assaulted. My first inclination was to treat her for shock. Within minutes she became increasingly animated and began to scream for help."

He continued, "I administered a sedative in an attempt to calm her down; it proved to be totally ineffective. It was at that moment that she pleaded for the nurses present to leave the room immediately. In an effort to calm her down I agreed to have everyone leave. She definitely wanted to speak to me in private. Ms. Cheramie immediately began to describe the events of that evening. She indicated that she was entertaining two individuals who agreed to pay exorbitant amounts of money for her services. She went on to say that she was told to deviate from her original trip to Louisiana and was forced to drive alongside them to Texas."

Mellings now turned to specifically address President Kennedy. "Within an hour of the drive these men began to talk about you sir! Their comments were decidedly uncomplimentary at first. Minutes into the conversation it became clear to her that these men shared a hatred for both you and your brother whom they claimed had betrayed them."

"Ms. Cheramie then described how the ride with these men changed dramatically when she attempted to defend the actions taken by your administration. Both men immediately "turned" on Ms. Cheramie and began to berate her. Their actions soon turned violent; they began to physically abuse her, telling her that she had no right to defend the actions of the Kennedys whom they considered to be hypocrites. They then tossed her out of the car and left her there for dead!"

"A passing driver witnessed the incident and immediately pulled over to assist her. The man did not get the license plate of the vehicle containing the two men but he did have the decency to drive her to the hospital. Apart from everything she had told me, Ms. Cheramie introduced a number of startling revelations that began to haunt me the moment my shift ended!"

We all looked on in stunned anticipation as Mellings recounted the most "telling" points of their conversation. "In a voice that began to tremble while speaking, Ms. Cheramie informed me that she had been told by both men that a bounty had been put on President Kennedy's life!" His face became flushed; he could hardly face President Kennedy as he spoke.

"Given the details of her conversation with these men, I immediately felt her story was credible and truthful. Given her emotional state, there was no doubt in my mind that she feared for her life because of the information that she had been made aware of. She began to calm down only after she had told me, in private, all that had happened to her that evening. It was as if a huge weight had been lifted off her shoulders. It was only after she was able to recant her ordeal to me that the morphine I had given her minutes earlier began to truly take effect. I had left her to rest. When I returned to check on her a few hours later she was gone. It may have been a blessing in disguise. Had she been there when those agents arrived, they would have probably disposed of her soon thereafter."

Dr. Mellings indicated that no one had given her clearance to leave, nor had anyone witnessed her sudden exit. It was as if she had vanished. It was clear however that Rose Cheramie had resigned herself to the fact that she would leave as soon as she was able to. Just as she had arrived in secrecy, she left in silence. He informed us that he had made a point to copy her emergency room file and called a friend he knew from the police department. A subsequent search of her address proved fruitless. Other searches on previous addresses for Rose Cheramie proved to be just as futile.

To say we were all in shock would have been an understatement. Robert did not utter a single word. President Kennedy began to speak in a soft voice seemingly resigned to the fact that the details described to him were accurate. The President then addressed him, "Other than your wife, have you told anyone about what Ms. Cheramie said to you?" Mellings nodded and responded by telling him that he hadn't divulged this information to anyone else other than his wife.

His story had a profound effect on everyone at the table. No one spoke for several moments. There was nothing anyone could say that would alleviate the sense of hopelessness we were undoubtedly feeling. His proclamation served as an apocalyptic warning of what was to come. Dr. Melling's story corroborated everything I had told them earlier that day.

Sensing the need to say something, Mellings tried to provide the only answer he could. "President Kennedy I am so sorry for having been the one to have to tell you this shocking revelation. I did not sleep at all last night knowing what I had been secretly told. I almost wish I hadn't been given this information at all. The most difficult aspect of this ordeal was the sense of helplessness I felt, knowing that there was nothing I could do to stop it!"

He continued, "Given what we now know to be true, are there any steps that can be taken to prevent what may happen to you? Robert looked at Mellings but did not say a word. I was immediately struck by the fact that he did not have a reply. I knew at that moment that neither of the Kennedy brothers had a response.

While his story was incredible, I couldn't help but think that every extra moment spent with Dr. Mellings took away from what little time we had left to formulate a plan which might prevent the events first prescribed by history. This same thought had undoubtedly crossed the minds of both John and Robert Kennedy.

The President stood up and proceeded to shake Melling's hand. Robert Kennedy did the same; both went to great lengths to thank him for the information he so willingly shared with them. Mellings then turned his attention to me and asked what my role was in everything they had talked about that night. President Kennedy quickly responded, "That sir, is a very special person who has helped us discover things we otherwise would have never discovered. My brother and I are both forever indebted to him!"

As John and Robert began to walk away from the table I glanced over to look at the doctor. The look on his face was that of someone relieved to have been able to discuss what had clearly been weighing on him for hours. I was coming to the realization that I was beginning to change the course of history. This one visit had "upped the stakes" in the effort to change the course of history forever!

We walked down the hallway to the front door and signaled to the Secret Service agents waiting outside that we were ready to leave. Within a few short moments the door opened and the three of us were escorted quickly into the car that awaited us.

The ride back to the White House was somewhat somber. Both men stared outside their prospective windows seemingly thinking about the new information brought to light. I myself stared out the window nearest to me thinking about what my next move would be, all the while I began to wonder about what was occurring back home.

CHAPTER 22

Upon our arrival several Secret Service agents, as well as members of President Kennedy's staff lined the hallway that led back to the viewing room we had previously used. I couldn't help but notice the "buzz" in the air created by our visit to Dr. Melling's house. President Kennedy closed the door behind us. Sensing there were going to be many questions asked about his visit that night, I sensed an opportunity.

I immediately told both men that I had to return back home to the future. I did not wait to explain my reasons for doing so, I simply closed my eyes only to find myself back home in my room again. Having heard my footsteps upstairs my father entered the room. The look on his face made it clear that a number of events had transpired during my recent absence.

He walked to the side of my bedroom window that faced the front of our house. He was careful to ensure that he kept to the side of the window so as not to be seen. He then motioned me to approach the other side of the window in the same manner. I moved my head to a position where I could slowly begin to see out the window. A vehicle was parked across the street. From its position directly underneath the street lamp, I quickly realized this was as a different vehicle from the one we had seen before. I was able to identify that there were two individuals in the car.

My dad then motioned me to move carefully away from the window. We now both sat at the foot of my bed. He began to describe how the vehicle had been parked in front of our house for the past couple of days. I asked my father if he had been in contact with Mrs. Donahue. He indicated that he last spoken to her two days earlier and that he had been unable to get a hold of her since then. I picked up my cell phone I had left on my nightstand. I immediately began to dial her number. I was somewhat startled as a man answered the phone. His voice was calm and polite; he identified himself as Mrs. Donahue's husband.

I immediately asked if everything was okay. He responded by saying that everything was fine and that Mrs. Donahue had gone to bed. I then asked him if the car that had been monitoring his wife was still parked outside their home. He hesitated for a moment, he then responded by saying that he had called the police and that the vehicle had since left. I told him I would call back later. I hung up the phone and looked at my father; he immediately sensed my concern over the conversation I had just had. I paused for a moment, thinking about what Mrs. Donahue had said to my father the last time we were together. Something just didn't sit right with me.

I began to think back once again to past conversations with Mrs. Donahue. It was at that moment I remembered how she had indicated to us that her husband was going to be away on business. As I relayed what I was thinking to my father, his demeanor began to change. Without saying a word the both of us made our way downstairs and into the car knowing full well that time was of the essence.

My father drove quickly towards Mrs. Donahue's house. I was suddenly overcome with a sense of fear and apprehension. This was the first real hint of actual danger, one that affected people I had been directly associated with! My father turned the corner slowly as we arrived. We now came to a complete stop. We both looked up in total disbelief. The vehicle that was parked across the street was now parked on her driveway. My worst fears were now confirmed; it was clear that the individual I had spoken to was not Mrs. Donahue's husband!

Without hesitation my father took out his cell phone and proceeded to call the police. He gave the police dispatcher Mrs. Donahue's address describing the situation at hand. If there was any doubt as to the gravity of the situation I now found myself in, it had all but disappeared! The dispatcher replied that she was to send a police car immediately. Moments later, the second of the two men exited the house in haste with a cellular phone in hand. Soon after, the mysterious vehicle and its passengers sped off.

This time however, instead of simply driving off in the direction it was parked, the car made a sudden U-turn and drove towards our car. I looked in utter dismay as the other car slowly passed us. It was a show of invincibility that was not lost on either one of us.

As the car drove past us I could plainly see that the windows of the vehicle were tinted thereby not allowing us the opportunity to identify the men inside. Soon thereafter, a police car arrived and pulled up in front of Mrs. Donahue's house. My father and I quickly got out and approached the police car. I immediately explained that I was the one who had placed the call to the police.

My father and I looked on as the police officers carefully and methodically entered the house. The officers walked in and began to look around for any sign of struggle. They called out Mrs. Donahue's name a couple of times. No one answered. They immediately called for backup as they proceeded to search the rest of the house for any signs of struggle. I slowly walked into the front foyer of the house and peered into the same kitchen we had all sat around hours earlier.

For all my accomplishments, they now paled in comparison to the harm I had indirectly caused to a woman whose only crime was to help me in my search for the truth. The front door now opened once more. To my surprise, Professor Osborne walked in. I immediately walked over to him and simply asked what happened?

He began to describe the events that had taken place hours earlier. "I had been with Judith last night, given the fact that the strange vehicle was still parked in front of the house. I then received a call from a university colleague asking if I could cover his morning lecture. He had covered for me several times so I felt I owed him a favor."

One of the two officers had a notepad in his hand. He began to take notes as Professor Osborne spoke. He continued, "I was gone for perhaps three hours. When I arrived she was nowhere to be found. I waited for her to arrive. I tried calling her several times on my cell but I couldn't get a hold of her. I waited up as long as I could but I fell asleep. When I awoke this morning she still hadn't arrived back."

The officer taking down the notes paused for a moment. "Professor Osborne, what time did you say you arrived back from the university?" He confirmed the time of his arrival to be about 4pm yesterday afternoon. The officer continued his line of questioning. "Did she say she had an appointment to go to?" Professor Osborne responded by indicating that she hadn't. The officer continued. "It is now 9pm in the evening, more than 24 hours since her sudden disappearance; can you explain to me why you haven't yet called the police department to report her as a missing person?"

My father and I now looked at one another, eager to see what Professor Osborne's response would be. He hesitated for a moment and indicated he was going to wait until morning in order to give her time to return home. The officer continued with his questioning. "Professor, would you consider Mrs. Donahue to be a close friend?"

Before he could answer, I indicated to the officer the fact that Professor Osborne and Mrs. Donahue had been close friends for years. The officer turned back to me and instructed me to allow the Professor to answer the question. Professor Osborne immediately acknowledged that he had been a close friend of her for many years. The officer hesitated for a moment to catch his thoughts and simply looked at Osborne for a couple of moments. He then finished off his notes. He thanked the professor for his help and asked he would be willing to come down to the police station to answer a few more questions.

Somewhat surprised by the officer's request, Professor Osborne responded by indicating that he was agreeable to answering the remainder of the officer's questions at the police station nearby. Two more officers then entered the house and immediately asked us to leave. As I stepped outside I looked back to see one of the officers point to both the front and back doors.

My father quickly approached me and pulled me aside knowing full well that we would both be questioned that evening. He made it clear that neither one of us could tell the police any details regarding her involvement in my research. One of the two original officers at the scene then approached us both and asked if we would be willing to come to the police station to give statements as to what occurred that evening. They agreed to have us follow them in their car to the station thereby avoiding having police cars follow us home. Professor Osborne followed as well.

The three of us were each questioned for about 25 minutes. The officers gave both my father and I their business cards asking us to call either one of them should we remember anything else about that evening. My father then spoke to the officers alone for a few more minutes as I waited. Professor Osborne had just finished answering questions as well. He approached me and asked what the officers had questioned me about. I couldn't help but feel something different about his demeanor. He seemed much more concerned about what I had told police rather than what may have possibly happed to Mrs. Donahue. I felt somewhat relieved as my father returned from his interview. Professor Osborne then insisted that I keep him updated as to how my journey to the past had progressed. I assured him that I would keep in contact with him. He then indicated that he had to meet with an associate and had to leave.

We got back into our car and made the slow drive back home. The drive back was eerily quiet. Neither one of us spoke during the initial few minutes of the ride. I kept thinking back to Professor Osborne's penchant for wanting to know what had been said during my questioning. My father finally broke the silence. "John I'm not sure what it is that these men want from you or Mrs. Donahue. One thing is for certain, you have information that is potentially threatening to these people; information that they do not want the public to know! They may also have custody of the one person that could potentially blow the lid on everything you have uncovered!

My stomach sank; it felt like the whole world had just caved in on me. Everything I had discovered and experienced over the past few weeks was now possibly compromised. "Do you think we should have told them about the fact that she had been followed and monitored the night before?" My father paused, as if thinking about it himself. "I'm not sure" he responded. "What I do know is this, if Mrs. Donahue was not safe, then neither are we!"

We quickly parked the car and walked inside as if to make sure everyone at home was okay. No sooner had we arrived; my mother came out of the kitchen with a concerned look on her face. "You two have been gone for some time. I want to know what is going on right this minute!" My father looked over to me for a moment. He then made his way beside her and sat down. He began to explain to her all the details of the events that had taken place over the past couple of days that ultimately led to the disappearance of Mrs. Donahue. As he finished I couldn't help but think that events now occurring in the present were somehow tied into the evidence that my research had uncovered.

Having listened to me intently, my father took my theory one step further. He explained that by changing the course of past events, the ensuing circumstances that followed would undoubtedly change the course of events in the present as well!

The telephone then rang; its ringing startled all three of us. My mother picked up the phone. "Yes, John is here, just a minute please." She hesitantly handed me the telephone. "Hello" I answered. The voice on the other end responded, "Is this John?" There was a pause for several seconds as the caller on the other end hung up. I put the phone down and did not say a word. The perplexed look on my face revealed everything I felt. It now became clear that events in both the past and the future were moving in a disturbing direction. I was running out of time in almost every sense. The importance of "righting" the events in the past suddenly took on a new importance given the fact that events in the present were now directly tied to those of the past as well.

As my parents spoke amongst themselves, I began to realize that I had to stop believing that I was solely responsible for the disappearance of Mrs. Donahue. It became apparent that there was no way I could have stopped the strange series of circumstances that had taken place. The most pressing question now was the identity of the two men that had followed us and were undoubtedly responsible for her disappearance.

The events that had unfolded over the past few hours now changed everything. My foray into the past now involved several other players, not the least of which was my family! Mrs. Donahue's life was now in grave danger simply because she agreed to help me. Suddenly, everything mattered!

My father approached me. "John, in the interest of safety I am taking the rest of the family to a safer location." He then got up and proceeded to make a phone call. My mother and I looked on as he carried on an in-depth conversation with another person. The conversation lasted several minutes. He then hung up the phone and hesitated for a few moments. "John, you need to return to the past in haste and do whatever you need to do to make things "right. Time is of the essence, you need to take care of this immediately. I will take care of things here in your absence. We will discuss things upon your return"

I looked at my mother. She had the look of someone who was unsure of what the future held next. One thing was certain: I had to return back to the past immediately. My ability to change what was happening in the present now depended on my ability to change what was happening in the past. My emotions then began to take hold of me. Perhaps it was the buildup of everything that was taking place around me.

I got up and hugged the both of them. My father softly whispered, "John, you will find your way! Just use the same judgement you have used up to this point and everything will work out." I acknowledged his advice and quickly made my way back to my room.

CHAPTER 23

I sat on the edge of my bed, the light in my room now shone brighter than ever before as if to tell me that the past now awaited my return. I closed my eyes only to find myself in front of John and Robert Kennedy. My sudden appearance no longer startled them. Before anyone could say a word the door to the room suddenly opened.

Jacqueline Kennedy walked into the room. As she closed the door I could see a throng of advisors now seemingly "camped out" in front of the room we occupied. It was clear that her arrival had a definite purpose to it. She immediately approached President Kennedy. Before he could say a word, she pulled him to a corner of the room. Given her somewhat raised voice I was able to make out their conversation. "John, what is going on, everyone is talking about your sudden absence that has coincided with HIS arrival. "Is there something you're not telling me that I should know?"

As she spoke I could not help but realize just how strong willed a woman she was. Everything I had read about Jacqueline Kennedy was true. President Kennedy, hesitant to divulge all that he had been informed of over the past 24 hours, simply stared at her. He now turned back to face both Robert and I knowing full well that we had overheard their conversation. Robert acknowledged his stare and then glanced back to me. From his facial expression it was clear he had decided we could no longer keep silent what she was now questioning.

The reality of the situation was not lost on either one of us; she was soon about to live out the events that fate had in store for her!

President Kennedy approached me and asked me to explain the details of what I had divulged over the past couple of days. I turned to Robert Kennedy who immediately nodded in agreement. I now sensed the similar apprehension felt by them hours earlier.

I quickly set up the projector and proceeded to play excerpts of the film we had previously viewed. I searched for several minutes and immediately rewound the film to the point which began with the arrival of the Kennedys at Love Field that fateful day in Dallas.

The film continued by showing President Kennedy's speech during the first leg of his visit. The President took a chair and sat beside his wife. He then held her hand in order to console her. Mrs. Kennedy's facial expressions turned from one of surprise to one of apprehension as she sensed the scope of the events she was about to witness.

No one spoke as the commentator described the last few frames of the Zepruder film including the fatal shot that killed President Kennedy. I could see Jacqueline cringe as she witnessed the shot that abruptly ended her husband's life. She looked on intently as the film continued to describe the efforts made by her in vain to get help for her husband who had just been mortally wounded.

Mrs. Kennedy suddenly shot up from her chair and demanded an explanation of the events she had just witnessed. "What is this film based on?" I quickly responded, "Mrs. Kennedy the images you have just seen represent the events that are about to occur mere hours from now unless we stop them from happening."

Seemingly choosing not to accept my explanation, she looked to her husband. "John, please explain what is going on. Where did this film come from?" The President spent the next few minutes explaining my arrival as well as everything else I had told them about their future events. While this was the third time I had shown my video evidence, Jacqueline's reaction to what I had shown her had a much more profound effect on me. The horror she witnessed and would have to relive for the rest of her life was something I now felt first hand. I slowly walked back to the projector and continued to play the movie.

The film continued by describing the events following the shooting of President Kennedy. She stared at the images of people crying outside of Parkland Hospital following the pronouncement of the President's death. The euphoria around the live footage of Lee Harvey Oswald's capture and subsequent death followed. Jacqueline was absolutely stunned by the events that unfolded before her.

The film once again turned its attention to the funeral of President Kennedy. The poignant images were climaxed by John F. Kennedy Jr.'s salute to his father. In my mind they were images that remained nestled in the mind of every American in the years that followed President Kennedy's assassination. They now had the same effect on Jacqueline.

She began to break down and openly wept as the images continued before her. Robert immediately asked me to turn off the projector. President Kennedy knelt beside her and began to console his wife. Robert simply looked down. Jacqueline's emotional reaction to the images she had just witnessed seemed to take a toll on everyone present.

I looked on as President Kennedy continued to console his wife. As he looked up, the image of his wife wearing a black veil symbolizing her husband's death, remained as an image on the screen! Jacqueline then raised her head and attempted to regain control of her emotions. She rose from her seat and walked towards the window nearest to her. She peered out the window for several moments then calmly wiped the remaining tears from her eyes.

Jacqueline continued to look out the window having now regained her composure. "According to what you've shown me, my husband is going to die in Dallas; we will be arriving there in just a few hours." She then turned to her husband. "Tell me there is a way of stopping this from coming true! Tell me this isn't going to happen!"

President Kennedy walked up to his wife and put his hands on her shoulders. She had the same look of total resignation that both Kennedy brothers had shown during their initial viewing of my film. I approached the projector and once again loaded the second film reel. I loaded the projector and paused for a few moments. I then turned to face the three of them. Given everything that was happening at home, events now taking place no longer afforded me the opportunity to waste what little time I had left with them.

"I know that this may seem somewhat inappropriate given what you have just witnessed, but time is of the essence if we are to have any chance of stopping these chain events from happening. There is one last element of the assassination I haven't yet informed you of, but it is the last piece of evidence that will leave no doubt as to the plans currently in place!

Jacqueline Kennedy turned to look at her husband, afraid of what lay ahead. He held her hand knowing full well that I was about to show them more images that would undoubtedly be difficult to accept. Robert walked over and stood beside them as a show of support. As with the previous portions of my film, this segment began with narration describing the conversation that had taken place between a Miami Police informant and extremist Joseph Milteer. The reactions of both John and Robert were immediate.

The footage described the conversation that took place between the two individuals. Subtitles on the bottom of the screen showed the conversations as each man spoke thereby making it totally clear as to what they were saying. As the segment reached its conclusion, I reached into my bag to reveal a folder full of notes and documents. I began to review the events that took place just prior to President Kennedy's visit to Dallas. I described how the President's advisors had cancelled his planned trip to Chicago.

Once again, I described the events that plagued President Kennedy's recent trip to Miami including the cancellation of the Presidential motorcade that had originally been the cornerstone of the Miami visit. I then took out another sheet of paper from my folder. This sheet was larger than the others I had taken out previously. I turned it towards them to reveal a map showing the layout of Dealy Plaza including an outline of the motorcade route.

I followed the route with a pencil pointing out where the buildings strewn along the motorcade were situated in relation to the route taken. I explained that the combination of the lax security arrangements, and more importantly the streets chosen for the Presidential motorcade, ultimately left President Kennedy totally vulnerable and proved to be fatal. From the looks on their faces it was clear that they had come to realize the correlation between the tape I had shown them and the security arrangements that were now in place in Dallas.

Robert Kennedy stood up and began to speak. "How is it that these lax security arrangements have been allowed to go on, especially given the information that this tape has warned of!" I approached him while addressing all three present. I described how many historians would later conclude that members of the Secret Service organizing President Kennedy's trip may have been unaware of the Miami surveillance tape. "Or they may have simply chosen not to pay much attention to it" responded President Kennedy.

The President walked over to the same window his wife had peered out of minutes earlier. We all looked on as he glanced outside for several moments. He then turned to face us. "It seems as if the venue for my assassination has been chosen; the only thing left is to put whatever plan they have in store for me into effect!"

The physical evidence presented through the film I had shown them now left no doubt in anyone's mind that the events it portrayed were to become fact. What was once days away was now mere hours away. Robert put his head down between his hands, seemingly resigned to the fact of the terrible fate that lay in store for his brother. He knew full well a similar fate was to await his own political aspirations, ultimately leading to a similar death.

Jacqueline Kennedy simply stared ahead with a blank stare. Tears fell down her cheeks, she made no attempt to wipe them. As I turned to walk back towards my chair Robert stood up. "We still have time to stop this from happening!" Jacqueline slowly stood up from her chair. In a low but audible voice she responded, "The motorcade, we have to stop the motorcade from happening!"

We all looked at one another. No words were exchanged. It seemed to be a viable solution. If we were to stop the cascade of events that would eventually lead to the assassination of President Kennedy, we would have to find a way to stop the motorcade! The real question was simply HOW? President Kennedy stood up and now turned to face the three of us. "I simply have to cancel the Dallas trip!"

Robert responded, now pointing to the agents waiting in the hall outside. "There is no way those advisors out there will allow us to cancel Dallas outright! We're still trying to recover from the fallout in Chicago. Canceling Texas would be even worse. Not only would it weaken our position politically, it would also undermine Lyndon's support in his own home state!"

President Kennedy turned and walked back towards me. He addressed me in a soft yet somber voice, "There are things you have to take care of back home." His comments startled me. I stared at the President but did not say a word. It was as if he was somehow aware of events that were unfolding in the future. Robert and Jacqueline were somewhat startled by the President's statement; his words were like a premonition of events that seemed to be unfolding at home. The President turned to look at me once more as if to suggest that it was imperative that I return back home immediately.

I acknowledged his request then walked back to my chair; I then slowly closed my eyes. As I opened them again I found myself back in my bedroom. The strange light that emitted from my closet continued to shine brightly. I slowly walked towards the side of my bedroom window. In the backdrop I peered out at the view of the sun as it began to set, its bright orange hue was a contrast to the light that shone from my closet. I walked across the hallway upstairs and made my way down towards the living room.

From the clock on the table I could see that it was 5:30pm, early evening. A sudden sense of worry began to overtake me as I quickly sensed that things were not as they had once been. Every blind in the house was closed. It soon became evident to me that the house had been left in this manner as if to suggest that no one was to be home for some time. Our house had been vacated; the question was for how long?

I continued to survey everything around me. There was no sign of any of my brothers and sisters, nor my parents. Our house, the place that normally housed our large family now stood empty. I had never experienced such an empty feeling before. Darkness slowly began to set outside. An eerie feeling came over me; it was as if I was not alone.

I walked slowly to the large window in the living room that faced the front of the house. I stood to the side of the curtain and carefully pulled the blind ever so slowly until I was able to see outside. My instincts were indeed correct. Across the street directly in front of my house now stood the dark colored vehicle my father and I had previously seen in front of Mrs. Donahue's house.

I could clearly make out the figure of one of the men I had seen before. The man threw out a cigarette he had just finished. I slowly closed the blind and stood by the wall beside the window. I turned my back to the wall and simply stared ahead. I then stared straight at the small mirror that lay on the armoire across the room. I began to make out a figure approaching the front of the house. It suddenly became evident to me that this person would be able to see me just as I had seen him through the same mirror.

I immediately slid over to my left; I could no longer see the person from the mirror. I now stood with my head pressed as firmly back towards the wall so as to conceal my presence as much as possible. The silhouette of an individual now covered the window. I now sensed the person outside peering inside the room. Seconds felt like hours as I did my best to remain as motionless as possible to avoid being seen. A few more moments passed, I could see that the individual outside had turned back.

After waiting a few more seconds I slowly turned and faced the side of the window. I carefully pushed open the blinds ever so slowly and peered into the darkness. The street lights had now turned on. The vehicle was parked underneath the street lamp located directly across the street. One of the two men leaned on the car beside the driver's side window that was now fully open. He turned to speak to the second man in the driver's seat.

It was clear that these men weren't going anywhere soon. What was also apparent was the fact that they had waited for my return home. I slowly made my way back upstairs to my room. I lay on my bed and simply stared ahead. I closed my eyes for several moments; tears now ran down my eyes as the complexity of the situation I now found myself in began to set it. A number of thoughts came to mind. I began to second guess everything I had done over the past few weeks.

Everything around me had come crashing down. It was like a bad dream was occurring! I now felt solely responsible for everything that was happening around me. The feeling of control that had been my trademark throughout had all but eluded me. I now felt alone not knowing what direction events were to take.

I closed my eyes for a few moments. Images began to immediately appear. John and Robert Kennedy stood with their advisors alongside Jacqueline. President Kennedy informed them that he no longer felt it was a good idea to include a motorcade in his trip to Dallas. I could plainly see the immediate uproar the President's request caused. Many of the advisors looked at one another caught totally off guard by the President's suggestion. A number of them asked him what had prompted his sudden change of heart with respect to the upcoming motorcade. Kennedy sited the changes that had been made in Miami.

He continued by explaining that, given the circumstances, he felt the motorcade was not a good idea. His assertion was met with outright resistance. As had been our fear all along, arrangements were already in place in Texas for the President's arrival. Once again my actions had begun to alter events in history; President Kennedy's request was a direct attempt to do just that. It represented a shred of hope that my efforts would not be in vain.

CHAPTER 24

As my eyes opened, I found myself staring at the same bright light that continuously illuminated from my closet. The door to the closet was not fully open. I then suddenly caught a glimpse of a note that was clearly taped to the side wall inside the closet. I got up and walked towards it. It was folded but was addressed to me. I carefully dislodged the note from the wall so as not to rip it in any way.

The note was from my father; its contents described how the mysterious individuals had staked out our home for several hours. He indicated that it was no longer safe for them to stay there. It went on to say that they had left and were not going to return until they felt it was safe for them to do so. The note continued with my father's hope that I was okay and that events in the past were occurring as I had envisioned. He left an e-mail address I could write to. I took the note and sat down in front of my computer. I typed in the e-mail address on the note.

I preceded to send a message to my father and asked if the family was safe. I continued by indicating that the mysterious vehicle was still parked in front of our house thereby making it still unsafe for them to return home. I ended my e-mail by describing the events as they had occurred during my latest journey to the past.

Moments later, I was startled by the e-mail notification sound that came from my computer. In the middle of the screen was the banner indicating that I had just received an e-mail. I immediately proceeded to open it. My father wrote back indicating that he and the rest of my family had left town for a few days. He informed me that the strange vehicle had been continuously parked in front of our home. He assured me that they had not been followed and were in a safe place.

He then began writing in bold letters so as to accentuate what he was now trying to say. I simply stared at the screen as the response came back. "JOHN, DO NOT EXPLAIN WHAT YOU ARE INVOLVED IN RIGHT NOW UNDER ANY CIRCUMSTANCE! JUST KNOW THAT WE ARE ALL SAFE. PLEASE DO ALL THAT YOU HAVE TO IN ORDER TO ENSURE YOUR OWN SAFETY!

I immediately acknowledge his warning. He then wrote back in bold letters again. "JOHN, IT IS IMPORTANT THAT YOU COPY OUR E-MAIL DOWN AND THAT YOU NO LONGER E-MAIL US FROM HOME! The message ended. I paused for a moment and began to simply stare ahead aimlessly. A host of thoughts soon overcame me. My family had now also been put in harm's way through my foray into the past.

Mr. Montgomery was right. These men he had spoken of had been monitoring everything I had been researching the past couple of months. The question was; who were they? Who had sent them? More importantly, were they sent to stop my actions in the past from occurring as planned? If so, did they have the means to do so?

I walked over and sat on the edge of my bed. I began to think about Mrs. Donahue, all the while wondering where she was and what had happened to her. I reached into the pocket of my jeans and took out the piece of paper containing Professor Osborne's cell phone number. I dialed the numbers and waited. Strangely enough it rang once followed quickly by a busy signal. I tried calling again making sure I had dialed the correct phone number.

The same busy signal followed again. I now realized this was the same carrier I was currently using. I dialed 611, the number used to contact them directly. Moments later an operator answered. I asked her to check the phone number Professor Osborne had given me. She put me on hold as she verified the number. She returned on the line and indicated that the number I had given her was no longer in service.

She went on further to say that this particular number had been activated for a mere three hours.

From the tone of her voice she seemed surprised by the fact that the number had been listed for such a short time frame. I asked her if this was common; she indicated that she had never come across something as peculiar as this. She asked if there was anything else she could help me with. I paused for a moment to collect my thoughts. On a hunch, I asked if she could tell me the precise time the number had been activated and subsequently cancelled. She replied that this was information normally privy only to the person holding the account in question.

I asked if she could wave this rule this one time. Before she could respond, I pleaded once more for her to help me. She hesitated for a moment and indicated that the number had been activated two days earlier. I then asked if she could give me the precise time it had been activated on the day in question. Upon checking, she replied that it had been activated at precisely 6:30pm on the day it was first activated.

I thanked her for her assistance and disconnected our call. I now crouched down in front of the foot of my bed and stared ahead. The time frame she had indicated occurred on the same evening Mrs. Donahue and I had met with Professor Osborne. Unbeknownst to us, we had arrived shortly after Professor Osborne had activated his account.

It was obvious that Osborne had taken out a temporary cell number to give to me. This subsequent number was immediately disconnected so as not be traceable. The obvious question was, WHY? Was he afraid to make himself readily available to me? What would have been the purpose of giving me a fake cell number if he knew it would be useless to me? I got up and made my way back to my computer.

I logged onto the website used to find local phone listings. I searched the University in Boston Mrs. Donahue had indicated Professor Osborne was currently lecturing at. Having found the main number I proceeded to call the University. An automated operator asked for the name of the staff member I was searching for. I pronounced Professor Osborne's name as clearly as I could. The operator indicated there was no match for the name selected. I pressed zero to speak to a live operator.

The operator soon answered. I asked her to connect me to Professor Osborne. She responded that there was no such staff member on her directory. I found this odd and grew increasingly suspicious. She then forwarded me to the Dean of the department I knew Professor Osborne had taught in.

"Can I help you? He asked. I replied that I was looking for Professor Osborne. The man on the other line hesitated for a moment. His voice demeanor instantly changed. "Professor Osborne? Robert Osborne? I now hesitantly acknowledged such, all the while wondering if something terrible had happened to him as well. "Robert Osborne's employment with this institution was terminated three years ago for conduct unbecoming of a staff member. What relation are you to him? I began to panic not knowing how to respond to his question and quickly hung up.

As I put my head down and brushed my hair back with my fingers, I began to perspire. Who was Robert Osborne? What indiscretion had he committed that led to his immediate termination? More importantly, was this same man I had divulged all my information to a friend or a foe? All signs now pointed to the latter.

I turned on my printer and proceeded to print off a copy of my father's last e-mail. As it began to print I put my head down for a few seconds. With my head leaned on my folded arms I turned to the side of the room which faced the closet. Suddenly, something felt strange. I cautiously walked to the side of my window where I felt I could not be seen from. I gently opened the blinds and looked across the house to where the mysterious car had been parked. Just then, the driver's side door opened abruptly and one of the two men stepped out. He was tall and wore a black overcoat. He quickly crossed the street and made his way to our front door.

From the bottom of the window I could also see that the second individual, dressed in a similar overcoat had already reached the veranda of our home. It was at that moment I realized they had discovered my movements from the light that shone in my closet. How could I have been so careless? I could hear the noise of the knob to the front door as it turned. I walked quickly towards the closet and proceeded towards the light. As I turned around I realized my computer had been left on. What if they were to look at the computer and see the internet address my father had e-mailed me from? Surely they would be able to trace my family's whereabouts! My first impulse was to shut my computer down.

I began to hear the noise of footsteps coming upstairs. I looked down at my computer and saw that the shutdown process had begun. I knew I had to leave NOW. I couldn't take the chance of having any of the two individuals witness my gateway to the past. Without hesitation I quickly closed the door to my closet until I could barely see through the small crack in the door. Moments later both men entered my room.

I peered through the small crack I had left open. I looked on as they pried through my desk hoping to find something that could somehow lead them to me. I could see that my computer was still in the process of shutting down. A yellow message window appeared on the middle of the screen. One of the two men had sat down before the computer and began to type in a host of prompts. The other man continued to rummage through my drawers looking for more clues as to what I had been working on for the past several months. The man in front of the computer then took out a cell phone from his pocket and proceeded to make a call. The other individual now stood by him and began to pan around my room, scouring it for any clue as to my whereabouts.

It was at this moment that one of the two men noticed the bright light that emanated from the closet I presently stood in. He slowly approached. Realizing I had only moments to escape, I quickly closed my eyes still holding the note my father had left me. I immediately found myself back in President Kennedy's office. Jacqueline stood a few feet in front of me but had not yet noticed my return. A sudden feeling of panic began to set in as I realized that one of the two men in my room would undoubtedly enter the closet I had just left.

No one else had gone near the strange light that signaled my return to the past on so many occasions. Was I the sole person with the ability to transcend time, or could anyone else journey back to the past? These questions consumed me for several moments as I began to perspire. I closed my eyes once more and followed the images that now consumed my mind. They were the images of what was now happening back home.

The first of the two individuals in my room now stood at the entrance to my closet. The bright light that still shone immediately caught his attention. He simply stared at it for a couple of moments surprised by its intensity. He then noticed the tape that had held the note my father secretly placed there for me. A portion of the note was attached to it.

The man ripped if off the wall. The second of the two men noticed the attention given to the closet his associate now partially stood in. The other individual handed him the tape and portion of the note still stuck to it. The man in the closet glanced around one last time and proceeded to walk in. He rummaged through several shirts and pants that hung from the shelves. He combed through some of the storage boxes that were present. Convinced that there was nothing of any significance he soon exited the closet.

I re-opened my eyes again and breathed a sigh of relief. Jacqueline Kennedy acknowledged my return and asked if everything was alright. I responded as such. Moments later John and Robert entered the room. Both had a concerned look on their face.

President Kennedy began to describe their latest meeting with advisors. The trip to Dallas was now hours away. Before he could go on, I informed them both that I had seen visions of the proceedings that had taken place during their meeting. "Mr. President, with all that has happened over the course of the past couple of days it is clear that there is no way to stop the motorcade that is planned for Dallas. It's been advertised long enough thereby making it impossible to change the route, let alone cancel it."

Robert responded, "If I remember correctly, from the film footage of the assassination you showed us, it seems the only way we can try and prevent the assassination attempt from being successful is to remove the ease to which the shooters had to assassinate the President." "I see what you are getting at", President Kennedy responded. He then asked me to rewind my film to the portion that dealt with the Zepruder footage.

I methodically rewound the film exactly to the point that the Zepruder film was shown. We now concentrated on the images before us. He asked me to play the same sequences over again a number of times concentrating on each frame of the movie. President Kennedy no longer appeared disturbed by the images of his own assassination. He seemed focused on the sequence of time between the initial shots and the fatal shot that would eventually kill him.

"If I remember correctly, the time frame between the shots was a mere six seconds." I acknowledged his accuracy. He then asked me to shut off the projector and proceeded to walk towards the nearby window. It was now pitch dark outside as he stared out. He seemingly spent several moments thinking about what his next move was to be. He then turned around and asked me to replay the Zepruder film once more. This time he began to speak as the film played. "After viewing this film footage the one thing that is obvious to me is the fact that the vehicle I was riding in left me vulnerable to shots that proved to be fatal."

He now turned his attention squarely at me as he continued to key on the factors that ultimately lead to his demise. "All your evidence points to the fact that the shots fired upon the Presidential motorcade were to come from different positions." I could not help but be enthralled by the words that the President spoke of; this was the oratory I had read about so many times during my initial research. To witness him speak with such passion and charisma was truly amazing. "What is the most glaring factor that "jumps out at you" as you watch this film? I turned back to the screen and proceeded to play the Zepruder film one last time. I turned down the volume on the projector and concentrated on the images before me. I was totally oblivious to the others around me.

A few moments later, a thought then came to mind. I turned

around and looked straight at President Kennedy. "The limousine! It was an open limousine!" The President smiled at me as if to acknowledge the fact that we had both reached the same conclusion. Robert stood from his chair and walked up to the screen in front of him. As he approached his brother slowly, Jacqueline stood up from her chair and looked over at the paused image of her husband moments before his assassination.

"John, that's the answer", he responded. "It's the only variable we can change. It's the only shot we've got to stop events as they were first meant to happen." I continued from his thought. "The plan to assassinate you is based on the premise that the assassins will have a clear shot at you. If we can remove this one variable, we may be able to thwart your assassination". Robert then added, "That's all well and good if we can "pull it off," the problem now becomes whether or not we can convince the organizers of the Dallas trip to make the change to the motorcade!"

President Kennedy quickly responded. "That's just it. We know about the warning signs that have been out there for weeks. I still don't know the full extent of the threat that caused the canceling of the trip to Chicago! We weren't really ever told the real nature of the threat that was posed on that trip; we were simply told that it would be a good idea to cancel it." He continued, "As far as I'm concerned, John explained it perfectly yesterday. One would think that the same care and consideration would be used during the Dallas visit; yet, as far as I can see there haven't been any real discussions of the security adjustments that have supposedly been put in place for this trip!"

I listened to President Kennedy as he spoke. The "air" of humility that had characterized his previous discussions had now been replaced with a definite swagger. It was clear the President was "on a mission" to save his own life and change the course of history forever. "As far as I'm concerned the security arrangement changes we have discussed here cannot be compromised in any way. If we are to change history then we have to change what was originally going to happen."

He continued, "Now, we can't stop the forces that are at work as we speak. Undoubtedly, these men are reviewing every aspect of their itinerary in order to ensure that everything is in place to carry out their plan and its success." Robert interceded. "We have to out-smart them. We have to ensure that our plan of action is put into place successfully if we are to have any hope of stopping the assassination from occurring!"

President Kennedy nodded in agreement knowing full well that his assertion was correct. Jacqueline simply looked on as the others continued to speak. Her expression was almost one of relief as if knowing that a definite plan was now being formulated that might have a chance to save her husband's life. I then turned to address them, "Mr. President if we are to put our plan in place we cannot wait until tomorrow to inform your staff of your wish to change the motorcade." Both brothers looked at one another in agreement. They made their way outside to meet with senior staff.

CHAPTER 25

Jacqueline Kennedy and I stayed back in the room. There was a slight air of uneasiness for the first few moments. I felt a knot in my stomach in anticipation of what was happening outside. I knew full well that our ability to stop the original course of events was now predicated on President Kennedy's ability to "sell" his staff on his prescribed change to the motorcade that was less than a day away.

Jacqueline arose from her chair and came to sit beside me. She put her hand on mine in an almost motherly fashion. "John, I can't thank you enough for what you have done. You have courage way beyond your years, and for that we are forever indebted." I smiled and thanked her for her kind words. Once again, I couldn't help but be captivated by the way she conducted herself. Her words of encouragement calmed the emotions that had previously taken over me. In a small way, I came to realize how my presence also proved cathartic to her state of mind as well.

John and Robert Kennedy re-entered the room moments later. "We have arranged for a meeting with all of the advisors and security staff involved with the Dallas trip in exactly 15 minutes." The look on the President's face made it clear that this meeting would serve as the turning point of my journey to the past and would ultimately determine whether or not our plan was to be implemented.

In my mind, there was simply no other way to stop the assassination of John F. Kennedy from happening, short of him simply not showing up! President Kennedy then walked towards me. "John,

I'm sure you understand that there is really no way for you to be part of this meeting." He then turned his attention to his wife. "It's going to be allright; we're going to make this work, one way or another". The two embraced one another for several moments.

It was the most poignant moment I had been witness to. It was the reassurance Jacqueline Kennedy needed, knowing there was now a chance to prevent the ordeal that both she and her husband would soon face if history was to occur as originally set out. President Kennedy looked up at the clock on the far wall; several minutes had now passed. The time had come for him and Robert to leave. Both men had been involved in a number of high level meetings before.

Robert Kennedy had "taken on" the mob and had come away unscathed. President Kennedy had risen above all else as the world found itself at the brink of nuclear Armageddon; he too had come away from it the victor. These two men were now on their way to perhaps the most important meeting of their lives. While the stakes during their previous meetings were high, they paled in importance to what was to take place in mere minutes.

They both realized the fate of their lives now rested on their ability to successfully convince their staff to make the vital change to the motorcade. If they were to somehow be unsuccessful, their future fates would be "sealed" in the annals of history forever.

President Kennedy approached both Jacqueline and I. He kissed his wife and, in a soft low voice reiterated to her that everything would work out. He then turned to me and insisted that I not leave the room for any reason. There seemed to be an underlying sense of purpose in his request. It served to remind me of the fact that my presence there still posed a threat to those powers with a stake in his assassination. He then turned towards Robert and they proceeded towards the exit.

President Kennedy opened the door and began to speak to a couple of the Secret Service men stationed outside. He pointed to me on a couple of occasions. It was clear that he wanted to ensure that my well being was not to be jeopardized during their absence. The door soon closed leaving Jacqueline and I to now await the fate of her husband's next actions.

There were a few moments of silence between the two of us. Jacqueline broke the silence once again. "John, I know I've said this previously but I can't thank you enough for finding the answers you've found and for having had the courage to try to save my husband's life. For that I am eternally grateful." Once again I was taken back by Jacqueline's uncanny ability to captivate whomever she spoke to. The tone of her voice as well as the words chosen served as more proof of the confidence and charm she exuded. I took solace in the fact that, for a few fleeting moments, "Camelot" was alive and well. It was embodied in the spirit that flowed from the personality of Jacqueline Kennedy. Not only had I witnessed it, I had actually been a part of it, if only for a brief time.

The door to the room suddenly opened again. The both of us stood up surprised that the meeting had adjourned so quickly. A Secret Service agent walked in and indicated that a situation required Jacqueline's attention. She looked at me and assured me she wouldn't be long. She left the room as the agent followed her out.

I sat back down in my chair and rested for several minutes. Once again, a sense of uneasiness suddenly came upon me. Within moments, a host of images began to appear in my mind. I now envisioned a large room with a large oval table. Around the table sat some thirty advisors along with President and Robert Kennedy.

I could see and hear the conversations that took place. The meeting had now been in session for well over 10 minutes and had already become "heated". Security advisors went through a host of arrangements they insisted ensured the President's safety. The advisor spearheading the security arrangements in Dallas then questioned why the President was suddenly critical of the security arrangements for the Dallas trip.

He rose from his chair and began a heated diatribe about John and Robert Kennedy's changed stance towards the upcoming trip. He went further to suggest that it was prompted by my sudden appearance and the subsequent closed door meetings that had taken place between us. He demanded an answer as to why the President's senior advisors were not present in any such meetings that had taken place. His comments caused an immediate stir in the room; it was apparent that his concerns were shared by a number of other advisors that were present.

President Kennedy's facial expressions now changed dramatically. He stood up from his chair and immediately took over the conversation. "Whatever discussions that have taken place between this individual and us are just that; strictly between us. Nor do I appreciate my top advisors questioning what the Attorney General and I do behind closed doors!" Every person in the room was caught off guard by the President's remarks.

There was a momentary hush in the room. Before anyone could respond to his comments, he continued. "Now, I don't know exactly what threat exists out there. I am however aware of the fact that the trip to Chicago was cancelled for security reasons. I also know that last minute changes to the Miami trip were made because of an apparent security threat. Gentlemen, we are not talking months ago, we are talking mere weeks. As far as I am concerned, there is a definite threat that still exists, one that I am not comfortable with. Now, I know how important this trip to Texas is, but I am sure as hell not going to leave myself or anyone else exposed to danger in any way."

A senior advisor stood up and insisted that there could no longer be any last minute changes to the Presidential motorcade. Enthralled by what he had just been told, the President stood up from his chair and slammed his fist onto the table. Once again, the reaction in the room was swift. President Kennedy, in a loud stern voice exclaimed, "Gentlemen, I don't care what last minute arrangements have to be made, I am riding in a closed limousine. It is not open to discussion either, that's an order!"

The images in my mind ended abruptly. I was then startled by the noise of the door opening. A Secret Service agent walked in. He indicated that I was to follow him to another room. I took a small step back and asked why he was being asked to do so. The man responded that he had orders from the President to have me moved. I sensed that something was not right with his request. From the corner of my eye I now stared at the bag that contained all the files as well as the second of the two films I had brought with me. If they were to somehow find their way into the wrong hands, the consequences could prove fatal. I wrestled with a number of excuses I could possibly use to prevent my exiting the room.

Just as he was about to reiterate his request, Jacqueline Kennedy entered the room. From his expression, it was clear that he was caught off guard by her unplanned arrival. She asked the agent what he was doing. He nervously replied that the room they were currently in had to be vacated in order to accommodate another meeting. She immediately stared at the film still loaded onto the projector. She then turned her attention to the agent and reminded him of the President's request that the room was to be left alone. She then insisted that she was unaware of any meeting her husband was to attend that evening. The agent turned and indicated he would go back to his superiors for more direction. I felt the weight of the world removed from my shoulders as he then closed the door behind him. I could only wonder what would have happened had she not interceded.

Robert Kennedy entered the room, trailing him closely was the President. He made sure to close the door behind him as he entered. Jacqueline immediately informed him of the agent's request. Both John and Robert appeared visibly concerned with the events that had just transpired. "It's becoming increasingly clearer that we can't have John stay by himself, he has to stay with us at all times!" replied Robert. The President then began to speak. "Robert and I were notified earlier this evening that Jacqueline, myself, as well as Mr. and Mrs. Connelly are to ride together in the motorcade."

He continued, "It would appear that the arrangements that have been put in place match the events John has shown us through his films. I have, however insisted that we ride in a closed limousine, much to their chagrin." Jacqueline stood up and approached her husband. "John, are you certain that this plan will work? President Kennedy tuned to face her. "As things stand right now, it's our only option. They won't cancel the motorcade. The parade route has been in all the papers for days, it's too late to change that too. It would seem that events are indeed happening just as John had described through his film. Our only hope is to change the one variable we can."

From everything I had reasearched, there was no doubt in my mind that trained hired killers awaited President Kennedy's arrival in Dallas. The response to this very real threat revolved around the premise that the President was to ride in a closed limousine. While the change would provide a greater challenge to those hired to assassinate him, it did not guarantee that our plan would be an unqualified success.

A thought then came to mind that posed an immediate threat to the success of our plan. I sat up and approached the three of them. I pointed out that the President had now informed those responsible for the security arrangements about the changes to the motorcade. It stood to reason that this information might somehow make its way to those involved in the assassination attempt on the President.

If my theory was correct, the individuals awaiting the President's arrival in Dallas would now undoubtedly alter their plans as well. These same individuals still had 24 hours to change their own plan of action in order to increase their chance of success, given the changes the President had now imposed on them. The President looked over to his brother; a look of concern had taken over his demeanor. Indeed, what I had just pointed out made a great deal of sense which threatened the success of our plan. By informing members of his staff of his proposed change to the motorcade, the President could very well have jeopardized his own future.

Robert stood up; he walked towards the President and began to talk to him in private. Within minutes, President Kennedy turned to Jacqueline and asked her to stay with me while he and Robert made one last attempt to talk to their advisors. As the two of them left the room I couldn't help but wonder about what was currently happening back home. I turned to look at Jacqueline who now stood looking outside the window of the President's office.

Sensing the opportunity before me, I immediately closed my eyes and reopened them only to find myself back in my room. I slowly and carefully peered into my room. It was now turned upside down. My drawers were thrown everywhere. Papers and sheets had been strewn throughout the hallway outside my room. I suddenly heard a noise coming from downstairs. I could hear portions of a conversation taking place.

I walked slowly towards the hallway, all the while being careful to make as little noise as possible. I had reached the foot of the stairs and was now able to hear the conversation taking place. "We must have missed a hiding spot somewhere! "How could we have? The other man responded. "We've turned this house inside out; if there was something here we would have found it." As the two men continued their conversation, I pulled around the banister and slowly walked down the first two steps. I cautiously bent down slowly to get a better view of them.

A third man came around the corner from the living room. It was none other than Professor Osborne! He was wearing a similar overcoat worn by the other strange men as well. He too wore leather gloves. His presence served as confirmation of what I had suspected earlier; Osborne was one of THEM! I felt goose bumps along both arms as I now had a clear view of the three men that posed the biggest threat to everything I was attempting to change in the past.

For a few moments I thought back to Professor Osborne's demeanor during his questioning at Mrs. Donahue's house. He had seemed somewhat evasive, but I hadn't figured it out at that time. Having now discovered his true identity, it all made sense. I couldn't help but feel a sense of betrayal knowing full well that he was aware of everything I had uncovered regarding JFK. Would his knowledge of what I had told him prove fatal to my plans of saving the President?

I leaned back slightly on the top of the stair with my right leg; it suddenly creaked. I immediately looked back towards the kitchen. Professor Osborne suddenly turned around, startled by the noise I had made. He then turned his head in the other direction. I could feel a bead of sweat pour down from my forehead as I tried in vain not to make any movement that might give away my presence there. A sudden feeling came over me; the feeling one would get when being watched.

I was now overcome with fear. I looked back to face them once more. The second individual now looked at Professor Osborne; he looked straight ahead towards the fridge. I quickly focused my attention to it. The reflection of my feet could clearly be seen on the small mirror that was held with a magnet on the fridge door. I stood still, not knowing what my next move should be. Suddenly, without warning, the three of them darted out from their chairs and began to run towards me. I immediately began to run back up the stairs.

I did not look back and ran as fast as I could towards my room. Just as I approached the doorway I tripped over one of the many sheets of paper strewn throughout the entranceway. I fell onto my stomach. I turned back; to my horror I now saw the first of the two individuals as he reached the top of the stairs. I quickly regained my feet. I reached the foot of my bed and simply stared at the light that once again shone from my closet. I immediately closed my eyes. Moments later I was relieved to find myself back in the room with Jacqueline I had left minutes earlier. I was able to simultaneously follow the events that continued to take place in both the present and the past.

The three of them now looked everywhere for any sign of me. They were completely startled by the fact that I had simply vanished before them. They continued to scour my room for a secret hiding spot or anything that would explain my sudden escape. I wiped the sweat that had begun to stream down my sideburns as well as my neck. I looked down at my watch; it was now 11pm.

President Kennedy was now mere hours away from flying to Dallas. A sudden sense of anxiety now overwhelmed me. Everything was coming to a climax, both in the past as well as the present. I hadn't envisioned events to turn out as they had. For a few fleeting moments I began to regret the day I stumbled onto the Kennedy assassination and everything it entailed. I now thought of how my own life had been turned upside down; how so many people I cared for and had come across had now been affected by my unlikely discovery.

What was once a blessing seemed to have turned into a nightmare; one that I was not sure I was ready for. I sat on my chair as Jacqueline continued to stare outside the window of the office. She then turned to me, having noticed the sweat that now poured down my face. She made her way towards the nearby desk and pulled out a small towel lying in one of the drawers. She approached me and softly began to wipe the sweat from my face.

She then asked what was wrong. Tears began to roll down from my eyes as I explained everything that had occurred at home over the past couple of days. The culmination of everything that had transpired had taken an emotional toll on me. She put her arms around me and tried to comfort me for several moments. A small couch was stationed beside the chair I had been sitting on. She walked me over to it and asked me to lie down. Exhausted both mentally and physically by what had transpired over the past few hours, I closed my eyes and fell into deep sleep.

Hours later I was awoken. It was still early in the morning and the sun was just beginning to rise. I looked down at my watch and saw that it was 6:15 am. As I gained full consciousness I began to hear a great deal of activity coming from the hallway outside. I got up, walked towards the door and proceeded to open it. I peered out into the long hallway outside. It was "alive" with the activity as several aides carrying folders and briefcases walked past. I was soon approached by two men each holding folders in their hands. One of them asked me if I had slept comfortably. I cautiously acknowledged that I had in fact slept quite well. The second of the two men then asked me to follow them to another room. I hesitantly walked towards them and followed them outside. I stared up at both men who simply looked at one another as the three of us began to walk down another of the many hallways that made up the White House. We had passed several other hallways when I suddenly realized I had once again left the bag containing all my material back in the room we had just left.

I turned and made my way back as quickly as possible. The two agents quickly followed me. As I turned the corner to the hallway I had passed earlier, I spotted two Secret Service agents. They were clearly startled by my sudden return. I did my best to try and conceal any concerns I had over the items left behind. I walked into the room and proceeded to pick up the bag that still lay beside the couch I had slept on. The two advisors had followed me back to the room. From the corner of my eye I picked up on the gesture that they gave one another as I grabbed my belongings, holding them as tighter as ever.

The three of us walked down the long hall that led to another area of the White House I had not seen before. We approached another room that was opened. As I walked in, I could see that this was a much larger room than the others I had been in. The door closed as the other two men left. I walked toward a nearby window and peered outside: it was a clear sunny day outside. I stared for several minutes looking at the activity taking place.

The door then opened behind me as President Kennedy walked in followed by a number of advisors each holding either a briefcase or a folder of some sort. Rather than being relieved to see me, President Kennedy seemed surprised by my presence there. He took me by the arm towards the window I had stared out of minutes earlier. "John, I thought I told you to stay in the room we were in before!"

Robert and several more advisors walked in. The room housed a large table in the middle with seating for at least twenty people. Moments later, a number of other advisors walked in and took their seats. The President asked me to sit down in a chair that was off to the side. This was clearly another milestone for me; I was now actually sitting in on a meeting between the President of the United States and his most important advisors. My euphoria would soon prove to be short-lived.

I watched as one of President Kennedy's advisors immediately stood up. "With all due respect Mr. President there are many among us here who have sat and watched a young man appear out of nowhere and suddenly take up virtually all of your time." I looked on in stunned silence as he continued. It became all too apparent as to why I had been brought here. The agent continued. "Over the past couple of days you and the Attorney General have spent countless hours in closed doors talking about God knows what. This has all come on the eve of perhaps your most important trip to date. Rather than spending the crucial remaining hours with your closest advisors, you have instead chosen to spend them with a "kid" whom no one has seen or heard of before. As your advisors, we have numerous questions we feel should be answered immediately. Who is this young man? Does he have a name? How do you know him? More importantly, why has he suddenly commanded so much of your time?"

No one else spoke as President Kennedy stared at the individual who now challenged him for an answer. I gripped the handles of my chair as tight as ever, my palms became sweaty. I realized the gravity of the situation before me; this was the first time President Kennedy was being taken to task about his time spent with me. Everyone present now focused their attention squarely on him.

President Kennedy seemed somewhat surprised, at first, by his advisor's comments. His expression changed as it had done so many times before over the past couple of days. He rose from his chair slowly, yet methodically, as if to give himself some time to collect his thoughts and decide what he was to say next. He then turned his attention squarely to the individual who now questioned his motives. "Mr. McCadam, you have come before me this morning, on the eve, as you put it, of my most important political visit to date."

Sensing the tone of the President's voice, the advisor interceded in an attempt to explain his line of questioning. "Mr. President I did not intend". Not allowing him to finish his sentence, President Kennedy quickly interceded. "No, you've made your points while asking your questions, I'm sure many of your colleagues share in your thoughts." He paused for a moment as he got up from his chair and proceeded to circle the table, making eye contact with a number of advisors he felt were sympathetic to him.

The sweat that had previously materialized on my palms and forehead now began to subside as I felt the President take over the situation. He continued, "While I can understand your curiosity behind John's sudden visit to the White House this week." All eyes were now focused again on me as the President had now made my identity public. "John is the son of a friend Robert and I have known since our college days. Earlier this week both John's parents were killed in a car accident leaving him the sole survivor. While the timing of his visit may be questioned, we felt we owed it to his parents to take care of him while arrangements for his custody were being finalized."

"Mr. President", continued the advisor, "You must admit that the entire situation involving this young man's sudden appearance here is strange, to say the least! Why are we only now being made aware the facts surrounding his arrival here?" President Kennedy quickly responded. "Gentlemen, I don't believe the President of the United States is required by any law to divulge the reasoning behind his actions. If there was any immediate danger to either the Attorney General or I, you can be sure that John would have been incarcerated immediately. Such was not the case therefore I did not see the need to divulge the circumstances behind his sudden arrival."

Another of President Kennedy's advisors stood up from his chair and began to address those around the table. "Mr. President, the purpose of this meeting is not to undermine the motives surrounding your recent time spent with this young man. However, the fact still remains that you have suddenly and inexplicably begun to question a number of arrangements that have been put forth for the upcoming trip."

President Kennedy walked towards the section of the table where the man sat and now began to address his comments as well. "You are obviously making reference to the questions I raised towards the motorcade. I have made quite clear my reservations towards the original plans for the motorcade given the circumstances that have transpired in other cities over the past few weeks. I reiterate those concerns to you now."

I looked on as the President's comments created a "buzz" throughout the room. The advisor rose from his chair a second time in order to address the President. "Mr. President, the decision to include an open motorcade in Dallas was decided on weeks ago and was confirmed again following the Miami trip. It was during this time that we all agreed that an open motorcade would be crucial in connecting with the large crowds we expect to be present along its route. The fact that you came to us yesterday insisting that we replace the open motorcade with a closed one, makes no sense to a number of us and only serves to undermine the whole idea behind the motorcade. Your sudden change of heart seemed to coincide with the arrival of John. Our question to you sir is WHY?"

President Kennedy wasted no time in responding. "I can assure you that my so-called sudden change of heart was, in no way influenced by his sudden arrival!" He continued. "In fact, I find it ridiculous that my top advisors would not take my concerns seriously given the indiscretions that have take place over the past few weeks. Gentlemen, when all is said and done we are talking about my safety and the safety of those around me. Isn't that what we are all here for?"

President Kennedy panned the entire room as he spoke. He left no doubt to the fact that his comments were meant for everyone present. "I want to make it clear that I expect each and every one of you to ensure that nothing goes wrong in Dallas, it's that simple." Not a word was said for several moments as everyone's attention was now focused on him. The door to the meeting room then opened as a female secretary indicated that Air Force One would be ready to take off within a few minutes.

President Kennedy approached me. A sudden feeling of uneasiness came to me as he began to speak. "John, I don't think its going to be possible for you to travel with us to Dallas. Your attendance at this meeting has caused enough of a stir as it is."

CHAPTER 26

I couldn't help but feel that the end of my journey was fast approaching. Not knowing if I would ever see him again, I approached President Kennedy one last time. Every emotion I had held back since my arrival in the past suddenly poured out. "Mr. President, please do everything in your power to protect yourself; your life depends on it." President Kennedy nodded in reassurance. An aide then called over to us from the door nearby, "Mr. President, we have to go".

I followed him as he and Jacqueline made their way towards the exit that would lead them to the tarmac that housed Air Force One. An agent then proceeded to escort me down the hallway back to the room I had previously slept in. I made my way back to the couch. I lay my bag down beside me. I stared straight ahead for several moments. A thought then came to my mind. I turned and reached down to grab the contents in my bag. Upon removing one of the two film reels, something immediately felt wrong.

One reel was now completely different from the other. I began to think back to the times I had switched reels. I then thought back to when Mrs. Donahue and I had originally picked up both reels from the videographer. I remembered back to my original concern as to how I was going to differentiate between the two films that had been converted. I remembered how the second of the two reels was much shorter than the first. The two reels before me now clearly did not match! I quickly loaded the larger of the two reels into the projector and anxiously turned it on. I was immediately relieved to see that the content was identical to what I had shown the Kennedys over the past few hours.

I continued to load the second of the two reels onto the projector. I anxiously began to play it. My heart instantly sank as the movie now playing served only to confirm what I had feared all along. The film playing was not mine. Someone had switched them in my absence! There was no doubt in my mind that one of the two reels had been removed from my bag while I had slept. More importantly, whoever took the film had ample time to study its contents. If this were in fact the case, then the plan to save President Kennedy was now in jeopardy!

The question remained; why had they taken and viewed the second film only? Perhaps those responsible wanted their discretion to go unnoticed. My whole world had been turned upside down. The element of surprise our plan had been comprised of had all but been eliminated. Worse still, President Kennedy was totally unaware of the fact that he was no longer the only one privy to the information surrounding his assassination. He thought he had now convinced those entrusted to protect him to make the one change that would give him a chance to survive the assassination attempt on his life. This had now been thrown into disrepute by those who had stolen my video evidence.

I put my head down and simply thought about all that had taken place. Why had I been so careless to leave such an important item exposed for all to see? I had to warn the President about what had transpired! I quickly approached one of several Secret Service agents stationed outside my room and informed him I had information for the President that was vital to his safety. He seemed hesitant to believe my story. I pleaded with him for several more moments until he agreed to take me to the President. We walked quickly through several corridors I had not seen before.

It took us several minutes to arrive at the area in which the President was to depart from. The exit doors were guarded by two more security agents. The agent that had accompanied me asked them to open the doors that led outside; as they did so I ran outside. I looked around but it was too late; he had already departed for Texas. I asked the security guards how long ago it had been since the President's departure. The security guard closest to us responded that the he had left a few minutes earlier. I put my head down and merely looked at the ground before me.

Two agents dressed in black suits soon appeared beside the security guards already present. "Son, the President has handed your custody over to us while he is away on his trip. Please follow us." I quickly indicated that President Kennedy had not made me aware of any such arrangements. The agent in charge insisted that the President had made his wishes clear to him just before he left. I knew right then and there that the request had not come from the President himself. He then ordered the security guards to escort me with them to another area of the White House. I followed them through another set of hallways. We soon arrived at a room that was much smaller than any of the rooms I had previously occupied.

"You'll be spending the next couple of days in this room until the President arrives back from his trip at which point he, along with his advisors, will decide what is to happen to you next." I quickly responded back, "Will I be allowed to leave this room?" The agent sneered back at me, "I'm afraid that won't be possible." I then asked, "For my own safety, am I in some sort of danger that I should be made aware of?" The man responded back, "the President simply wanted to make sure that you were kept safe during his trip." I responded back to him, "If I am in no immediate danger then why am I being confined to this room? Am I being kept as a prisoner? I don't believe this would be the President's wish to have me kept in this fashion."

Angered by my insistence, the agent glared back at me. He then walked up to me. "Son I don't know what sort of power you think you command here, but I can promise you this, it will prove to be short lived!" Chills now ran through my arms as his comments reverberated through my mind. It was clear by his tone that the protection President Kennedy had offered me was tenuous at best.

I turned and proceeded to leave with the other agent who merely stood and observed my expressions throughout. They were flanked by the two other security agents. As the door closed behind them, I could see that a security guard now stood watch in front. I walked back towards the chair that was off to the side. Any doubt as to whether someone had viewed my film had all but been removed. I was no longer a guest in the past; I was now its prisoner! One chilling fact became evident to me. If President Kennedy were unsuccessful in his attempt to prevent his own assassination, I would remain a prisoner in both the past and present.

Thoughts began to swirl in my mind. I had to somehow get to Dallas in order to warn the President of the events that I was certain he was yet unaware of. I wasn't sure what my next move should be. The President was a couple of hours away from arriving in Texas. Once again, I found myself in a race against time. I put my head down and began to piece together every detail of the President's fateful trip. As I sat there, every subtle detail of the trip came back to mind once more.

The President's trip to Texas began on the morning of November 21, 1963. President Kennedy arrived at San Antonio that day at 1:30pm. The Kennedys were greeted by Vice President Lyndon Johnson and Governor Connally of Texas. I watched as a planned motorcade through San Antonio went off without a hitch. President Kennedy waved to the adoring crowds that greeted him. Knowing what I now knew was destined to happen in history, I couldn't help but wonder how the events in Dallas came without warning. The Presidential entourage was to arrive in Dallas having participated in three planned motorcades through the largest cities in Texas without incident.

I rose from my chair; I hadn't taken more than three steps when I noticed that it was pitch dark outside. I walked up to the window and stared out into the darkness that now surrounded the evening sky. It was confirmation of the fact that the same amount of time it had taken for the events of that day to have occurred in my mind had now passed. I looked down at my watch. It was now 11pm on the evening of November 21, 1963, the eve of the assassination of President Kennedy.

It seemed as if everything was indeed going to transpire as history had first prescribed. I had done everything in my power to warn

President Kennedy of his impending doom. It seemed in all likelihood that my efforts may have been in vain. I peered out once more into the darkness. Consumed by everything that had taken place over the past few hours, I made my way back to a couch located on the far corner of the room. Knowing full well that I would undoubtedly fall asleep, I grabbed the bag containing the films and my notes and began to clutch it under both my arms. I soon fell into a deep sleep.

Hours soon passed as I slowly opened my eyes. The quietness of the room I had been in had suddenly been replaced with the sounds of people that now surrounded the landscape around me. As things slowly came to focus I awoke to the realization that I now found myself in the middle of a crowded walkway. The street was alive with hundreds of people who walked by. I looked up momentarily and was immediately overwhelmed by the intensity of the sun that shone brightly. As had been the case so many times before, I found myself in a totally different place.

Having acclimatized myself to where I now stood, I made my way to a diner across the street. I simply stood and watched as a number of people sat in the rows of seats before me. It was clear that the President's impending arrival had brought thousands of people to Dallas. A waitress approached me and told me that it would be several minutes before I was to be seated. I felt somewhat uncomfortable as several people sitting in nearby booths now began to stare at me. It seemed the different style of clothing I wore had not gone unnoticed.

Several other people began to line up behind me hoping to sit in the first available booth. A few more minutes passed when the couple in the booth immediately in front of me now got up and proceeded towards the cashier to pay their bill. Having noticed the booth now vacated, the waitress walked towards me; she motioned for me to follow her to the empty booth. As I approached, I spotted a man who had been sitting by himself in the booth next to mine. As I walked past him, he proceeded to grab his jacket having now finished his breakfast. I quickly noticed that he had made no attempt to pick up the newspaper he had been reading as he walked towards the cashier to pay for his meal.

I took a glance over at the lineup of people waiting to be seated. Sensing that my chance was slipping away I quickly got the attention of the waitress and asked if I could take the booth the other man had just vacated. Somewhat surprised by my insistence, she sat me down and proceeded to bring me a menu. I picked up the still folded newspaper and opened it. I didn't know where to begin. Before me was the front page of the Dallas Morning News. Its headlines declared that President Kennedy was to arrive in Dallas that morning. I looked at the date of the newspaper; it was dated November 22, 1963. The numbers and letters seemed to jump out at me as if to get my immediate attention. My facial expression had undoubtedly caught the attention of those near me.

The waitress soon returned and asked if everything was okay. She then asked me if I was ready to order. I told her I needed a few more minutes to decide. I waited for her to leave and unfolded the newspaper once again. I began to read a few of the headlines that graced the ensuing pages. A thought immediately came to mind as I flipped back to the front page. Chills ran down both arms as I now realized I was looking at the same newspaper I had stumbled on back home weeks earlier. While I had read the same headlines before, to now read them on the morning of President Kennedy's visit to Dallas gave more credence to their importance.

I folded the newspaper and held it underneath my right arm as I now proceeded to leave the diner. I spotted a bench nearby and made my way towards it. I detached the newspaper from under my arm and threw it in the garbage can beside me. It seemed that fate had taken a turn for the better. Once again, I had been given the chance to seize the opportunity now before me.

I looked down at my watch; it was now 9:30am Dallas time. The rain that had fallen in Dallas the day before had given way to an overcast sky. The weather forecast had changed, it now called for sunshine in time for the President's arrival. From an organizer's perspective, one could not have picked a better day for the Presidential visit. For the many people who now began to assemble in Dealy Plaza that morning, they were undoubtedly ecstatic about the conditions for the President's visit to their city.

I got up and began to walk for several minutes. The sights and sounds around me were incredible, to say the least. While I had seen pictures in books and on TV, to now see it in person was indescribable. I simply tried to consume everything around me. I came to a nearby bench and rested for a moment. I put my head down, closed my eyes, and waited for the images that would soon fill my mind. As had been the case before, I once again began to follow President Kennedy's every move.

On the morning of November 22, 1963, Kennedy attended a breakfast at the Texas Hotel he had stayed at overnight. He later addressed a crowd in a nearby parking lot. Kennedy enjoyed outside appearances and answered a host of questions from those who had assembled to meet him. It was during the conclusion of the impromptu session that I witnessed a conversation I had otherwise been unaware of. I couldn't make out what was being said between President Kennedy and the individual he was speaking with. It seemed however, that the conversation had become somewhat animated.

Jacqueline turned and looked at her husband. She then turned to the other individual her husband had been talking to. Within minutes of the conversation, President Kennedy boarded Air Force One on route to Dallas. What had not been lost on me was the fact that the images I was now witnessing were ones I had not seen before at any time during my research. They were far more explicit and detailed. They did however suggest that I was nearing the conclusion of all that I had anticipated.

CHAPTER 27

Air Force One touched down at Love Field in Dallas at 11:40 am Central Standard Time. Governor and Mrs. Connally and Senator Ralph W. Yarborough had traveled together with President and Mrs. Kennedy. Vice President Lyndon John had arrived 5 minutes earlier on Air Force Two; they were there to greet the President and the First Lady upon their arrival.

I opened my eyes once more. I got up and began to walk across the street. It was as if I had been here before; I began to identify each of the buildings I passed by. All of them were familiar to me. I now stood in Dealey Plaza, the place where the attempt on President Kennedy's life was soon to take place! I continued to pan the area one more time. Situated to the right of the Texas Schoolbook Depository Building stood the grassy knoll, the place many historians considered to be the origin of the fatal shot that ultimately killed President Kennedy. Unbeknownst to those around me, the places and buildings around us would soon become landmarks to one of the worst crimes ever committed in America.

I looked down at my watch. It was now 11:45am Dallas time. Images flashed suddenly in my mind as I continued to follow the events now taking place. President and Mrs. Kennedy were greeted by a large crowd of spectators who had gathered to catch a close glimpse of them. Secret Service agents had formed a cordon in order to keep onlookers as well as members of the press from blocking their passage through the crowd. As President Kennedy walked amongst them, he approached the line of vehicles that made up the motorcade. I looked on as President Kennedy's attention shifted to the set of cars that awaited him. There, in the middle of the motorcade, stood the Presidential limousine.

Jacqueline immediately picked up on her husband's concern; she too now turned her full attention to the TOPLESS limousine that was parked ahead. I looked on as President Kennedy tried to conceal the panic that had undoubtedly set in, having realized that the crux of his plan to prevent his own assassination had now been compromised. He and Jacqueline continued to shake the hands of several more onlookers as they proceeded to the end of the reception area.

President Kennedy quickly pulled a couple of his aides aside and questioned why he was to now ride in an open limousine. They explained to him that a number of his aides felt the logistics through Dallas made it impossible for them to change the nature of the motorcade. The President's inquiry now turned to anger. He demanded to know who had been responsible for the change. It was now 11:50am. Unaware of the conversation now taking place, several Secret Service agents approached the President insisting that the motorcade had to begin in earnest.

The same agent that had questioned President Kennedy during their last meeting soon interceded. He reminded President Kennedy of the fact that a number of Dallas newspapers had advertised that the President was to ride in an open motorcade through the streets of Dallas. Knowing that he had now reached the point of no return, the President turned to Jacqueline; neither one spoke but they were both well aware of the ramifications that an open limousine now posed. The forces that had lobbied all along for history to repeat itself had seemingly prevailed in their attempts to do so.

The President and Jacqueline reluctantly entered the Presidential limousine along with Mr. and Mrs. Connally. Everything I had read about for weeks on in was now unfolding before my eyes. The pilot car driven by members of the Dallas Police Department led the Presidential motorcade, followed by several vehicles including the open Presidential limousine. A number of Dallas police officers rode on motorcycles as further escorts to the motorcade.

They left Love Field at precisely 11:50a.m. It drove through a number of lightly populated areas on the outskirts of Dallas. On the direction of the President himself, the limousine suddenly stopped. President Kennedy stopped to acknowledge a sign that asked him to shake hands with the many onlookers that had lined the streets in an effort to catch a glimpse of him. I couldn't help but wonder what the President and First Lady were thinking as they rode through the streets of Dallas, minutes away from making history. Given all that he knew, he was still adamant in recognizing those that that had made the effort to see him. Perhaps it was his way of leaving his mark on all those he came in contact with during his short tenure as President.

I looked down at my watch and saw that it was now 12 noon, a mere half hour before President Kennedy was to arrive. I turned once more to look over at Dealy Plaza. As I did so, I focused my attention to the many individuals who now lined the streets of Dallas. I then panned over to other areas of the Plaza where a host of individuals stood obstensively to catch a view of the approaching motorcade. I turned my attention to the infamous grassy knoll I had read about throughout my research. My attention was now focused squarely on a vehicle parked behind the knoll; it was parked over the boulevard directly behind the grassy knoll area.

I noticed what appeared to be an object emanating just behind the picket fence. My attention was now fixated on it. Was it merely the shadow made by the fence itself? I walked a few steps to my right in order to try and get a better view. I continued to concentrate my attention on the object and kept my eyes on it for several minutes. A second shadow then appeared. My inner suspicions were in fact correct. Two or more individuals now stood behind the grassy knoll.

I quickly made my way to the centre of the plaza. It was now 12:10 pm. I walked methodically, looking around once more at the landmarks before me. They were no longer at a distance and now took on a new meaning. A number of things swirled in my mind as I thought back to some of the details I had read about during my research into the assassination. I began to recognize a number of individuals I had read about throughout my research into the assassination.

A mere 20 feet across from me now stood Marian Mormon, waiting for her opportunity to take photos of the President. I stared at her for several moments hoping she would not notice my stares. I made my way towards a slightly hilly portion of grass that lined Dealy Plaza. A host of people stood by, some were seated on the grass. I panned the area near the grassy knoll one more time. In the corner of my eye, one person immediately caught my attention. I walked slowly towards the individual I had now grown infatuated with.

A family was seated on the grass area in front of the knoll eagerly awaiting President Kennedy's iminent arrival. I had not taken my eyes off them as I approached. The father of the four had noticed my stare and simply stared back at me. I quickly put my head down as I passed by them so as not to attract any further attention. It felt as though we had made a connection with one another. I finally glanced back in an effort to get a better look at the individual who had originally garnered my attention.

Having now had the luxury of a closer look at the subject of my attention, I suddenly realized that the person was none other than a young Mrs. Donahue. I simply stared at her, the resemblance was uncanny. To see her some fifty years earlier was surreal. She stood beside her father with a look of exuberance one would expect from a child waiting for the moment everyone was anticipating.

Having now noticed my stare, she glanced back at me and simply smiled. It was as if she was somehow aware the connection her and I would share in the future. She glanced at me several more times. Not wanting to further attract her father's attention, I turned away from her. A sense of uneasiness overcame me, knowing full well the effect President Kennedy's assassination would have on her in the years that followed. The individuals I had now come into contact with only served to highlight the relevance of the setting that provided the backdrop of the assassination.

I made my way across the street. I took one last look at Mrs. Donahue's family, all the while thinking about the crucial role she was to play in my attempt to prevent the assassination of the President 50 years later. To now see these people in person happily awaiting the President's arrival, unaware of what was to happen in due time, was difficult for me to accept. As I walked past them I noticed several other families sitting on the grassed area also patiently awaiting the President's arrival.

I now stood in front of a series of steps bordered by a large curb which overlooked the street. A man stood on the curb holding a movie camera. Beside him stood a woman ostensibly there to make sure he did not fall from where he was perched. He panned Dealy Plaza with his projector filming the building as well as the large crowds eagerly awaiting President Kennedy's arrival. It was at that moment that I became witness in person to the making of perhaps the most compelling piece of film footage shot in the 20th century.

The man I stood in front of was non-other than Abraham Zepruder. He was about to capture the assassination of the President as it took place. The relevance of Zepruder's film could not be underestimated. It was to be at the crux of all those who would chose to revisit the assassination of President Kennedy. The site line Zepruder had chosen gave him the perfect position to shoot the film that would go down in infamy; one that would make him a household name for decades to come.

It felt overwhelming to be in Dealy Plaza with all the figures so important in history. Along with the apprehension I felt was the surreal realization that the President's arrival was only minutes away. A sudden feeling of bewilderment began to creep in. It was as if I had missed something. It was now 12:25, five minutes before the arrival of the President.

I turned back to look at Dealy Plaza now behind me. I began to stare once more at some of the landmarks I had looked at from the triple underpass minutes earlier. I walked across the plaza and looked straight up at the Texas Schoolbook Depository building. I counted up the six floors from the bottom of the street and began to look at the windows up top. A handful of windows were open. I sat down to ponder my thoughts on a nearby bench.

I closed my eyes in order to watch the images of what was now occurring elsewhere. The two men I had witnessed before had knelt down on their knees and were now in the process of opening two separate briefcases. History was indeed repeating itself. I reopened my eyes in order to refocus on everything around me. I found myself once again staring squarely at the large crowd that had now assembled along Elm St. I looked down at my watch once more; it was now 12:28pm.

There was an "air" of anticipation as the motorcade was approaching. I could hear some people in the crowd telling others around them that the Presidential motorcade was in view. Time was running out for me. I looked over once more at Abraham Zepruder. He began to film President Kennedy's arrival as the motorcade slowly approached him. I then turned to track the progress of the motorcade as it slowly made its way towards us.

The motorcade was now within a few feet of us. It was close enough for me to see the smiles on the faces of both President Kennedy and Jacqueline Kennedy. Their demeanor had clearly changed from the previous times I had witnessed them as first set out in history. Their smiles were "strained" at best. Both of them knew full well that shots were about to ring out in Dealy Plaza. The President turned to look at the grassy knoll area he had now just passed. Was history to change given the information both of them were now privy to?

President Kennedy turned his attention to the upper floor windows of the Texas Schoolbook Depository Building. In true Presidential style he stared at the window he suspected housed the assassins hired to kill him. It was a sign of defiance that did not go unnoticed by me. The conspiracy to murder was now in full force.

I quickly looked down at my watch. It was now 12:29pm. The cheering amongst the crowd assembled had increased to an almost fever pitch as the Presidential motorcade was directly in front of us. I stood about 20 yards away from where Zepruder was filming the approach of the Presidential limousine. Time was of the essence. Trying hard not to get noticed, I quickly walked past the spot Zepruder was filming at. I began to wiggle my way to the front of the crowd.

I suddenly began to feel that I was once again being watched. I immediately looked to my right. Directly across the street stood the two mysterious men that had dogged me throughout the past few weeks. They were now joined by Professor Osborne who had positioned himself at the front of the crowd assembled directly across from me. I looked on nervously as they panned the area where I now stood. Once again, the resolve of these men was unfathomable. My every contingency was factored into everything they did.

From their perspective it only made sense that I would be present at the moment of the assassination attempt on President Kennedy. They had found me once again. Before I could move back into the crowd behind me, I spotted Osborne pointing at me. The three of them began to make their way to the front of the crowd so as to cross the street towards me. I made my way back into the crowd of people I stood by. I ducked and continued to maneuver in and out of the people around me. I looked at my watch one last time; it was 12:30pm.

Osborne and the other two agents had now made their way to my side of the street. I tried to camouflage myself in the crowd so as not to be seen by the three men pursuing me. Osborne spotted and led them as they methodically made their way towards me. A loud sound then rang out. The firecracker type sound that emanated from the first shot fired was one that I was all too familiar with. It startled everyone around me. The sound had momentarily stopped Osborne and the other agents dead in their tracks.

The attempted assassination of President Kennedy had indeed begun; there was no turning back now. We had all now stopped to view history in the making. Time stood still as the events slowly progressed. Before I could collect my thoughts, a second shot rang out which caught the attention of many more people. I turned once more to look at the Presidential limousine. Governor Connally was surprised by the second shot that had been fired closer to his general direction.

I looked in horror as both President and Jacqueline Kennedy tried desperately to duck down so as to avoid being shot a second time. They were indeed trying to change the outcome of history. Two police motorcycles began to accelerate towards both sides of the limousine.

Just as they attempted to do so a second shot hit the President.

The sense of euphoria I had felt seconds earlier quickly dissipated as I now saw him grimacing in pain. He had indeed been shot; he knelt over in pain. I desperately tried to move closer to determine where and how badly he had been shot. I could however see that he was still moving. To this point, he had not been mortally wounded! Jacqueline screamed for the nearby Secret Service agents now approaching the limousine to help her husband; all the while she screamed out that her husband had been shot. Panic began to set into the crowd closest to the Presidential limousine. It was now obvious to everyone present that they were in the line of fire.

President Kennedy was hardly moving. While he had attempted to avoid being shot, he was still susceptible to an attack from above. My immediate reaction was to look up at the Schoolbook Depository Building off to my left. From my vantage point, I couldn't make out whether shots had been fired there! As I paused to recompose myself, what immediately became clear was the fact that President Kennedy's actions to protect himself had in fact delayed the sequence and timing of events as originally unfolded. The assassins that had been hired to kill him were well aware of the fact that they would not get another chance. They were undoubtedly adjusting to what had occurred in an effort to finish the job they had been hired to do!

I turned back to see that the three agents had resumed their pursuit for me. Osborne was the lead person now a few feet away from where I stood. The fatal shot had not yet been fired. Time was running out for all of us. I had to do something if I was going to some way prevent the final sequence of events from happening. Sensing that my captors were closing in on me, I pushed away some of the people in front of me and ran towards the street stopping directly in front of the Presidential limousine.

The limousine squealed and swerved to avoid me. The Secret Service agent closest to the front of the Presidential limousine immediately grabbed me, knocking me to the ground. My shoulder hit the side of the curb directly in front of the grassy knoll area. The Secret Service agent had hit his head on the same curb. He lay on the ground and could not recover from the fall he suffered. I looked back in an effort to follow what was now happening with the President's limousine.

A Secret Service agent had collapsed "spread eagle" over both the President and the First Lady. He did not move; a bullet had pierced him in the back during the attack. A second Secret Service agent sat over the end of the limousine desperately looking around in all directions in an effort to locate the precise area of where the shots had been fired from. I then watched as the Presidential limousine sped off at a high rate of speed. I was suddenly overcome with a sense of fear.

What I was witnessing in person seemed to match the images I had seen both in my mind and on film as it originally happened in the past. I now sat there powerless, all the while wondering how badly President Kennedy had been hurt. Had my efforts been effective enough to have saved him?

CHAPTER 28

Panic had now consumed everyone in Dealy Plaza. Many of the images I had first seen in film were now transpiring before me. Families were strewn throughout the grassed area; many were still on their stomachs while others had begun to get up having sensed that the gunshots had ended.

I spotted Mrs. Donahue walking by quickly, all the while holding her father's hand. They began to walk away from the picket fence they stood near. It had become the focus of the attention by Dallas Police officers that now combed the area. Amidst the panic that had ensued, a number of police officers ran toward the grassy knoll with guns in hand. The entire scene was one of utter chaos. It was all happening in front of me just as I had witnessed so many times before.

The police officers present seemed overwhelmed as they attempted to control the frenzied crowd around them still in shock with what had just occurred. I made my way to the curbside and sat down; as I did so, I closed my eyes once more and watched the other events unfold in my mind. The two men at the sixth floor of the Depository building had now disassembled their rifles. They made their way quickly yet calmly down the steps of the building towards a back exit.

The men behind the grassy knoll quickly made their way to their parked vehicle. This was the same vehicle I had seen parked there. They slowly drove away so as not to appear suspicious to the officers that were converging onto the area. Just as the images ended, an officer immediately grabbed me and placed me in the back of his police car cruiser. He closed the door and stepped out for a few moments. I could hear a number of police officers as they spoke on the police band; they spoke to one another confirming which areas of Dealy Plaza were to be secured.

Information began to filter in regarding the individuals that had been shot during the assassination attempt. They included President Kennedy, Governor Connally, as well as the Secret Service agent injured during the assassination attempt. I waited with baited breath for word on the condition of the President. The police radio confirmed that the Presidential limousine had arrived at Parkland Hospital and that all three wounded individuals had been transported to Emergency to be treated for their injuries.

The officer returned a couple of minutes later. As he was about to open his door, he was met by Osborne and the other two agents. They spoke to him for several moments. I now looked on as Osborne carried most of the conversation with the officer. The second of the three agents glanced over at me. I could see him listening to the conversation still taking place, all the while glaring back at me. The conversation between them had now become animated. It was clear they wanted to take me with them. The officer was clearly not in agreement with their request. Thankfully, he had not yet relented to their repeated request, despite their persistence. The argument that had ensued now ended.

Osborne and the other two agents stood in front of the police car as the officer opened the door. Just as he entered the car, I began to plead with him. "Officer, those agents you have been speaking with are not whom you think they are! They have been pursuing me for quite some time! I beg of you, please do not hand me over to them. My life depends on it. I will answer all your questions at the police station. I will tell you everything you need to know." I continued to plead with him as Osborne continued to look at me with the corner of his eye so as not to conceal his interest in our conversation now taking place.

The officer then turned to face me directly. "Son, I don't know who you think you are but I can tell you that you are in a 'heap' of trouble. They claim to be part of the CIA!" I quickly pleaded to him once more. "Officer, if you hand me over to those men, I will surely die. I won't live to tell the truth regarding the reasoning behind my actions of today. If you want to know the real truth, you need to keep me away from them!"

The officer turned back to face the three individuals and caught another glimpse of me in his rear view mirror. It was clear he was debating in his mind what his next move should be. He grabbed the microphone to his radio. He radioed in the fact that he had apprehended the suspect wanted for questioning, all the while continuing to focus his attention on me. He told me to sit still as he proceeded to step back out of his vehicle. I looked on as he approached the three men he had spoken to earlier. Once again, an argument ensued. The second of the two agents now became incredibly animated and began to point to me repeatedly as he spoke. Osborne glanced over to me once more in disgust.

It was clear the three agents were not prepared to accept the fact that I was not going to be handed into their custody. The officer then returned back to his car. He began to ask me what my name was and where my parents were. I was unprepared for his line of questioning and hesitated for a few moments. I remembered the excuse President Kennedy had used to explain my sudden appearance during the meeting with his advisors. I responded by telling him that I was in Dealy Plaza alone. He seemed surprised and somewhat skeptical of my story. He was about to ask me another question when the police band came on again.

Officers stationed in front of Parkland Hospital described how Governor Connally had suffered a gunshot wound to his wrist but was now in stable condition. More details of the Governor's condition and injuries followed. Word came that Lee Harvey Oswald had been apprehended in a nearby movie theatre. We began to slowly drive off towards the police station nearby. I looked on as the three agents quickly made their way back to their car. I assumed that they would follow us to the police station.

We arrived and made our way to the officer's desk located at the back area of the station. I was immediately asked to sit in front of his desk. The station was abuzz with all the events that had transpired that day. The officer indicated that he would be back in a few minutes. Knowing that we had been followed back by the other agents, his absence became increasingly worrisome for me. I looked around at everything that was happening around me. The police station was chaotic given everything that had transpired that afternoon. Moments later, the officer returned. He held some papers in his hand. He then notified me that he could not find any information on me anywhere in his records.

He immediately asked me why I had run in front of the Presidential motorcade. I quickly responded by telling him that I simply got caught in the euphoria of the moment and wanted to get closer to see the President. Once again, I could tell he wasn't convinced with the reasoning behind my actions that day. He asked me to remain seated while he checked another lead that could possibly help discover my identity. As I continued to look around me, it seemed for the moment that my presence there seemed to have gone unnoticed by the other officers present. Their focus now centered on capturing those responsible for the attempt on President Kennedy's life.

I didn't want to tempt fate. There was no information traceable to me, nor would anyone be able to find any information about me. I stood up from my chair to see the outer waiting room of the station. I suddenly caught a glimpse of Professor Osborne alongside the other two agents now speaking to another officer. The three of them stood out, being the only ones wearing suits. Eluding their pursuit of me was virtually impossible. Given the animated conversation taking place, it was clear they were not leaving the police station without me.

Having barely eluded their capture before, I knew I had to get out of there before they found me! I got up from my chair and walked gingerly towards the door that led to the stairs. It seemed to be the only way out. I now feared I would be seen by the other officers present. I then noticed a water fountain located beside door that led to the staircase. I approached an officer sitting at the desk beside me and asked if I could use the water fountain. He nodded that it was okay to do so. I got up and slowly walked toward the fountain. I proceeded to get a sip of water.

As I bent down, I could see that the officer I had just spoken to had been approached by another policeman. Sensing my opportunity, I quickly opened the door beside me and slowly entered the stairwell beside me. I turned back and carefully looked through the small meshed glass of the stairway door. Within moments, Osborne and the other two agents had entered the back office I had just vacated.

I could now see them as they vehemently asked where I was. The officer then pointed to the water fountain I had just used. I quickly moved away from the window. I heard a commotion coming from the other side of the door as they now converged towards me. Without hesitation, I ran as fast as I could down the stairwell. I could hear the door to the stairwell open as several officers, including Osborne, followed me down the same stairwell.

I soon approached the exit door that led to an alleyway. I quickly made my way out and turned towards the first street on my right, adjacent to the station. It led to another alleyway at the end of the street. I quickly turned the corner, stopped for a moment, and peered back at the street I had just passed through. I looked on as officers ran towards the alleyway I now found myself in. I then spotted a taxi cab parked across the street. I carefully crossed the street and walked quickly towards it.

A police car drove by with its lights flashing. I immediately turned to face the other way. I could still see the flashing lights as their shadow emanated throughout the street. I reached the cab and quickly sat in the back seat. Startled by my sudden arrival, the cab driver immediately asked me what I was doing inside his cab. From the front windshield of the car, I could visibly see a host of officers quickly searching the area for my whereabouts. Amongst them was one of the two agents I had seen with Osborne. Seconds later Osborne followed with the other agents and several other police officers.

The cab driver once again asked me why I had entered his cab. I continued to watch the officers from the corner of my eye as they came closer towards the cab. Panic began to overtake me as I politely asked the driver if he knew where Parkland Hospital was. Sensing my anxiety, he snapped back that he was well aware of the location of

Parkland Hospital. Overwhelmed by a sense of impending doom, tears ran down both my eyes as I politely asked him if he could take me to the hospital.

The driver stared at me, having now sensed the panic that had overtaken me. I immediately told him that my parents had been seriously hurt in an automobile accident and were now being treated at the hospital. I pleaded for him once more to take me to them. He then turned around and proceeded to start his car. My story had indeed worked. The car began to move slowly ahead. We soon passed two police officers who were scouring the area for my whereabouts. I quickly put my head down as they passed by my window.

I looked up again and noticed the taxi driver staring at me through his rear view mirror. He seemed surprised by my actions. We now drove past the two officers stationed outside. I slowly lifted my head up high enough to look out the window. As we drove away, in the distance I could see Osborne and his partners stare at our cab as we moved out of their view.

The fear that had engulfed me began to subside as we turned the corner and onto the adjacent street away from them. I looked out the rear view mirror one last time so as to be reassured that I had eluded Osborne once again. I asked the driver how long it would take to get to the hospital. He replied by indicating we would arrive there in less than 10 minutes. I sat back in my seat and noticed him once again staring at me through his rear view mirror. I looked out the window and began to look at everything around us. The numerous cars parked along the streets we drove past were a reminder of the era I was now a part of.

The clothes worn by the people we drove past all represented a piece of nostalgia I had seen before in photos. I then looked ahead and noticed that the cab driver was paying a great deal of attention to his rear view mirror. He now divided his attention to the traffic in front as well as the traffic behind him.

"Those officers we drove past in the alleyway where I picked you up, were they looking for something? I hesitated for a moment. "I don't think so?" He continued. "Are you certain? They sure looked like they were looking for someone. I say that because the vehicle behind us has been following us since we left." The calm I had felt for those few minutes now suddenly dissipated. I glanced back at the rear window. We made a turn onto the next street, the vehicle behind us turned to follow.

The car following us was too far away for me to be able to make out who was driving, but there was clearly only one passenger. I looked once again at the rear view mirror. The cab driver noticed my stare. "Don't worry, there are no police cars following us; if that's what you're afraid of." He continued, "Look son, I don't know what the police want from you. I didn't 'buy' the story about your folks, given the number of cops looking for you. At this point I don't really care because you seem like a nice kid." I smiled back at him. I then turned my attention back to the rearview mirror to see if the car that had been following us for the past few minutes was still behind us.

We soon pulled up to the emergency entrance to Parkland Hospital. I opened my door and walked up to the driver's side window. I reached into my pocket and pulled out two quarters I knew were still in my jean pocket. I handed them to the driver, all the while telling him that it was all the money I had. He looked down at the two quarters I had given to him and stared at them for several seconds. He looked at me somewhat bewildered. He then looked up and proceeded to give me back the money I had offered for the ride there. He told me I didn't owe him anything. "Take care of yourself kid. I hope everything turns out ok." I thanked him for his help.

As he drove off, I opened my hand and looked down at the two quarters I had given him. One of the two quarters was turned over showing the year it was minted. Both quarters had been minted in the year 2013, fifty years from the time we now found ourselves in. I put them back in my pocket and slowly turned to look at the vehicle that had been following us. The driver of the vehicle was no longer in the car. I suddenly heard the squeal of several vehicles that had just made the turn onto my street.

I quickly ran to the entranceway of the hospital directly in front of me. I opened the door and peered out of its meshed glass window.

Osborne and the other two agents stepped out of the patrol car they had arrived in. They immediately pointed to the hospital. Once again, they had anticipated my every move! I could now hear them as they, along with several officers made their way towards me. How was I going to elude them this time?

I quickly walked along the small hallway in front of me. It soon led to a much larger hallway that was strewn with people having arrived at the emergency section of the hospital. Two police officers stood across the hallway from where I now stood. One of them caught a glimpse of me. He began to stare at me for several seconds; I tried carefully not to stare back. I glanced back at him for a split second. It soon became clear he was trying to figure out where he had seen me before. He motioned over to his partner who also began to stare at me with some interest.

Realizing my identity may have been compromised, I quickly turned away and walked slowly back around the corner towards the emergency hallway I had first entered in. A round mirror was placed at the top corner of the hallway so as to see traffic coming from both directions. From it I could now see that the officers had begun to make their way towards me. I turned the corner and began to run as fast as I could towards the adjoining hallway in the hospital. I suddenly stopped dead in my tracks. There at the end of the hallway stood Dr. Mellings. I simply stood and stared at him for several seconds.

I looked on as he noticed my stare. The expression on his face was one of total surprise. I glanced back at the mirror located at the corner wall that separated the hallway I had walked passed. I could now see that the officers had now almost made their way to me. I turned back towards Dr. Mellings. He looked at me as if to motion me towards him. The two officers had almost reached us. I spotted a door which led to an electrical room. I quickly ran to it and turned the knob of the door. I prayed that it wasn't locked. To my relief, the door was indeed unlocked. I quickly made my way into the small room. From the small crack of the door left open I could see them as they ran down the hallway in an effort to find me.

Beads of sweat ran down my forehead as I waited several seconds until I felt safe enough to exit the room. I made my way around another adjoining hallway. Behind me, I heard the commotion of Osborne and the others. I could hear a voice of someone calling out my name. I quickly looked behind me; the others hadn't caught up to me as of yet. The voice called out for me once again. Without warning, agent Montgomery suddenly exited out of the door beside me that led to the stairwell nearby. He pulled me inside the stairwell. He quickly motioned for me to keep to the side of the window casing of the door.

We stood on both sides of the window. I looked on as Osborne and the others stormed by along the hallway we had just vacated. I could hear them speaking to several of the nurses and doctors, asking if any of them had seen me. Pointing to a photo of me, Osborne asked each and every staff member if they were able to identify me.

Agent Montgomery pulled me up and motioned me to follow him up one flight of stairs. We quickly made our way up the flight of stairs that led towards the door to the second floor. "President Kennedy is on this floor. There are two Secret Service agents guarding his room." He continued, "We don't have much time. Osborne and the other two agents will be here soon. They know that you will try to get to President Kennedy. Getting into his hospital room is the only chance you have to get to safety. The question is, how do we get you in there?"

Montgomery thought for a few seconds. He now looked back at me. "I am going out there, you have to stay here. I will cause a diversion. I will then yell out your name. That will be your signal to come out. DO NOT leave until I call out your name! Do I make myself clear?" I nodded in agreement. "John, if I am unsuccessful in doing what I have to do, you need to get out of here as quickly as you can. You will be trapped in time, but you won't be a prisoner in it. If Osborne and the others get to you, you will be lost forever!"

As grave as his assessment was, I knew agent Montgomery was right. If I was unable to reach President Kennedy, my fate would be sealed. He put his right hand on my shoulder and smiled at me. It was at that moment that I knew I might never speak to him again. I watched as he took a deep breath and proceeded to make his way into the hallway just outside our door. I hid behind the door until it fully closed. I then listened on as he was immediately questioned by the police stationed outside the door to the President's room.

I carefully peaked through the meshed window of the stairway door. Seconds later, I pulled my head back as agent Osborne and the others with him arrived. I could hear the instant commotion that now took place. Osborne immediately asked the Secret Service agents present to check Montgomery's credentials. I looked on as one of the two police officers then grabbed Montgomery by the arm and began to hold him. The second of the two officers approached Montgomery as well. It was clear to me that they were in the process of apprehending him.

I looked back at the stairwell now before me. Montgomery had made it clear that I should escape the moment I realized his plan was not going to work. I continued to stare ahead for several more seconds simply contemplating what my next move should be. I was still unaware as to whether or not President Kennedy had survived his injuries. It was at that moment that I realized that my life would be doomed if I were to turn back and leave.

Sensing I had only seconds to spare before Montgomery was arrested and taken away, I burst out of the stairwell I was in. I made a run for the door that led to President Kennedy's room. Osborne immediately grabbed me by the arm. Two officers had already begun to walk Montgomery down the hallway. Hearing the commotion behind him, Montgomery turned to look back at what was happening behind him.

One of Osborne's two associates now approached me as well. I began to scream at the top of my voice. "LET ME GO", I yelled several times. The door to President Kennedy's room suddenly opened. To my utter amazement Robert Kennedy stepped out. He was followed by two Secret Service agents that had heard the commotion outside their room. He immediately realized it was me. "John", he yelled out. "Mr. Kennedy" I replied. He then looked at Osborne. "What the hell is going on here?" Osborne did not move a muscle. Kennedy now pointed to me. He then demanded that I be released immediately!

Osborne did not make a move. Robert now walked up to him and stared at him directly. "I'm not going to ask you again, release him now!" The decibel level of his voice had reached a fever pitch. His eyes did not flinch. Osborne's associates now turned to look at him as well. He acknowledged his stare. Both men now released their hold on me. Sensing that I now had one chance, I pointed to Montgomery. "Agent Montgomery should be released as well; he's with me!" Osborne and the other agents now looked at one another. Their plight had seemingly gone from bad to worse.

Kennedy was somewhat surprised by my request, having had no knowledge of who agent Montgomery was. He then ordered the officers to remove the handcuffs off him. They did so immediately. Montgomery now made his way towards us. One of the two officers attempted to remind the Attorney General that I was wanted for questioning by Dallas police. "For what?", replied Kennedy. The officer hesitantly responded that I was being questioned for my actions in Dealy Plaza. Kennedy did not allow the officer to finish his response and replied back. "This young man's actions probably SAVED the President's life!

CHAPTER 29

Kennedy's stern reply immediately silenced both officers. He pulled me lightly on the shoulder and the two of us accompanied him into President Kennedy's hospital room. As we walked in, Robert asked the police officer stationed in the room to wait with the others outside. Somewhat surprised by Kennedy's request, he immediately complied.

With the door to the room still opened, the Attorney General pointed to Osborne and his two associates. "I want these men apprehended and brought to FBI headquarters in Washington immediately!" I watched with great satisfaction as the three men were handcuffed and escorted out. Robert approached me and asked if I was okay. I quickly replied that I was, now that I was in his care. He then turned his attention to agent Montgomery. Montgomery was visibly nervous as he began to address Robert.

"Mr. Kennedy, it is an honor to meet you. I've read so much about you." Kennedy responded. "How are you involved in all of this?" Montgomery turned and looked at me as he answered back. "I'm here to make sure this young man finishes was he started." The door slowly opened and Jacqueline entered the room. She was pleasantly surprised to see that I had returned. She then turned to face Robert. A tear now flowed from her right cheek. I felt an immediate sense of apprehension. She then announced that the President's injuries had been deemed to be non-life threatening. She described him as being stable.

An overriding feeling of relief filled the entire room as everyone present breathed one huge sigh of relief. My efforts had indeed been successful in thwarting the assassination of the President. I glanced at agent Montgomery. He immediately smiled, seemingly acknowledging that my efforts had indeed saved President Kennedy's life. Robert walked over to me and shook my hand. "Well done son. Our entire nation owes you a debt of gratitude. On a personal level, I want to thank you for saving my brother's life. I promise you neither him nor I will waste the 'second chance' you've now given us." Jacqueline then walked towards me and reached over to kiss me on my cheek. She then put her mouth to my ear and softly whispered. "Thank you for saving my husband's life. I will never forget what you have done for us."

Everyone in the room now stood in silence. Not knowing what to say, I simply acknowledged her appreciation. The door to the room then opened. To my utter dismay, Dr. Mellings entered the room with another doctor. His serious demeanor was tempered for a brief moment as he glanced over to me. The irony of the moment was not lost on me. As fate would have it that day, he was the lead doctor that had treated President Kennedy.

He approached both Robert and Jacqueline Kennedy and began to update them on the President's condition. The look on both their faces was one of total relief. It was clear the President was to make a full recovery from the injuries he had suffered during the assassination attempt on his life. I could only catch parts of the conversation now taking place. I could, however make out the fact that President Kennedy was to be brought back to his room within the hour. It was confirmation of the fact that he had now cleared every hurdle in his recovery from the injuries sustained during the assassination attempt on his life.

Mellings and Robert smiled for several moments. It was clear that the sense of relief they felt was shared. Dr. Mellings had indeed exorcised the sense of hopelessness he had felt days earlier! He began to make his way towards the door along with the other doctors. As he approached the door, he stopped for a moment and looked over to me one last time. He smiled for a moment, as if to acknowledge his role in having saved the President's life.

As Mellings exited the room, Montgomery approached me. "John, I have to make a phone call. I just wanted you to know how much of a pleasure it has been to work with you. You should never take for granted what you have done here." He continued, "You alone have single handedly changed the course of history for ever. What you have done in a short time will be felt for generations to come. I'm just glad I was able to play a small part in your success!" Agent Montgomery's accolades were genuine and poignant. I couldn't help but feel that there had been an underlying message in what he was trying to express to me. He then made his way outside.

Extra chairs had been brought in for all of us to sit on. I sat on my chair and leaned my head back on the wall beside me. I thought back to the kind words he expressed. Emotionally drained by everything that had transpired, I fell asleep for the better part of an hour. I was later awoken by the sound of the door opening. President Kennedy was being wheeled into the room. He was still unconscious from the anesthetic they had given him during his operation. I looked on as a series of doctors and nurses attached him to a host of different monitors. It was clear the patient they now worked on was different from any other. Robert was then summoned by some of the aides now stationed outside.

Several minutes soon passed. Agent Montgomery had still not returned. Somewhat concerned by his absence I began to worry about his well being. I asked one of the guards stationed in the room if he had seen agent Montgomery. He indicated he hadn't heard from him since his departure. I once again rested my head against the wall beside me and dozed off only to soon be hearing someone calling out my name. I slowly opened my eyes as I heard the voice of the President. Robert and Jacqueline stood alongside his bed. They both smiled at me so as to reassure me that everything was going to be ok.

President Kennedy asked me to stand beside his bed. As I approached him he held out his hand to shake mine. He thanked me for the actions I took in Dealy Plaza that ultimately saved his life. "John, it took a great deal of courage and conviction to do what you did, you saved my life. For that I thank you." I thanked the President for his kind words. "Mr. President I would not have been able to live with myself had I not been successful in saving your life. History had been cheated once and I couldn't let it happen again."

The television in front of the President's bed had been on all along. The news of the attempt on President Kennedy's life consumed the coverage on television that day. We all looked on as Walter Cronkite anchored the coverage of the arrest and subsequent questioning of Lee Harvey Oswald. Reporters swarmed Oswald asking him a barrage of questions.

The door to the hospital room suddenly opened. A senior advisor to the President walked in. He insisted that he had to speak to them in private without my presence. I turned to face the President, fearful of being separated again. Robert sensed my fear. He immediately informed his advisor that I was to wait directly outside his room and was to be guarded there while they spoke. The advisor seemed surprised by the President's insistence as he escorted me outside. With his back to them, he glared at me almost as a sign of defiance to what the President had just ordered him to do. I looked down as the door closed behind me, not wanting to make eye contact with any of the several agents and officers that had congregated in front of the President's hospital room.

Several minutes passed. I could hear the argument that had now ensued inside the room behind me. The advisor questioned Kennedy's insistence in practically "harboring" a criminal, as he put it. He insisted that I be kept for questioning so as to determine the reasoning behind the actions I had taken in Dealy Plaza hours earlier. President Kennedy vehemently denounced his suggestion, making it clear that my actions were directly responsible for having saved his life. As he put it, the courage I had exhibited should have been recognized, not chastised.

The door to the room opened again as the advisor walked out, he glanced at me as I reentered the room. Upon entering, I immediately concentrated my attention to the continuing coverage of Oswald's apprehension and subsequent arrest. I then turned back to face President Kennedy once again. "Mr. President, whoever is responsible for Oswald's involvement is now witnessing what we are now seeing. With every attempt and every question asked of Oswald, they must be undoubtedly concerned about what he may say about the assassination attempt on your life." Robert continued on my point. "No doubt, they may still attempt to silence Oswald, even though the attempted assassination failed. Once again, time was becoming a factor. In less than 24 hours Oswald was to be transferred out of the Dallas Police station he had been held in.

As history would have it, Ruby would undoubtedly be waiting to silence Oswald forever. President Kennedy eased himself forward and continued to look at the television monitor before him. I stared at him, noticing the intensity on his face as he continued to stare at the images before him. He then broke the silence. He turned squarely to his brother who now stood in front of him. "We have to somehow get to Oswald before THEY do."

Everyone in the room was surprised by President Kennedy's statement. It seemed he felt he owed Oswald the same second chance he had been given in having had his own life spared. Robert looked at his brother. "Jack, do you think it's a good idea at this time to have the Attorney General meet with the man accused of trying to kill you so soon after?" The President responded. "Robert, the man does not have much time left, I was given the gift of a second chance at life; do we not owe him the same opportunity?" Not a word was said for several seconds. President Kennedy's comments resonated with everyone in the room. In true Kennedy fashion, he responded in the way only he could, with compassion and grace. Perhaps he himself was unsure as to what role Oswald actually played in the assassination attempt.

The door to the hospital room opened. Another advisor asked the President what his wishes were with respect to dinner. Kennedy looked up at me. Not turning back to face him, the President informed him that he was to have dinner brought into the room for everyone present. Robert approached the advisor and spoke to him privately for a couple of minutes. The other man was visibly surprised by what Kennedy had now requested. A few minutes now passed, the door to the room opened and several trays of food were brought in. I spent the next half hour or so dining with them.

The four of us did not speak much, seemingly fixated with the continuing coverage of the questioning that was taking place between Oswald and members of the Dallas police dept. Robert seemed particularly predisposed with what was to happen next. He then approached me, informing me that a car was parked outside the hospital waiting for us. I quickly realized where our next visit was to be. I reached into my bag and removed several sheets of papers. I carefully folded them and stuck them into the front pockets of my jeans. I turned back to President Kennedy; the President nodded and then smiled back at me. It was acknowledgment of the fact that I would know what to do next.

I followed Robert out to the hallway outside. It was now full of advisors and security. An advisor came up to the Attorney General and asked to speak to him privately for a moment. I stepped back so that the two could talk amongst themselves. A feeling of uneasiness came over me once more; I waited as they now spoke. The conversation between the two quickly intensified. As their voices grew louder, I could plainly hear that the conversation revolved around the purpose of our upcoming meeting with Lee Harvey Oswald! Robert briefly turned back to look at me as he continued his conversation with the other man. A few minutes passed, he approached and asked me to follow him. We made our way to an awaiting car. A second car followed closely behind us as we drove back to the same police station I had escaped from hours earlier.

The Attorney General's entrance into the station caused an immediate stir among the officers present. It was clear that Robert Kennedy was not your average visitor. As we continued down the hallway that was to lead us to Oswald, I couldn't help but muse at the events that were now taking place. These were all events that were not preordained by history; their outcome was still to be determined. Kennedy immediately notified those present that he and I were to meet with Oswald in a private room.

Two police officers flanked on both sides by Secret Service agents accompanied us down the hallway and down a set of stairs that led to a private room used to question prisoners. The room contained only one table and three chairs. I sat and lay my bag down beside my chair. Robert stood by his chair nervously anticipating the arrival of Lee Harvey Oswald. It was clear from his facial expression he too did not know what to expect.

I opened my bag and began to sift through the pages of files I had brought with me. I then placed a host of them on the table before me. The door now opened; an officer walked in followed by Lee Harvey Oswald. Oswald walked slowly as his feet were shackled together. His hands were handcuffed behind his back thereby making it difficult for him to move around. Robert approached the officer standing beside Oswald and instructed him to reposition Oswald's handcuffs with his arms in front of his body. He then instructed the officer to remove the shackles placed around Oswald's feet.

As had been the case many times over the past couple of days, I now found myself staring in person at one of the most recognizable figures of the 20th century. I felt the same feeling of amazement I had felt after having met the Kennedy family. The officer seemed caught off guard by Kennedy's request. Oswald was clearly surprised by the fact that he now stood before the Attorney General of the United States. Kennedy's gesture of good faith did not go unnoticed by Oswald. The officer did as instructed.

Kennedy asked Oswald to sit down in the chair provided for him. He then politely asked the officer to leave us alone in the room. The officer once again did as he was told and immediately closed the door behind him. Robert began to explain to Oswald why we had requested to meet with him. Oswald interceded quickly and asked what the present condition of the President was. Robert responded by informing him that he was in stable condition and resting comfortably in hospital. He indicated to Oswald that we were aware of the planned assassination attempt on the President. He made it clear how he was well aware of the fact that others may have been responsible in the conspiracy to assassinate the President.

Oswald's demeanor suddenly changed. Kennedy's apparent support of Oswald's innocence provided an immediate sense of relief for him. I continued where Kennedy had just left off. I pulled out the newspaper articles that showed the headlines of JFK's death as well as the subsequent capture of Oswald. He was totally caught off guard by what he was seeing. I explained how my presence there had changed the way history had unfolded. I proceeded to explain to him that the headlines before him were the actual headlines of the newspapers that described events as they were originally set out in history.

I picked up the copy of the newspaper with the headlines announcing Oswald's death at the hands of Jack Ruby. I took out a second photo from a magazine that had revisited the Kennedy assassination many years later. The photo was a still shot of the exact moment that Ruby shot Oswald. His face turned white, he was now totally speechless. Robert and I looked at one another knowing, full well how Oswald must have been feeling at that precise moment. Oswald's reaction mirrored Kennedy's own reaction upon learning his fate. Kennedy then continued to outline everything that was to happen to him in due time. He described the events that led to the attempted assassination, as well as the actions taken by me to stop the assassination.

Oswald began to address the both of us. "Where do we go from here?" I got up from my chair and approached him. "Mr. Oswald, tomorrow morning Jack Ruby will be among those waiting as you are transferred from your current location to another jail. Mr. Ruby's sole purpose will be to silence you forever."

Robert then addressed Oswald and continued where I had left off. "Mr. Oswald, given the information we have revealed, you need to decide the steps necessary in order to prevent your own assassination. We have given you the information you need in order to do just that." Oswald glanced over to me just as Kennedy finished. He paused for a moment to collect his thoughts. "Mr. Kennedy, what do you think my outcome will be with respect to the charges that have been brought against me?"

Kennedy paused for a moment to carefully consider his response to Oswald's question. "Mr. Oswald, at this point no one else has been taken into custody for the attempted assassination of my brother, nor do I anticipate that changing. The fact remains, you shot and killed a police officer. The Dallas police department has the person it feels is responsible. The American public will undoubtedly support the case for the person responsible for the assassination attempt on their President as well as the murderer of a Dallas Police officer. I cannot sit here and tell you what the result is going to be once your trial is over. No one can predict which way a jury is going to rule. I can however promise you that I will do everything in my power to ensure that you are guaranteed proper representation along with a fair trial. The rest is up to the jury to decide."

Oswald put his head down for a moment as if to collect his thoughts. He then put his head up and looked at Kennedy once again. He reached out to shake Robert Kennedy's hand. Kennedy quickly acknowledged his gesture and proceeded to shake Oswald's hand. It was a measure of respect and gratitude Oswald now felt for the Attorney General. Oswald then turned his attention to me. He nodded to me as if to thank me for my role in trying to save his life. Moments later, Kennedy signaled for the guard to take him back to his cell. I did not take my eyes off Oswald as the guard escorted him out. The look on his face was that of someone still uncertain as to what his fate was yet to be.

CHAPTER 30

It was now Saturday afternoon, less than 24 hours before the attempted assassination of Lee Harvey Oswald. We made our way back to the hospital. As we entered the President's room, Jacqueline informed us that the he had experienced some discomfort and was advised by his doctors to rest.

I sat in one of the chairs as Robert met with several advisors. Something inside of me now compelled me to return to the future. It was the same energy that had allowed me to transcend time so many times before. I closed my eyes to once more find myself back in my bedroom. I was immediately struck by the fact that everything had changed since my last trip home. Everything in my room was back in its place.

I walked towards my window and slowly pulled back the blinds to see if the strange vehicle was still parked in front of our home. To my utter surprise the vehicle was no longer there. I carefully made my way down the stairs where I suddenly heard footsteps coming from the kitchen. I froze for a moment, not knowing what to do next. The noise did not sound like a commotion of any sort. I slowly made my way downstairs and approached one of the two open entrances to the kitchen. To my surprise, both my parents were in the kitchen.

I pulled my head back and began to rub my eyes. I turned back and looked into the kitchen again. I then caught the attention of my father who called out to me. "John, what are you doing? Why are you hiding behind the wall?" I stared at them both and hesitated for a moment.

"When did you both come back? I asked "Come back, from what?" replied my father. For the first time I found myself at a loss for words. Neither one of them seemed to be aware of what I was referring to. "Don't you remember having to leave home because of the two men that had staked out our house over the past few days?" My father became visibly concerned by my comments. "Strange car, what are you talking about?" It was clear he was genuinely unaware of what I was referring to.

It now seemed pointless to try to explain my journey back to the past. Yet, something inside was telling me that my father would have the answer to the only question that now mattered. I asked my parents to describe to me how history had unfolded in relation to John F. Kennedy. My father was surprised with my sudden curiosity as to the outcome of President Kennedy's life. He responded by telling me that Kennedy had survived an attempt on his life in 1963. His affirmation only served to confirm the fact that my actions in the past had indeed changed the course of history.

It all began to make sense. Not only had my actions affected the past, their repercussions affected the present as well. The strange men that had haunted my family, and were responsible for the disappearance of Mrs. Donahue, were no longer present. There was still something that didn't quite "add up". I excused myself and made the short trek to the library.

I approached the front door and proceeded to walk in. As I did so, I glanced over to the head librarian's desk. Mrs. Donahue was not there. I walked around and tried to look for her to no avail. A friend from school tapped me on the shoulder and asked where I had been. I told him that I had been a way for a few days to visit relatives from out of town. I caught a glimpse of Mrs. Donahue. As had been the case so many times, she was helping a student find a book.

I walked slowly towards her as she approached her desk. I stood in front of her but did not say a word. Sensing my presence she asked if I needed some help. It was at that moment that I realized she was unaware of the fact that I was the person responsible for saving President Kennedy's life. As far as she knew, the altered version of the attempt on President Kennedy's life was one that ended on a positive note. The tragic events as originally prescribed by history had all been wiped away through my actions in the past.

For some strange reason though, something inside of me now told me that she was somehow aware of the fact that I had an important role in history. What it was, she wasn't able to figure out, but I sensed something inside of her told her such. I then responded back, "No thanks, you've already helped me enough." She immediately pick up the 'hint' of sarcasm in my voice. I thanked her and made my way to the exit. As I exited, I took one last glance back at her, relieved at the fact that she was now ok.

The fact that Mrs. Donahue was alive and well was further proof that everything was as it always had been. I took the short trek back home I had made so many times over the past few weeks. I rounded the corner of the street that now led to my house. Just as I turned the corner I heard my name being called. I stopped dead in my tracks. I slowly turned my head to now face the person who had called my name. As I turned to face the entranceway to the park, there stood agent Montgomery. I quickly made my way towards him. He now began to approach me as well.

"Mr. Montgomery, you're alive!" He immediately nodded to acknowledge such. "I thought something had happened to you!" "John, I'm sorry I left without warning, but I had to leave. Once President Kennedy's condition became stable, I knew my very presence in the past could only cause more harm than good." I replied back to him. "I needed to update you on all that has occurred here since we last saw one another. I want you to know that everything is as it always was. My family, Mrs. Donahue; as far as they're concerned, it's as if nothing ever happened!"

Montgomery replied, "Everything is back to normal because YOU made it that way. Your actions in the past not only saved the President's life, it also saved the lives of all those who helped you in your journey to the past. Had you not been successful in saving President Kennedy's life, the forces that would have ensured the repeat of history would now be present and the lives of millions would now be different. Your actions in the past, and the affects they have had assured that 'good' triumphed over 'evil'.

He continued. "I, along with Mrs. Donahue would have been lost forever. Your family and all that you have known would have disappeared for ever. Your life in the future would have failed to exist! As it stands, Osborne and those like him are no longer present in the past or the future. Your actions sealed their fates. It's as if they never existed." I quickly responded back, "But, in the stairwell, you said my life was doomed if I left. Was that always the case?"

"John, everything hinged upon whether or not President Kennedy had succumbed to his injuries. Had he died, I would no longer have been there to help you. I couldn't take that chance. You do, however need to know that there are still events occurring in the past that you need to be witness to; if only to provide closure for everything you have done. They are events that need to take place in order to create a balance between the past and the future. You will understand once you witness them for yourself."

He then smiled and hesitated for a brief moment. It was at that moment that I knew there was still one last missing piece of the JFK puzzle I hadn't yet discovered. "John, you need to go to the past one last time. The saving of President Kennedy's life is only the beginning of what is to come!" He smiled at me one last time seemingly satisfied that I would soon discover for myself everything he had alluded to. I put my head down for a moment then turned to face Montgomery once more. "Will I ever see you again? He smiled. "I think there's a good chance you will." He then reached out his hand to shake mine. He turned and walked away. I continued to stare at him as he exited the park.

My journey to the past had now come full circle. My actions had changed events in the future as well as the past, albeit in a positive way. For all those who had been involved in what had taken place over the past few weeks, it was as if nothing had occurred. I had truly been the focal point of a real-life fight between good and evil. Osborne and Montgomery were the players involved in the race for time. The stakes involved meant President Kennedy would live or die based on which side was able to help or prevent me from saving his life.

As far as those involved in the future; apart from Montgomery, history had taken place as it was first set. I now felt totally at peace knowing that those around me previously affected by my actions were now safe. The light that had shone brightly so many times before now shone brighter than ever. As Montgomery had predicted, the past was calling me back one last time. I continued to stare at the light still emanating and closed my eyes. Moments later I found myself back in the hallway in front of President Kennedy's hospital room.

I walked past the Secret Service agents and aides that once again lined the hospital hallway. I was oblivious to their stares that greeted me as I walked past them. The two agents posted directly outside the room now made no attempt to block my entry into the President's room. Everyone in the room acknowledged my return. President Kennedy immediately brought my attention to the television in front of us. There before us in black and white stood a number of reporters and police officers awaiting the arrival of Lee Harvey Oswald.

The four of us stared intently at the small television screen. Oswald arrived handcuffed, flanked by police officers on both sides of him. The officers escorting Oswald were the same ones I had seen before. We all stood silent as Oswald began to take the methodical walk toward the car that was waiting to transfer him to a different cell. Time seemed to move slowly as Oswald approached the area where Jack Ruby now stood. As Oswald continued to walk ever closer to Ruby I concentrated my attention on him. Ruby simply stood there seemingly waiting for the precise moment to approach Oswald.

Ruby made his move and lunged at Oswald. It immediately became apparent to us watching that something was wrong. We looked on in horror as events seemed to continue just as we had viewed them before. President Kennedy glanced over to his brother. Ruby fired a shot as he lunged at Oswald, who had not made any attempt to protect himself from what he knew was coming. Oswald moaned and grimaced in pain. Everything was as it was 50 years earlier. Nothing had changed.

We all watched in utter dismay as officers converged on Ruby in an attempt to remove the gun from his hand. Chaos ensued as Oswald was immediately placed onto a stretcher and wheeled into an ambulance. Our attention was now fixated on the television as events continued to unfold. Reporters on site described the scene as one of total pandemonium. To now witness what was transpiring in person instantly brought chills to me.

I turned to look at the President. His expression was one of shock. Robert was clearly stunned by what had transpired, his eyes remained fixed at the television before him. Jacqueline held one hand over her mouth, horrified by what she had just seen. President Kennedy immediately asked the officer still stationed inside the room to leave at once. As he exited the room, I could hear the commotion in the hallway outside as details of what had just transpired made their way throughout the hallway.

We continued to stare at the television monitor as reporters described what had just occurred. I looked on as Ruby was immediately handcuffed and escorted out by several police officers. The door to the President's room opened as a couple of his advisors relayed to him the latest information regarding Oswald's condition. The President asked me to wait outside for a few moments as he and his brother spoke to their advisors. I began to contemplate how and why Oswald had made absolutely no attempt to protect himself from the attempt on his life we had warned him of.

Several minutes now passed. I could only speculate as to what President Kennedy's advisors were briefing him on. A few minutes later the door opened. Robert escorted the advisors out and asked me to come back inside. He then handed me a sheet of paper which contained a suicide note that had been found in Oswald's jail cell. In it, Oswald apologized to his wife for everything he had put her through over the past few days. The note ended with Oswald telling his wife that he would always be with them in spirit and would watch over them forever.

I sat back in my chair and took several moments to digest all that had happened. I began to think back to all the articles and books I had read on Lee Harvey Oswald throughout my research into the Kennedy assassination. To the best of my knowledge no such suicide note had been mentioned in anything I had read regarding Oswald's death in 1963. The simple fact remained; this note had never existed. The one question that now mattered was simply, why? Why had Oswald not made any attempt to spare his life? More importantly, if he felt his life was not worth saving, why did he leave a suicide note?

I thought back to the conversation Robert Kennedy and Oswald had during our meeting with him. I remembered the question Oswald posed to Kennedy regarding his chances of being acquitted of the charges laid against him. Kennedy had been up front and honest with Oswald. He could not guarantee Oswald that he would not go to jail. I remembered Oswald's reaction to the realization that he could very well spend the rest of his life in jail, away from his family. The more I thought about it, the more it became apparent to me that Oswald had made the decision that he did not want to spare his life. He knew full well that there were no guarantees that he would be able to prove his innocence. The Attorney General had been unable to give him the reassurance he so badly needed.

Robert broke the silence in the room and questioned out loud why Oswald would make such a drastic decision, knowing full well that the information given to him made it possible for him to spare his own life. President Kennedy responded, "Lee Harvey Oswald knew that his life had already changed forever. Given the fact that he was unsure of whether or not his innocence would be proven, he probably felt that neither he nor his family would be safe as long as he was alive and in jail!" Robert added to the President's assertion. "Given the information we gave him, he probably felt comfortable knowing that he had at least been given the opportunity to leave his family with an explanation of what had happened. It was something that he would otherwise not have been able to do; it probably brought "closure" to his life."

I began to think about what I had thought about during my last trip back home. I had wondered how everything had gone back to normal at home. Everything seemed "too clean" at the time. It all made sense now. With Oswald's death and Ruby's subsequent imprisonment, all the remnants of evidence had been taken care of. Ruby would once again go to prison and would later die a man with a secret he had already proven he would never divulge.

The fact that President Kennedy actually survived the assassination attempt on his life now eliminated the need for Ruby to divulge what he knew. Oswald's death proved to be the catalyst, thereby ensuring that everything would now carry on as it should, both in the past as well as the future. In the end Oswald dictated the ending to his life on his terms. Agent Montgomery was indeed correct. I had to view Oswald's death in real life so as to realize that everything had indeed fallen into place.

We spent the remainder of the afternoon watching coverage of the events that took place that fateful day. Early into that afternoon the official word came in announcing that that Lee Harvey Oswald had succumbed to the wounds inflicted on him by Jack Ruby. I continued to watch the events on television, all the while amazed at the fact that I was now watching history as I had first viewed it on film. I then noticed President Kennedy staring at me. I glanced back at him and smiled. My gesture was greeted with the same response. Not a word was said between us.

Once again, President Kennedy's smile seemed to be hiding something else. I then glanced back at Robert, who had now focused his attention to his brother. The three of us seemed to be thinking the same thoughts. Jacqueline was oblivious to what was happening, still concentrating on the coverage of the Oswald assassination press conference being held by doctors at Parkland Hospital.

I began to think back to what I had thought about during my last visit to the library. There was an almost somber tone to what I knew we were now thinking. It was at that moment that I began to realize that my time in the past was nearing its end. I had completed all that I had gone back to the past to accomplish. Everything had now fallen into place given what had transpired over the past couple of days. As was the case for Montgomery, I began to feel that my continued presence there would only serve to make things worse. It was only a matter of time before the FBI and CIA would begin to take a greater interest in investigating my true identity.

I sensed that both President Kennedy and Robert Kennedy had come to the same conclusion. The look on both their faces revealed just that. I walked over to President Kennedy and stated the obvious, "Mr. President, I think it's time that I leave the past and let the future unfold as it should." Jacqueline Kennedy turned her attention to me, now totally ignoring the television before her. It was at that moment that I let her know what I truly felt for her. "It has been a pleasure making your acquaintance. You truly personify what pageantry is really about."

While I could see that she was grateful of the compliment paid to her, it was clear by her expression that Jacqueline Kennedy was deeply saddened by the fact that she knew I had to leave. "John, I share your sentiment, you are a very special person. I can't thank you enough for having saved my husband's life." In my short time with her, Jacqueline left a lasting impression on me, one I would not soon forget. The accolades she had been afforded by historians were truly justified.

I paused for a moment to think about how my actions had changed her life forever. She was totally unaware of the path she would take following her husband's assassination and her subsequent remarriage that would follow. The time that followed her husband's death, as originally prescribed by history, saw Jacqueline Kennedy move towards a life of obscurity that would ultimately take her and her children on a different path.

I then turned my attention back to John and Robert Kennedy. I had truly enjoyed every moment spent with two of the most recognizable figures in American history. The Kennedy name was to be entrenched in the annals of American history for years to come. My actions had only served to ensure that this was to continue. While I had changed the parameters to which the future was to now play itself out, there was no doubt in my mind that the second chance given to both men would not be wasted. I came to the realization that I would change the course of history for both men were I to divulge any further hint of what lay ahead in the future.

From the look on their faces it was evident that my conclusions were shared by both men. Robert then asked if I was privy to information regarding their future. I simply smiled, knowing full well that he already knew the answer to his own question. The mood in the room now became more somber with each passing moment as it became increasingly apparent that my time in the past was approaching its end. President Kennedy asked both Jacqueline and Robert to help him up. With their assistance, he carefully propped himself up on his bed. The President reached out his hand to me; I immediately put out my hand to meet his and we simply shook hands one last time.

"John, my family and I are truly indebted to you forever. I cannot thank you enough for having saved my life. I can assure that we will do everything in our power to use the second chance you've given us to make the RIGHT decisions that will benefit all Americans both at home and abroad!" It was at that moment that I realized I had been given a "once in a lifetime" opportunity few others could only dream about. To be able to spend time with true icons in the annals of American history was unbelievable. To make such a difference in their lives was truly remarkable. I turned away from them for a moment sensing a tear now streaming down the side of my face. I had come to the realization that my miraculous journey into the past was now nearing its end.

CHAPTER 31

The images of those around me quickly faded as I closed my eyes for the final time. I fell into the deepest sleep which seemed to last for hours on end. I dreamt about all the all the events that had taken place over the past few days. I revisited the assassination attempt on President Kennedy, including the meeting with Oswald and his subsequent assassination at the hands of Jack Ruby. Things began to feel increasingly strange. The events I was now witnessing in my mind felt different. It was as if I was now viewing these same events from a totally different perspective. As I came back to the present I began to awake from the deep sleep I had been in.

Everything around me slowly came into focus. Having realized that I had awoken, the woman sitting beside me quickly rose from her chair. "John, how are you feeling?" I looked up at her for a moment, all the while struggling to gain focus on the person who now stood beside me. She grabbed my hand and slowly began to squeeze it. She then gently brushed the hair on my forehead back and smiled at me. "I think this is the longest I've ever seen you sleep." Startled for a brief moment, I responded that I felt quite sore. I tried to prop myself up. I immediately winced from the pain I felt in my side. I pulled the sheets down a few inches to reveal the huge bandage wrapped around my entire ribcage area. She now gently placed her hands on the bandage in an attempt to help relieve some of the pain I felt.

The door to my room then opened. Moments later Robert Kennedy entered the room. He seemed relieved that I had awoken.

Jacqueline immediately asked if he could help her prop me up. He quickly walked to the other side of my bed. The two of them carefully grabbed me from underneath both my arms and proceeded to lift me up a few inches, just enough for me to sit up comfortably in my bed.

The door to my room then opened once more. Robert McNamara walked in. "Mr. President, it's great to see you awake; I hope you are feeling better. For a while there, the doctors treating you weren't sure you were going to pull through! I turned away from them and stared at the window beside me. It was at that moment that I realized the situation I now found myself in. Jacqueline grabbed my hand. I turned back to face her. "John, are you alright, you seemed confused." I smiled at her, hesitating once more for a few moments. "I'm alright; I guess it takes a while for the sedatives they gave me to wear off." She smiled back at me. I turned to look at my brother. He smiled back at me somewhat relieved that I had seemingly regained my senses.

McNamara then continued. "Mr. President, I wanted to update you on what has transpired over the past few hours. As you well know, Jack Ruby is in jail and has been charged with the murder of Lee Harvey Oswald. He is being questioned as we speak. We are also following several "leads" by witnesses who heard shots being fired behind the grassy knoll area as well as the 6th floor of the Schoolbook Depository building. Police haven't arrested anyone as of yet, but we're confident that progress will be made to find those that may have been involved in your assassination attempt."

McNamara's reference to the assassination attempt on my life served as final confirmation of the fact that my life had been spared by the events altered in the past. I turned to look at my brother Robert. He quickly acknowledged my stare. Robert sensed the fact that I was trying to piece together everything that had changed over the past several hours. With Oswald's death, it seemed likely that the identity of those directly involved in the assassination attempt on my life would never come to light.

I then turned and faced the wall in front of me. Having seemingly tuned everyone else out around me for a few moments, I asked about John. McNamara then spoke, "Oh yes, John, the young man that ran in front of the motorcade. We have several agents scouring the immediate area looking for his whereabouts as we speak. His disappearance caught us totally "off guard". He left your room and said he would return in a few minutes. The entire floor had been secured by Secret Service staff; he just simply vanished!" McNamara continued, "He couldn't have gone very far. We'll find him, sooner or later."

Although he was steadfast in his assertion, I knew his efforts would prove to be fruitless. I turned to look at my brother Robert once more. He seemed as unsure as the others around him. I wondered in my mind if he was cognizant of the events that had transpired. More importantly, was he aware of the younger John and the actions he had taken to save my life?

As I turned my attention away from him, sudden images started pouring into my mind as I began to daydream. The events that had taken place over the past few hours began to race in my mind quickly. I was able to see all the events and individuals I had recently come across. As was the case earlier I began to view a number of events I had not seen before. I found myself retracing many of the events that had taken place during my childhood. Yet, as I recounted these events I began to witness other events that seemed to parallel the memories I had originally known to be true.

It was as if my past had held two different paths of events that had come together to make up my current life; they were the events that had been altered in order to change my fate. It was at that moment that I realized my life had ostensibly been part of two different universes that had been brought together to create a new ending , not only in my life, but the lives of those closest to me. This explained everything. Montgomery had indeed been correct. I had to come to the realization myself. My past had been altered by history through the parallel events in my life. Although he had known this to be true all along, he also knew that this was something I would soon discover for myself.

My life as a child growing up, along with everything that had encompassed my research into JFK and my subsequent journey into the past, occurred just as my current life was unfolding. It ultimately lead to my swearing in as President. What I had now come to discover was what Montgomery had known all along. He could not divulge the elements of my life that I now knew to be true simply because my knowledge of these events prior to their occurrence would have jeopardized their outcome.

The only thing that didn't quite make sense was the fact that it seemed that no one else, other than my brother Robert, had made the connection between the younger John Kennedy and myself. Perhaps the unlikelihood of my transcending time made it impossible for anyone to believe that John and I were one in the same, even if the facts pointed to this. In truth, I myself found it hard at first to make this same connection.

Moments later, I was shaken by my wife Jacqueline. "John, are you alright? You seemed to dose off again. Startled for a brief moment, I answered that I was fine. I then caught the stare of my brother Robert once again. Robert expressed, "I don't think the President has had enough time to fully heal. I think its best that we give him some time to rest." Jacqueline immediately acknowledged my brother's assertion. Everyone in the room now made their way out. She turned back and looked at me once more as she followed the others out.

Now alone again, I glanced at the window beside my bed. The sun had now begun to set; as it did so it began to shine ever so brightly. It was eerily similar to the bright light that shone so many times in my bedroom. I knew at that precise moment that I was being summoned one last time to view the events that would surround my life in the years to come. The serenity I now felt allowed me to rest and follow the last set of images I would dream of.

I made my way to the librarian's desk located at the centre of the library study area. There stood Mrs. Donahue. It seemed as if she had anticipated my return. She immediately asked me to follow her back to the internet station as usual. It was obvious she had visited this site before and knew exactly what she was searching for.

The internet site she had come across encompassed a number of interesting facts about my childhood and education. I looked on as she began to read on the history of the private school I had been enrolled in for the past 4 years. She then pointed to the information she knew was forth coming. Having not turned away from the screen, she asked me to take out my student card. She asked me to read the first 4 digits of my student number. I immediately read them out to her. She then asked me to look closely at the information on the screen.

There before me was John F Kennedy's school records. His student number was identical to mine. It was the piece of information that provided the final proof that President Kennedy and I were indeed one and the same person. The fact that she had suspected this to be true served as further confirmation of what I had myself suspected. Many of the events that had taken place during Kennedy's life as a child mirrored the events that had that had taken place in my life. I lay back in my chair and stared aimlessly thinking about everything we now knew to be true.

Mrs. Donahue looked at me and put everything into perspective. "John, your life has mirrored that of President Kennedy's, separated only by years in time. Everything that has happened in your life has been duplicated in the past through his life. Fate had dictated that your lives would cross between the past and present in order to ensure the injustice originally prescribed by history would not cut your lives short, thereby changing the course of history forever. If what I am thinking is correct, you will meet up with the past and will assume your life as set out in history given the changes you have allowed to happen. Your actions have assured that your own life will carry on through him."

I was somewhat shocked by the fact that she had been able to surmise what I had already discovered for myself. In truth, she had lived through the events I had myself come across during my foray into the past. More importantly, she was well aware of the ramifications my actions had caused. The overriding message she now bestowed on me was that my life had been pre-ordained!

"John, given everything you know and have gone through, you need to take this "second chance" you have been given and make the most of it. You need to do everything in your power to change things for the better!" I nodded so as to assure her that I would. Those around us looked on as we embraced one another, possibly for the last time.

"Good luck with everything you are about to do "Mr. President." I acknowledge her words of encouragement and made my way to the exit.

As I approached the exit doors she stood by her desk and simply smiled back at me. It was the last time I would ever see her in person again. I took the short route back home for the last time. The fear that had transcended over me for so long had now been totally wiped away. I felt a sense of peace and serenity I had never felt before. I now knew where my future path would take me.

Although I began to wonder how and when my current life would eventually meet up with my future, I knew things would fall into place in due time. Mrs. Donahue's synopsis of the situation I now found myself in served as the final piece to the puzzle I had waited so long to finish. The story of my life was now complete. I began to follow the events that I myself would be responsible for. They were events that were to take place in my current life.

I was sworn in as President for a second term in 1964. In my second inaugural speech as President I spoke about the continued fight for civil rights in America. I described America's role throughout the world and reiterated the fact that America would intervene where necessary to stop the spread of communism. I spoke of America's role throughout the world, making it clear that American lives would not be put at risk for needless wars fought in other parts of the world. The backdrop of Vietnam was clearly a factor in the message I now proclaimed to the world.

As I delivered my speech, I glanced over to my brother Robert. We were now the co-authors of the many elements that would help shape both the domestic and foreign policy of America for years to come. I also spoke of America's continuing quest for space. I explained the importance of affirming the promise I had made four years earlier of landing a man safely on the moon. Given all that I now knew to be true, it was a promise I would keep before decade's end.

America's policy as it pertained to Central America changed dramatically during my second term as President. America's hard, yet careful stance involving the events in Vietnam proved successful in "curbing" our involvement in the war between North and South Vietnam. Although a number of Americans lost their lives during the war in Vietnam, thousands more were spared. While many in the military community questioned our stance in Vietnam, our decision to do so helped save the lives of many Americans abroad.

Perhaps the most telling example of how history had been forever changed was best illustrated in the enactment of the American Equity Rights Law passed during my second term of office. The Equity Rights Law, introduced in March of 1965 was the most important piece of legislation introduced by my administration. It was passed on Sept 10, 1966. The Equity Rights Law introduced a number of sweeping changes that furthered the cause of equal rights for African Americans not seen since the abolishment of slavery itself. It declared the segregation as illegal and immoral, and severely punished those individuals and institutions that supported it at any level. Americans of all colors and creeds rejoiced the law as the last step towards true freedom and equality. My brother and I had truly laid the foundation for the cause of civil rights in America for decades to come.

The Cold War, perhaps the greatest threat to mankind during my tenure as President, was a focal point in my foreign policy portfolio. As was the case so many times before, I was determined to make the most of the "second chance" I had been given to change history. The process began with a series of meetings with allied countries, including Great Britain and France. The purpose of these meetings was to introduce a broad spectrum of initiatives whose sole purpose was to put pressure on the Soviet Union. The pressure was aimed on several fronts.

The first was centered on the immediate reduction of nuclear weaponry throughout the world. A conference with U.S allies was held in Bordeaux, France on April 5, 1964. It concluded with the Bordeaux agreement between Western powers to immediately reduce their nuclear arsenals by 50%. The reduction in arms was to be completed by the fall of 1964. It was also agreed that a meeting was to be arranged that same year between the United States and the Soviet Union. Its sole purpose was to convince Soviet premier Nikita Khrushschev to match the commitment given by Western allies in Bordeaux. The result was the Moscow agreement signed on Dec 7, 1964. With this agreement, the Soviet Union agreed to match the commitment made by Western powers in Bordeaux months earlier. The reduction of the Soviet nuclear arsenal by 50% was to be completed by May of 1965.

The Bordeaux and Moscow agreements were landmarks in history. By placing limits to the nuclear arsenal held by countries in the world, it effectively put an end to the Cold War. This was accentuated by my subsequent trip to East Berlin in the fall of 1965. The location chosen was historic. The East Berlin conference began on September 10, 1965.

Given the worldwide acceptance of the efforts made through both the Bordeaux and Moscow agreements, the Berlin Wall was seen as the last remnant of the Cold War. Through my exhaustive efforts in the months that passed since Moscow, Soviet premier Krushschev agreed to attend as a mediator alongside myself and the leaders of both Eastern and Western Germany.

Like the Moscow conference held less than a year earlier, the Berlin conference was extended an extra day. The resulting Berlin agreement of Sept 14, 1965 was as historic as the two recent agreements that preceded it. Acting as the spokesman of the Western world, I proposed a truce between East and West Germany made possible through the introduction of comprehensive economic measures. A crowd of thousands "crammed" the area surrounding both sides of the Berlin Wall as I delivered the speech that announced to the world the newly signed Berlin agreement. It was at this speech that I declared myself a citizen of a "unified" Germany.

The final set of images now flashed before me. My brother became President-elect on November 14, 1968. The effects of the policies and legislations put forth during my second term in office served to catapult the Kennedy popularity that assured my brother's rightful place as President following my second term.

Robert Francis Kennedy was sworn in as President of the United States on Jan 20, 1969. His inauguration was met with great fanfare. It was the first and only time brothers would follow one another as President. Once again, history had been made.

Jacqueline and I stood closely by as Robert read the oath of office in front of thousands. The pride I felt was trumped only by the sense of accomplishment I felt, knowing full well that the events now before me were the culmination of all that had occurred years earlier in Dallas.

Robert Kennedy's policies followed where mine had left off during my second term as President. His stance towards civil rights, along with his stance on America's involvement in Vietnam made him the overriding choice for President. The end result of all this was a truce declared between North and South Vietnam on December 12, 1970. The United States played an instrumental role in the negotiation process between the two neighboring countries.

The truce between the two countries lasted only two years, culminating with the takeover of South Vietnam by North Vietnam in April, 1972. The net result of this, however was the saving of thousands of American lives that would have been lost had events taken place as first set out in history.

In the spring of 1969 talks began between newly appointed President Robert Kennedy and the leaders of both East and West Germany for the unification of Germany. By the fall of 1969 East and West Germany reached an agreement that unified the two countries together to form a unified Germany.

He continued the fight for civil equality that I had championed so vigilantly during my two terms in office. He also exacted the same energy towards man's ongoing thirst for knowledge about outer space. Less than a year after taking office, Robert and I stood together alongside the successful Apollo 11 crew days after having successfully returned to earth from the moon's surface. It was a moment in time made possible only through my actions in the past.

My journey was indeed complete. I was back in my rightful place as President. I now felt the strange need to close my eyes once more. It was at that moment that I began to view the last remaining set of images that would serve as closure to my life.

I looked on as the President of the United States was being sworn in. Jacqueline and I were now in the latter stages of our lives. We stood beside our son John F. Kennedy Jr. as the 45th President of the United States. The timing of his ascendency to the Presidency had not been lost by those throughout the world who had cherished the legacy that both Robert and I had left. It was only fitting that the son of a Kennedy, so entrenched in the cause for civil rights, would follow the footsteps of the first African American President.

My son's speech seemed to usher in the same sense of promise and pageantry that previous Kennedy inaugurations had evoked. Every element and promise he outlined during his speech was met with loud cheers from the many thousands of onlookers present. My son was every bit a Kennedy. His inauguration served as final confirmation of the effects that my actions in the past had on the world for years to come. The legacy of my efforts years earlier had now transcended the 20th century!

I continued to follow the events that took place on that historic day. My son had finished his speech and now waved at the huge crowds assembled before him. He stared at the several large screens that were now focused on me. It was at that moment that my son turned and saluted me. His salute was a new piece of history that served to join the past with the present. Thousands cheered and chanted for the newly inaugurated Kennedy. I then looked on as he, unbeknownst to his advisors, slowly made his way down the stairs that lead to the crowd before him.

From the reaction on his face, it now seemed that he had picked out someone from the crowd; he now made his way to greet him. The Secret Service agents assigned to protect him quickly scrambled to set up a perimeter around the newly appointed President. It was clear that this was not part of the original planning of the inaugural ceremony. I looked on as the agent in charge advised my son that they had not been given the opportunity to create the logistics required to assure his protection.

He made his way through to the crowd before him. Several Secret Service agents had already cleared a walkway for him. President Kennedy slowly walked down the makeshift pathway that had been made for him. He shook the hands of the many onlookers who had now scrambled to catch a glimpse of their new President.

I looked on as my son walked towards the Washington monument. He approached the man who had caught his attention. "Mr. President, it is an honor to meet you in person." My son responded. "Do I know you? You somehow look familiar, although I don't think we've ever met!"

"Mr. President, my name is Robert Montgomery Jr. Years ago our fathers shared a special relationship. It was an important journey that helps to explain why the both of us are here!" My son hesitated for a moment, surprised by Montgomery's comments. He then collected his thoughts. "I remember my father having spoken about your father. He never fully explained all that had occurred between the two of them, but he always impressed upon me the importance of their relationship."

The Secret Service agent beside President Kennedy turned to whisper to him. My son turned to face him and softly responded back. "I have time for this man." The agent, surprised by his response, took a step back seemingly having realized the importance of the conversation now taking place. My son then turned back to face Montgomery once more. "I'd like to have you over at the White House in the next day or so once things have "settled" into place. We have many things to catch up on."

Montgomery quickly acknowledged his invitation. My son then turned to one of the two aides standing beside the Secret Service agents. "Make sure you speak to Mr. Montgomery and make all the necessary arrangements for us to meet." The aide immediately acknowledged his request. My son faced Montgomery and with a stoic look declared, "We could use another good man in Washington!" They smiled at one another, having realized that they had now forged the same relationship their fathers shared years earlier.

THE END

Purchase other Black Rose Writing titles at <u>www.blackrosewriting.com/books</u>
and use promo code PRINT to receive a 20% discount.

CPSIA information can be obtained
at www.ICGtesting.com
Printed in the USA
LVOW01s0833101215
465803LV00006B/61/P

9 781612 965802